P9-DXT-337

ST. MARTIN'S

MINOTAUR

MYSTERIES

DEATH TAKES UP
A COLLECTION

SISTER CAROL ANNE O'MARIE

St. Martin's Paperbacks

*To the Sisters of St. Joseph of Carondelet
in gratitude for their encouragement and
support of Sister Mary Helen and
her many escapades.*

DEATH TAKES UP A COLLECTION

Copyright © 1998 by Sister Carol Anne O'Marie

All rights reserved. No part of this book may be used or reproduced in any manner whatsoever without written permission except in the case of brief quotations embodied in critical articles or reviews. For information address St. Martin's Press, 175 Fifth Avenue, New York, N.Y. 10010.

Library of Congress Catalog Card Number: 98-21148

ISBN: 0-312-97193-1

Printed in the United States of America

St. Martin's Press hardcover edition/ September 1998
St. Martin's Paperbacks edition/ December 1999

St. Martin's Paperbacks are published by St. Martin's Press, 175 Fifth Avenue, New York, N.Y. 10010.

10 9 8 7 6 5 4 3 2 1

Sunday, March 16

❧❧❧

Fifth Sunday of Lent

If Sister Mary Helen didn't know better, she'd swear that she was standing in the Klondike and not on the steps of St. Agatha's rectory in San Francisco's Sunset District.

"What in the name of heaven is keeping them?" Sister Eileen, her companion, stamped her feet to keep warm. "Ring again."

The raw wind off the Pacific Ocean swept up the boulevard, swirling into the staircase, raising goose pimples on Mary Helen's legs. "Now is the time we could use those long serge habits," she said, glad that she'd worn her heavy black wool coat and remembered her gloves.

Mary Helen pushed the small button of a doorbell. The two old nuns listened to the melodious ring of chimes echo through the seemingly empty building.

"Maybe we should have called before we came." Eileen's eyes cut from her hands, which held a large loaf of Irish soda bread wrapped in green cellophane, to Mary Helen's face.

The words *as I suggested*, hung in the air between them. Mary Helen knew that Eileen had too much style to actually say them.

But, just in case, she deftly changed the subject.

"Just look at all those cars." Mary Helen pointed to the row of automobiles parked diagonally on the avenue in front of the rectory. "Maybe they're having a meeting."

"Or a St. Patrick's Day party," Eileen suggested brightly, "in which case, our Irish bread is not a moment too soon."

"Please hurry up," Mary Helen urged the phantom door answerer. She was tempted to ring the bell a third time. Eileen and she had spent all weekend delivering festively wrapped loaves of Irish soda bread to Mount St. Francis College benefactors. Frankly, they were tired. Monsignor Joseph Higgins at St. Agatha's was their last stop before heading back home to the college. Both of them were looking forward to putting up their feet and relaxing for a few minutes before dinner.

Usually the nuns delivered home-baked goods to their benefactors at Christmastime. This past Christmas, what with the murder of their prominent alumna Gemma Burke and the bizarre death of library staff member Angelica Bowers, nothing had been "as usual."

"Everyone gives 'goodies' at Christmastime," Sister Cecilia, the college president, had argued logically. "People might really appreciate them more at an off season like . . . like. . . . "

"St. Patrick's Day!" Sister Therese, who insisted that her

name be pronounced "trays," chimed in helpfully. Then, without hesitation, she'd volunteered Eileen to oversee the project.

"Isn't that always the way," Eileen had fumed. Although she didn't mention it, Mary Helen suspected that her friend would have been even more upset if she hadn't been suggested.

Eileen was the only one of the nuns who was actually Irish by birth. Even though she'd been in the United States for well over fifty years, she was still considered their expert on all matters Hibernian, including, of course, soda bread.

"I haven't baked a cake of it in years," Eileen had fussed. Mary Helen, however, noticed how quickly she was able to find her mother's old recipe. With the help of Ramón, the college pastry chef, and very little trouble besides, she had orchestrated the baking of dozens of plump, raisin-filled loaves of soda bread.

Young Sister Anne was responsibile for wrapping the round loaves and tying up each one of them with a perky gold bow and a sprinkle of plastic shamrocks.

In Mary Helen's opinion, the paper gave the bread a rather unappetizing hue. But Eileen, always the optimist, had said, "We can just thank God, old dear, that she didn't decide to put green in my batter!"

Sister Mary Helen still was unable to figure out how it had fallen to their lot to deliver the bread, but it had. And they were almost finished. If someone would just answer the front door!

Mary Helen was about to ring the bell for the third time when Charlotte Wixson, St. Agatha's parish secretary, inched open the heavy wood-paneled front door. Mrs. Wixson, who

3

wore a thick Kelly green sweater with an enormous rolled collar, blinked at them over the door chain.

"Come in, Sisters," she said, as if she wasn't quite sure whether or not they should. Clumsily, she slipped off the chain.

"I didn't expect to see you here on a Sunday afternoon," Mary Helen said, happy to step into the warmth of the rectory foyer, at last.

"I'm here for the emergency meeting," Mrs. Wixson whispered and pointed toward a closed door. If Mary Helen remembered correctly, it was one of the doors which led into the priests' dining room.

"Why don't you two go into the kitchen," Mrs. Wixson suggested, nervously running her finger under the collar of her sweater. "Eve can fix you a cup of tea and I'll tell Monsignor Higgins you're here. I'm sure he'll welcome a break."

Letting the last three words drift over her shoulder, Mrs. Wixson disappeared behind the closed door. The two nuns were left standing in the entry.

"Do you think we should just walk into Eve's kitchen?" Eileen whispered.

Sister Mary Helen shrugged. Eve Glynn, the housekeeper, had been at St. Agatha's rectory for as long as almost anyone could remember.

"She came with the kitchen," generations of young assistant pastors had quipped.

Eileen knew differently. "Eve came with Monsignor Concannon," she had once explained to Mary Helen, "when he was appointed pastor of the old St. Agatha's, before they built the new church. Must be nearly forty years ago now.

4

"Eve was a spinster cousin of his from Galway. Although Eve wasn't her name then. She had one of those Gaelic names with all the e's and i's like Eibhilin or Eadaoin which are difficult for Americans, even San Franciscans, to pronounce. The monsignor himself called her Eveleen. You know, after the first woman . . . in the rectory anyway. Later it was somehow shortened to Eve."

Sister Eileen had taken a breath and Mary Helen was glad. It was really more than she wanted to know about the history of Eve Glynn's first name.

"Anyway," Eileen had continued, "she was a relatively young woman, used to hard work, and very dedicated to God and to the priests and to the Church. Not necessarily in that order." Eileen had raised her bushy eyebrows to make her point. "When Monsignor Concannon passed away, Eve simply stayed on and on and on."

"The many faces of Eve," years of assistant pastors had teased. These same curates were never quite sure which one of her faces they would be shown.

"A sweet tongue is seldom without a sting to its root," Eileen had said of Eve, quoting yet another of her "old sayings from back home."

Although Mary Helen had never felt the sting of Eve's tongue, she didn't doubt it existed. There was something vulpine just behind the housekeeper's pale blue eyes that led Mary Helen to believe that Eve was probably well deserving of her reputation.

"Knock, knock," Eileen called through the closed kitchen door. "May we come in?"

"Yes! Come in! Come in! Welcome!" Eve sang out cheerfully. Mary Helen heard the scurry of soft soles across the linoleum.

"I'm just brewing a pot of tea," the housekeeper chirped in a tone that made it clear she was doing anything but. "Push the door open and come in."

The moment they stepped into the enormous stainless-steel kitchen, Mary Helen realized that Eve must have been eavesdropping on whatever was going on in the priests' dining room. The self-conscious way the housekeeper's eyes avoided the pantry door, which opened into it, confirmed her suspicions.

"We'll have to keep our voices low," Eve whispered. "Big meeting going on in there. Heaven help us!" Her pale eyes rolled heavenward.

Although Mary Helen was unable to make out any of the words, she could hear the buzz of voices, like angry bees caught in an empty mayonnaise jar. Clearly, it was coming from the next room. She wondered crazily whether or not the monsignor was the one left holding the jar.

"But that's not your worry, now is it?" said Eve, rounded by years of her own good cooking, and gave a carefree shrug. "Sit down! Sit down! You must be frozen on a day like this." Her lips pulled tightly over her teeth into a rigid smile. "It's as cold as charity out there on the avenues."

Eve's kitchen, on the other hand, was toasty warm. Actually it was hot, maybe even a little cloying. The windows were covered with moisture. Mary Helen's bifocals steamed up almost immediately.

"Sit!" Eve repeated, pulling back two chairs, then handed Mary Helen a tea towel to wipe her glasses.

Shedding their gloves and heavy coats, the two nuns settled themselves at the cozy kitchen table set by a triptych of windows. In the center, one enormous, delicate pink rhododendron bloom floated in a glass relish dish. Both nuns admired its showy beauty.

"They grow like weeds in the rectory garden," Eve said, setting a plate of warm oatmeal cookies next to the flower. "White ones, red ones, pink ones. My sainted cousin, Monsignor Paddy Concannon, couldn't seem to get enough of them." Her eyes misted over.

Pouring three generous cups of tea, Eve sighed, placed the teapot on a trivet, and joined them. "So you brought soda bread, I see," She pushed a heavy thumb into its corner to test for freshness. "I suppose you had that Chinese cook at the college make it."

Eileen's back straightened. "Ramón is not Chinese," she began. Mary Helen could tell from the touch of the brogue creeping into her voice that Eileen was pitching for a battle.

Eve must have noticed it, too. Quickly she put a finger to her lips. "Like I said, Sister, they're right in there." She nodded toward the pantry door. "In the dining room. The whole parish council!" she whispered. "On a Sunday, no less! It can't be good news!" Eyes dancing, she took a sip of her tea and swallowed it with satisfaction.

"I like to stretch out and take a little snooze on a Sunday afternoon before I go out. Sunday night is my one night off, you know. But there'll be no such thing today." Her weary sigh fooled no one. A team of Clydesdales couldn't have hauled her out of the kitchen and into her bedroom.

Before Eve could continue, Monsignor Joseph Higgins

burst through the pantry door. Since he was what was known as "smoked Irish," his face was usually tan. This afternoon it was gray. From his Roman collar to his jawbone, his neck was streaked bright red, almost as if someone had tried to strangle him. He seemed to fill the entire kitchen, which wasn't a surprise.

Joseph P. Higgins—no one knew what the "P" stood for—had what many called "presence." Even though he was not an exceptionally tall man, perhaps five ten or so, with his full head of icy white hair, sharp blue eyes, and a booming voice, he seemed to fill any room he entered.

"Well, well, look who's here," the monsignor said in a volume worthy of the whole of St. Agatha's Church, let alone the rectory kitchen.

He stuck out his hand. A diamond cuff link sparkled in his French cuff. He gave off a spicy, fragrant aura. "It's the good Sisters," he said with forced cheer.

If I were a dog, my hackles would have risen, Mary Helen thought, watching Eileen take the pale, offered hand. Why does that expression always do that to me? How can something which is supposed to sound like a compliment come across as such a put-down?

Before she could analyze it further, it was her turn to shake the monsignor's soft, warm hand.

"Won't you come into the dining room?" he asked earnestly. "Mrs. Wixson tells me that you brought some home-baked Irish bread. It's perfect timing, Sisters. I'm certain you already know some of the members of my parish council from the college or wherever. We're having a meeting. Most of us could use a break, I'm sure."

The color was beginning to fade from his neck. "Eve, will you serve us," he ordered, his eyes flashing. Not waiting for her reply, he turned on his highly polished heels and led the way back to the dining room.

Just before the pantry door swung shut behind them, Mary Helen caught a glimpse of Eve. Flat, slippered feet far apart, head lowered, her eyes blazed like two match flames. They fastened on the back of the monsignor's finely tailored black wool suit jacket. Mary Helen winced. If looks could kill, she thought, turning to face the crowd in the priests' dining room, at this moment Monsignor Joseph P. Higgins would be a dead man.

❧❧❧

Six pairs of eyes, sharp as needles, pinned Joe Higgins the moment the priest re-entered the dining room. Slowly, the three men at the long mahogany table rose. This reflex politeness was the only sign Mary Helen had that the council members even noticed that the nuns were with him.

"Teatime," the monsignor called out with false gaiety. "These nuns from the college just dropped by with Irish soda bread. I told them that I thought we'd welcome a break."

From the expressions on the other faces in the room, Mary Helen felt sure that he was using the pontifical "we."

The monsignor, with the "ho, ho, ho" of a tired Santa Claus, made remarks about "perfect timing," and "all needing a change of subject," while he pulled two chairs from their resting places along a brocaded wall. No one moved to

9

help him. Deliberately, he flanked one chair on either side of his as if he were protecting his bastion.

Just our luck, Mary Helen thought, feeling the anger in the six pairs of eyes spread out to encompass them, too.

"Sit, Sisters, sit," Monsignor Higgins insisted.

Obediently, they sat. Mary Helen smiled uncomfortably.

In the thick silence, the monsignor cleared his throat. Nervously, he ran his hand across his red neck. "While we wait for Eve to bring in the refreshments," he said, "why don't each of you introduce yourselves?"

With a quick, nervous movement, he nodded toward clearly the oldest person in the room. "Why don't you start, Fred?" the monsignor suggested, looking to his right.

Fred, who Mary Helen judged to be about her own age, reddened. "Fred Davis, Sisters," he said in an amazingly strong clear voice. His face was long and narrow with paper-thin fair skin. The red-rimmed eyes bulged slightly behind wire-framed glasses. "I'm the head of this parish's finance committee," he stated flatly. Dropping the pencil he was holding onto the tabletop, Fred Davis spread out his large knuckled hands, as if he were about to resign.

"And a wonderful job he's doing, too," the monsignor added too quickly, then chuckled.

His blue eyes jumped to Fred's right and landed on a bony woman, carefully dressed, even if a little out of style. Her auburn hair was neat and short, almost manicured. "I'm Deborah Stevens," the woman said. Her eyes, the color of Hershey's kisses and glinting with anger, avoided the monsignor's. She beamed in on the nuns.

"I'm Ms. Deborah Stevens." In a high, slightly nasal

twang, she emphasized the "Ms." "Chairperson of the outreach committee."

Although the muscles in her square jaw were still working, it was clear that Ms. Stevens was not going to say another word.

"Really, I don't know what I'd do without Debbie," the monsignor declared, gesturing to the woman to her right.

"I'm Tina Rodiman." The slight young woman scooted to the edge of her chair, rocking precariously back and forth. She squeezed her small bejeweled fingers together. "My husband, Tony, and I are in charge of the parish bingo. Tony's at our son's soccer game today. He's the coach. He had to be there." She sounded apologetic. Nibbling at her waxy red lower lip, her spider lashes, heavy with mascara, fluttered over her penny-colored eyes. "They call us the 'Two T's.'" She giggled self-consciously and pushed an errant brown curl off her forehead.

Quickly Tina looked toward her right, leaving Mary Helen to wonder what other things the "Two T's" were called. "Tweedle Dum and Tweedle Dumber" were the first two names that popped uncharitably into her mind.

The gentleman to the right of Tina Rodiman didn't even look up. Instead, he continued to slump lazily in his chair, one elbow propped on its back. Rhythmically, he bounced his pencil eraser on the tabletop. He appeared to be studying his long legs, which stretched out under the table and ended in extraordinarily large scuffed brown shoes.

"George Jenkin, here," he said in a throaty growl. "Communications."

Clearly not today, Mary Helen thought. She studied his

fish-white face for a moment before turning toward one of the two people in the room whom she did recognize, Sister Noreen, the principal of St. Agatha's School.

Today Noreen, who was usually placid and friendly, looked as if she would burst into tears if she spoke.

Not willing to take the chance, Mary Helen spoke up quickly. "We know Sister Noreen, of course," she said with a reassuring smile. "Sister is a regular at the college enrichment programs."

From behind her owl-eyed bifocals, Sister Noreen blinked her appreciation. Her round, dumpling face was almost as gray as her hair. Her chubby hand flew up to her mouth as if, at any moment, she might be sick.

What in heaven's name is going on here? Mary Helen wondered, quickly shifting her attention to a stocky man wearing a tweed jacket and a bright tie. "And, of course, we know Professor Komsky," she said.

For many years before his recent retirement, Nicholas Komsky had been a renowned history professor at San Francisco State University. During that time both Eileen and Mary Helen had met him at numerous higher education meetings. The two nuns had always found him to be a good man, pleasant and well met, if a bit officious on occasion.

In an exaggerated show of deference, Nicholas Komsky bowed his head toward the two nuns. "It is always my pleasure to see you, Sisters," he said, running his fingers through his full head of white hair. Because of the hair and his wild white eyebrows, Eileen always said that he reminded her of an aging Albert Einstein. "I am currently the chairman of the parish liturgy committee," he said.

Despite the facade of friendliness, behind his horn-rimmed glasses, the professor's blue eyes shone as hard as glass. Clearly, Nicholas Komsky was enraged about something.

"Are you enjoying your retirement?" Sister Eileen asked, in what surely was an attempt at conversation.

"I was," Komsky said, staring pointedly at Monsignor Higgins.

Suddenly all the anger in the room seemed to rise up like an atomic mushroom cloud to the Waterford crystal chandelier, then slowly fall out over all the people at the large dining room table.

Mary Helen waited for the explosion. Happily, the only boom she heard was the pantry door.

"Your tea!" Eve Glynn announced, putting down the tray with a grunt. The china cups rattled in their saucers and the teaspoons jingled. "I'll get the rest," Eve said and left again.

Sister Noreen, seeming to regain some of her composure, stood and began to pass around the cups. This time, Eve swung through the pantry door, rear end first. "Enjoy!" she said, placing a plate of bread, a cube of hard butter, and a crystal dish containing a lump of berry jam next to Sister Eileen.

Mary Helen studied the bread. A chill crept up her spine. The way that Ramón's perfect soda cake had been hacked made her wonder crazily, who Eve really wanted to slice.

Eileen, on the other hand, didn't seem to notice. She was helping Noreen serve, monsignor first, of course. She chatted happily about the merits of sesame seeds versus no sesame seeds in the batter as she tried to interest the others in a slice.

"No, thanks," Debbie Stevens said politely while Tina Rodiman simply shook her head.

"I won't be able to eat my dinner," old Mr. Davis complained when Eileen extended the plate of soda bread in his direction.

At least, the professor took the plate from Eileen's hand, but he passed it off, as if it were hot, to George Jenkin.

George, looking pale, put it down in front of Sister Noreen, who simply stared at the roughly cut bread.

Like a game of musical plate, Mary Helen thought. Apparently the anger and tension in the room had robbed everyone of an appetite. Actually, she didn't feel much like eating either.

"Well, if none of you are hungry, pass it my way," Monsignor Higgins said with a hearty laugh.

Woodenly, Noreen passed the plate to the monsignor.

"Thank goodness someone has an appetite," Eileen said cheerfully. Apparently, she was unaware that hers was the only voice in the room.

The pantry door banged open once more and Eve came into the dining room. Her slippers scuffed in the silence. "Forgot these," she said, placing a silver tray holding a Belleek creamer and sugar bowl in the center of the table. Beside them, looking as out of place as the catsup bottle on the Hearst Castle dining room table, was a twelve-ounce plastic honey bear. Its Kelly green plastic top was still on.

Stiffly, the group began to pass the sugar and cream. The butter and jam went to the monsignor. Debbie Stevens stirred honey into her tea. "Sticky as usual," she mumbled when she picked up the honey bear.

"I'll just rinse it off," Sister Noreen offered helpfully.

"I'm right here," Debbie snapped, her brown eyes still angry. "I'll do it."

Without looking at Eve, she shot into the kitchen. In the silence that followed, they could hear the water from the sink.

"It's about time she did something around here," Eve mumbled. The remark was clearly meant to be overheard.

Smiling, Eve waited for Debbie to vacate the kitchen before she re-entered it.

All around the room, the sipping sounds seemed extraordinarily loud. To her credit, Eileen tried several times to serve up a conversation. Both Monsignor Higgins and Sister Noreen made valiant efforts to help her keep the volley going. Although no one was actually rude, each of her attempts hit the ground like a spiked ball.

The moments dragged on awkwardly. To distract herself, Mary Helen eyed the group. Tina Rodiman's cup had her waxy red lip prints all over one side of it. George Jenkin downed his cup in two thirsty gulps while Debbie Stevens took baby sips as if the tea were bitter medicine.

The monsignor, seemingly oblivious to all the tension around him, added a large dollop of honey to his tea and Mary Helen wondered absently if the man had diabetes. Or was he on a diet? Maybe she should try honey, too, if it had fewer calories.

She was thinking of asking the monsignor to pass the bear when Fred Davis cracked his large knuckles. The sound sent shivers up her spine and she reached for the sugar, which was closer. When she'd finished with it, she passed the

Belleek bowl over to Professor Komsky, who absently traced designs in the sugar with the edge of his spoon.

This is what torture must feel like, Mary Helen was beginning to think, when George Jenkin pulled in his long legs. Straightening up in his chair, he cleared his throat, put down his empty teacup, and made a great show of studying his wristwatch.

Now, that's communication for you, Mary Helen thought, pushing back her own chair. "We know that you have things to do," she said, setting her cup back in its saucer. "We'll just be on our way now and let you get back to them."

On her right, Monsignor Higgins struggled to stand.

"Don't even bother to show us out," Mary Helen insisted.

"Thank you all for your time," Eileen added politely, "and happy St. Patrick's Day!"

Mary Helen couldn't remember when the two of them ever made a quicker exit. Their only delay was Eve Glynn at the front door.

"I've seen a happier scene at a deathbed," Eve said. With a delighted smile, she closed and locked the door behind them.

Once outside, the two nuns stood by the convent-owned Chevy Nova. Mary Helen felt the laughter bubbling up. "I thought we'd never get out of there alive," she said. "I was beginning to wish Sister Cecilia would send out a posse looking for us."

"What in heaven's name do you suppose was going on?" Eileen whispered as if she expected the nearby calla lilies to be bugged.

"I, for one, don't want to know," Mary Helen said. Her eyes scanned the avenue, which ran downhill all the way to the beach. The winter sun hovered egg-yolk yellow just above the horizon, turning the cloud-banded sky into a study in pastels.

"Whatever it was, that little tea party gave the old expression 'cut the tension with a knife' new meaning," Eileen said, rolling her large gray eyes.

Nodding, Mary Helen unlocked the car doors. The wind blew open her coat and twisted her skirt around her legs. "To tell the truth," Mary Helen called across the top of the Nova, "I felt like a character right out of one of those locked room murder mystery plays. You know the ones I mean."

Eileen chuckled nervously. "I know exactly the ones you mean, old dear," she said. "But I was having a difficult time deciding if the victim was dead, or if the victim was just about to be killed."

❧❧❧

Impatiently, Monsignor Joe Higgins picked up the receiver on his bedroom intercom. "What is it, Eve?" He tried not to let his anger spill out on her. No good would come of it.

What happened this afternoon wasn't her fault. Or was it? Someone had spilled the beans, hadn't he? Or she? It could just as well have been a she.

Nervously, he fingered one of his cuff links. The diamond was heavy and felt smooth to the touch.

"I was just wondering, Monsignor," Eve began in that soft, servile voice of hers which didn't fool him for a minute. "Are you going out for supper this evening, or would you like me to fix you a cold supper before I go?" she asked, continuing her annoying charade. "Sunday night is my night off," she added unnecessarily.

For God's sake, after twelve years of living in the rectory with that woman, he knew Sunday night was her night off. He visualized her with her pale blue eyes staring pitifully at him through the finger smudges on her glasses. She would be wearing that silly-looking hat to cover her hair, which Lady Clairol helped her keep dull and brown.

He wanted to slam down the receiver, tell her to get out of his rectory, but he didn't. It would do him no good. Her cousin, the Reverend Monsignor Padraig Concannon had a few old friends left—secretly Joe Higgins called them the Irish Mafia—who had nested in the archbishop's ear. If it came to a showdown, Joe Higgins knew that he would be the one sent packing.

"No thank you, Eve," he said, holding his voice in check. "If I don't go out, I'll just fix myself a little something later on." He felt a sharp cramp in his stomach.

"Oh, my!" she said. Her inflection infuriated him. Was she implying that he might drink his supper? If so, she had him mixed up with her "sainted cousin." Drink had never been Joe Higgins's problem. He had plenty of others without adding alcohol. And Eve well knew it! That was one of the problems with Eve. She knew way too much about everything.

"Eavesdropping Eve!" a flip young assistant pastor had dubbed her once. Shortly after, the priest was sent to a remote parish in Tomales Bay, whose mission church was a round-trip of more than twenty-five scenic, but narrow and winding, miles.

"It's a fit," Monsignor Concannon had declared when the priest was reassigned. "The lad is young and he needs more to keep him busy than wondering who's eavesdropping."

Joe Higgins shed his black suit jacket and the black broadcloth rabat that covered the front of his shirt. The skin on his neck felt warm and prickly. He wondered if he was coming down with something. Mrs. Wixson had been out with the flu one day last week. Maybe he'd picked up the bug.

Tonight, Joe had a tentative date with his friend and classmate, Monsignor Ed Singleton. They had planned to have dinner at Chez Michel's, a sleek new restaurant on North Point, just up the hill from Ghirardelli Square. Joe was hoping it would be a kind of celebration, if he lived through the afternoon, which he obviously had. Now, he was looking forward to Chez Michel's famous purple potato fries.

Even Ed seemed worried about this afternoon's meeting with more good reason than he knew. Joe had been careful not to tell him everything. Ed was such a straight arrow. But tonight he intended to come clean.

In fact, he thought he might ask Ed to hear his confession. That way, if Ed got scruples about whether he should go to the archbishop with what he knew, his hands would be tied. Joe snickered. Or, at least, his tongue would be!

Besides, Ed was a canon lawyer. If there was a way out of this mess, he'd know it. Maybe it would be wiser to telephone Ed and have him come to St. Agatha's for dinner. The purple fries could wait. You never knew who was sitting next to you in a restaurant and what he or she might overhear.

Joe would send out for Chinese. He knew the number of Yet Wah's by heart. They could eat in his study and gab all night if they wanted to. Eve was out. The other priests in the rectory knew better than to bother him when his suite door had the DO NOT DISTURB sign on its handle.

A tingle ran down Joe Higgins's right arm. Odd, he thought, slipping into his sports shirt. Maybe with all that tension and sitting this afternoon, he had pulled something. Tomorrow morning he'd play golf. He could scarcely wait to use the brand-new set of clubs he'd bought himself. Top of the line, he thought, remembering with pleasure the smell of the leather bag.

He hadn't done too badly for a bare-assed kid from Bernal Heights. "Genteel poverty." He always referred to his up-bringing that way. In his more truthful moments, he knew there had been nothing whatsoever genteel about his family's poverty. His father drank what little money he made while his mother cleaned other people's houses. Joe and his three brothers slept in the same bed, two at the head and two at the foot.

When he'd entered the seminary on a scholarship, he thought he'd died and gone to heaven. Not only did he have his own bed, but he had his own room.

He wasn't the only kid there on a scholarship, but he was the only one so poor that he didn't even have a middle name. It bothered him. Ed had suggested he choose Patrick in honor of the co-patron of the archdiocese. Joe leaned more toward Peter, the first pope. They had settled on just plain "P," and kept everyone guessing.

Joe Higgins poured himself two fingers of Cutty Sark and took a swallow. The liquid burned his mouth. He'd call Ed. Tell him he wasn't feeling up to snuff and that they'd eat at St. Agatha's.

Without worrying, he left the message on Ed Singleton's answering machine. Ed was so conscientious that he checked his machine every hour. Joe wondered who called his friend. Sometimes, he himself would go for days without a message. That was the joy of being an excellent administrator, he told himself, and of insisting that your associates each carry his own weight.

The monsignor took another sip of the scotch. He was having a little difficulty catching his breath. He sank into his plush tan leather chair, another gift, to himself from himself, courtesy of the second collection.

Joe Higgins closed his eyes. For a moment, he wished he still enjoyed a relationship with Debbie Stevens. Although she had been much more appealing when she was Sister Mary Deborah.

Out of the convent, she seemed a little frumpy. Maybe dowdy was a better word. He didn't remember her being quite so bony either, when she was a nun. Nor so bitchy.

If this afternoon was any example, Debbie had turned into a regular A-number-one bitch! He was smart to have broken things off. In his position, his name couldn't be linked to a woman—to any scandal—if he wanted to climb. And Joe Higgins did! He wanted it so bad he could taste it. Monsignor Higgins, Bishop Higgins, Archbishop Higgins, Joseph Cardinal Higgins!

He held up his glass of scotch in a proposed toast to his well-deserved rise. A ray from the setting sun shot through one of the bay windows in his study and touched the edge of the crystal highball glass. It threw a rainbow on the wall and Joe studied the colors with fascination. The kid who was once happy to have a jelly glass for his powdered milk now drank out of Lismore Waterford!

Maybe he should have served scotch this afternoon when the nuns from the college came instead of that mediocre tea Eve always produced. It's impossible to swallow the stuff without a heavy dose of honey, Joe thought, taking a generous pull on his drink. The scotch burned on its way down. Was he getting a sore throat?

What a piece of luck the nuns' arrival had been! He was just beginning to feel cornered when he heard that doorbell. He was hoping it was an emergency sick call. He'd have to go. No one, not even Fred Davis, would expect him to stay at a meeting when someone was dying.

Fred Davis! Joe Higgins visualized those knobby knuckles of his turning white. What had the old fool called the parish ledger? Creative bookkeeping? Fred had no idea just how creative Joe Higgins could get.

The nuns' arrival was even better than a sick call. They were the "good Sisters" from the renowned Mount, and he was considered a benefactor. This time he took just a sip of his scotch and swallowed it slowly.

Hot damn, what a deal! One scholarship a year from St. Agatha's. It cost him nothing. Today it had saved his hide. At least, for a while.

Even that pea brain Tina Rodiman was beginning to get suspicous. It was impossible to tell what Nick Komsky thought. Just because he looked like Einstein didn't mean he had a brain like Einstein, Joe Higgins consoled himself.

Sister Noreen was no problem. Imagine the nerve of her following him to his suite after the meeting. Telling *him* to come clean. Who did she think she was? He was the pastor. He had set her straight. She'd been so upset, she'd forgotten her antacid tablets in his room. Joe Higgins chuckled and closed his eyes. They burned. Plump, jolly old Noreen was scared to death of scandal. Unless he had her all wrong, Sister Noreen was taken care of.

Jenkin was the one who worried him. The monsignor would bet his brand-new Porsche that George Jenkin was the one who had alerted the other council members. That big, tall drink of water looked harmless, like a balding Gary Cooper.

I should have known better than to get a media person on my team, especially one who likes his drink. Joe Higgins sniffled. His nose tingled. Jenkin's the snake! He's the viper in my bosom! Joe was convinced of it.

First thing tomorrow morning, he'd turn the production of the parish bulletin over to Mrs. Wixson. She could fit it in if she cut down on the time she spent drinking coffee with Eve Glynn in his kitchen.

He'd call George Jenkin and thank him for his dedicated service to the parish. All he had to do then was wait until the whole unfortunate affair blew over. In two weeks, no one would even remember that they'd met.

Joe Higgins sat up with a start. The room was dark. His mouth was furry. I must have dozed off, he thought, reaching over to turn on the lamp. And no wonder. This afternoon's meeting had been exhausting. The light on his message machine was blinking. Odd that not even the ringing of the phone had awakened him. No doubt the message was from Ed Singleton. Ed would be wondering what had happened. Joe picked up his glass. He'd just finish his drink, then call his friend.

Numbness spread through Joe's hand. It must have fallen

asleep, too, he thought. Unable to keep a tight grip, the delicate crystal slipped through his fingers. He watched helplessly as it bounced once, twice, three times on the rug.

"Thank God," he said aloud, when it came to rest on the thick shag. All at once, tears rose in his eyes. He felt the same relief he had once felt as a small child, saved from the licking he would surely get if he broke one of Mum's glasses.

What was wrong with him? He shook his head. He was no longer that Joe Higgins, Joe the butterfingers. Now he was Monsignor Joseph P. Higgins, pastor of St. Agatha's, one of the largest and most affluent parishes in the entire Archdiocese of San Francisco.

A sudden spasm shot through his entire body. His mouth burned. Nausea swept over him. What was happening? Should he call Ed Singleton or should he dial 911?

Shakily, Joe rose from his leather chair and took a step forward. The telephone seemed miles away. He needed the toilet.

Wiping his eyes, he staggered toward his bathroom. The room blurred. Only the white of the toilet itself was clear. His legs were too rubbery to hold him up. Lowering himself to the floor, he crawled forward feeling the cold of the tiles under his palms. Crazily, he wondered if the knees of his good pants were getting soiled.

Reaching out, Monsignor Higgins hugged the base of the toilet and vomited. Retching, he vomited again and again.

Slowly fear replaced the emptiness he felt. What was happening to him? He gulped in short, nervous breaths. Even holding tight to the rim of the toilet bowl, his body swayed. Frightened, he sat on the floor and leaned against the wall to keep from falling. Most of the feeling was gone from his arms and legs. They were numb and heavy. The rest of his body felt as if a thousand pins were sticking it.

This can't be happening to me, Joe Higgins thought, struggling to breathe. His ears were ringing. It can't be!

"Oh, God. Oh, dear God," he prayed earnestly, "be merciful to me. Be merciful to me, a sinner." All at once, a blinding light shone in his eyes. Its radiance blotted out everything else.

❧❧❧

Even after Sister Mary Helen soaked in a hot tub and said five decades of her rosary, she was still wide awake. Turning on her bedside lamp, she reached for the latest Linda Grant mystery. Halfway to the nightstand, her arm froze. If I start reading I'll be up until dawn, she thought, listening to the night sounds creaking in the convent hallway.

The central heating belched, then went on. The temperature must have dropped. She'd never get to sleep now with that blasted heater on! Everyone knows people sleep better in the cold, she fussed. Or, at least, they should.

Throwing back the bed covers, she got up and lifted her soft turquoise robe from its hook in the closet. Her best bet was to get herself a glass of warm milk and maybe a buttered graham cracker to go with it.

Quietly, Mary Helen made her way down the dim convent hallway. No lights shone under any doors on either side. It must be late if even young Sister Anne's room was dark. Mary Helen squinted at the dial of her wristwatch. She was almost certain it read quarter of twelve.

Loud ragged snores came from behind old Sister Donata's door and echoed in the silent hallway. It was amazing Donata didn't wake herself up. She crept past Sister Therese's room. Not surprisingly, Therese was talking in her sleep. In a steady, unintelligible prattle, she seemed to be driving home her point.

Reaching the staircase, Mary Helen took a firm hold of the banister and made her way down.

Once at the bottom, she paused to listen. The grandfather clock in the Sisters' Room ticked noisily and the filter in the fish tank bubbled in rumba rhythm.

There was another sound, the sound of someone or something moving. The noise was coming from the kitchen. Ignoring the shiver of fear skittering up her spine, she moved forward warily. Surely it must be one of the other Sisters who couldn't sleep either.

"Yoo-hoo?" she whispered, approaching the swinging door that led to the kitchen. She didn't want to scare whoever it was to death. Unless, of course, it was a burglar. "Yoo-hoo?" she repeated.

"Yoo-hoo, yourself, old dear!"

Eileen, Mary Helen thought with relief. "Why aren't you asleep?" she asked, pushing open the door. Her eyes smarted in the room's sudden brightness.

With her faded pink chenille bathrobe pulled tightly around her, Eileen stood at the stove stirring something in a saucepan. Her short gray hair stood up around her head like a halo and made Mary Helen wonder what her own looked like.

"I'm not asleep, most likely, for the same reason you aren't," Eileen answered. "Shall I add some milk for you?"

"Please." Mary Helen pulled out a stool and sat at the tiny kitchen table. With satisfaction, she noted that the graham crackers were already there.

"I can't seem to get that meeting at St. Agatha's off my mind." Mary Helen buttered one double cracker for Eileen and one for herself.

"Me, neither." Eileen tapped her spoon on the side of the pan.

"What do you suppose it was all about?"

"I've no idea. But you could cut the tension in that dining room with a cleaver," she said, placing the mugs on the table.

"I was more afraid that they were about to cleaver one another." Mary Helen sipped her milk. Eileen must have added just a drop or two of brandy. The liquid felt warm and comforting all the way down.

"I've never seen either Sister Noreen or Professor Komsky so upset. I can't imagine what was going on." The recent highly publicized scandals involving the Catholic clergy in San Francisco popped unbidden to her mind. "Or maybe, it's more that I don't want to imagine."

Eileen leaned forward and patted her hand. "Have no fear, my friend, nothing travels faster than bad news. We'll find out soon enough what it's all about, whether we want to or not."

❧❧❧

Back in her own bed, Mary Helen began to feel drowsy at last. The drink helped, of course, but somehow knowing that Eileen was awake and stewing helped to relax her, too. Maybe there was some truth in the old adage, "Misery loves company."

She snuggled down under the covers, feeling no compunction whatsoever for turning off the thermostat. All the Sisters would sleep better, even if they didn't realize that it was she they had to thank for it.

Mary Helen pulled her comforter over her ears, burying herself in its warmth like "the grain of wheat" in this morning's gospel. John's words jumped into her sleepy mind: "Unless a grain of wheat falls to the earth and dies, it remains just a grain of wheat. But if it dies, it produces much fruit. . . . The man who loves his life will lose it. . . . "

Inexplicably, the familiar words filled Mary Helen with sudden compassion. She ached for all those out there in the darkness and the cold who would lose their lives on this chilly March night.

Have mercy on them, O Lord, she prayed earnestly. Tears burned her tired eyes. Have mercy on them all, but especially on those who will die alone this night and who have no one else to pray for them.

Later she would say that she had known something sinister had happened. But, really, that night it was only a feeling.

Monday, March 17

❧❧❧

Feast of St. Patrick,
Apostle to Ireland

Despite her late night, Sister Mary Helen awoke on Monday morning feeling "full of beans." She hadn't thought of that expression in years although her father had often used it. And this morning it fit her feelings perfectly. She was in high spirits, and why not? Today was St. Patrick's Day, a day of celebration, even if you weren't Irish. But especially if you were!

Before she left her bedroom, she checked to make sure that her plastic shamrock was pinned straight on the lapel of her navy suit. She slipped a chain with a large Celtic cross over her head for good measure.

Even the Bay Area microclimate, as the forecasters were calling the weather these days, seemed to be observing the feast. Walking across the campus toward the chapel, she watched the sun rise, clear and vibrant, over the East Bay hills. Any wisps of fog that even thought of settling in were quickly dissipated in its path.

She paused and savored the sight of the sun bouncing off the steel towers and decks of the Bay Bridge. It was a beautiful bridge. Not only was it considered one of the seven engineering wonders of the world, but it was the only bridge in California, or maybe in the entire country, for all she knew, blessed by a pope!

Never mind that he was Cardinal Eugenio Pacelli when he blessed it in 1936. Shortly after, he did become Pope Pius XII.

Along the path, grape-colored hyacinths were bedded between daffodils with bright coral cups, snapdragons, and perky gold and black pansies. Lucy, the new head gardener, is wonderful, Mary Helen thought, stopping to breathe in the fragrance of a lilac. The woman was turning the holy hill, as generations of wags had called it, into a miniature Filoli, that well-known garden jewel south of the city.

More power to her! Although Sister Therese had complained that the hedge letters MSF which Lucy had planted on the side of one of the hills were a bit ostentatious, even she couldn't find fault with the dazzling colors and floral tapestries the woman was creating.

Most of the nuns were already gathered in the chapel for morning Mass by the time Mary Helen arrived. Quickly, she slid into the pew beside Eileen, whose gray eyes were a little bloodshot, but not too bad, considering. . . .

Sister Anne, decked out in Kelly green pants and a green-and-white printed top, took her place next to the altar and began to lead the nuns through a chorus of "Great and Glorious St. Patrick."

Anne always liked to practice the hymns before Mass. That way, she was almost sure that the group would be able to get through them once Mass started. Even so, on far too many occasions she was left singing a solo.

Despite their best efforts, the nuns were having trouble following along. The ancient hymn sounded so out of place with Anne's guitar accompaniment. Even Anne must have noticed. Before anyone realized it, Sister Cecilia slid onto the organ bench. Suddenly the chapel swelled with deep, resounding chords. The nuns, feeling more comfortable, filled the rafters with their voices.

Poor Father Adams, mistaking the practice for the opening hymn, rushed onto the altar. Sure that he was late, the priest made the sign of the cross. "In the name of the Father and the Son and the Holy Spirit." With an enthusiastic "Amen," the Mass in honor of St. Patrick began!

True to form, Father Adams finished Mass, including a short homily on the saint's life and accomplishments, in under thirty minutes. Had Patrick not lived to the ripe old age of seventy-two, Father might have done it in twenty-five.

Picking up her book for the closing hymn, Mary Helen wondered what Ramón had baked for breakfast. She was hoping for raisin scones.

With a flourish, Sister Cecilia struck the opening chords of "Faith of Our Fathers." Before Anne could start the singing, a white-faced Sister Therese hurried up the side aisle and slipped onto the main altar. She handed Father Adams a small piece of paper and left as quickly as she had come.

The color drained from the priest's face, leaving him as white as his chasuble. Still studying the slip of paper, he raised one hand for attention. Sister Cecilia let her fingers slide from the keyboard. All eyes were on him.

Clearing his throat, Father Adams said, "Your prayers are asked for the repose of the soul of Monsignor Joseph P. Higgins, pastor of St. Agatha's." He paused while a collective gasp spread through the small congregation.

"His housekeeper found him this morning," the priest continued. "Apparently, he died some time during the night."

"Who died?" old Sister Donata turned and asked in a stage whisper.

"Monsignor Higgins from St. Agatha's," Mary Helen mouthed.

"What did he die of?" Sister Donata inquired.

Mary Helen shrugged. "Father didn't say."

"Am I wrong, or didn't you just deliver Irish soda bread to the poor man yesterday?" Donata asked, a twinkle in her soft brown eyes.

❦❧

The telephone rang four times before Inspector Dennis Gallagher picked it up. "Homicide," he said, then looked across his desk at his partner, Kate Murphy. "Would you repeat that?"

Kate couldn't remember ever seeing his face get so furiously red so fast. And that was saying something! The two homicide detectives had been partners for nearly eight years and Gallagher was not a man noted for his patience.

Kate, herself, would never be considered a paragon of forbearance, either. If anything, she was a match for him. Maybe that was why the two of them managed to get along so well for so long.

Actually, at first glance, Gallagher's flaming face frightened Kate, especially when he clutched the phone receiver with one hand and struggled to unbutton his shirt collar with the other.

Is he having a heart attack? Kate wondered, mentally running through her CPR training. She scanned the near-empty Homicide detail and was glad that, at least, O'Connor was still at his desk in case she need help.

"Are you sure?" Gallagher roared into the receiver in disbelief. Listening to the answer, he groaned and yanked to loosen his bright green tie.

Relieved, Kate realized that it was the message and not the muscle that was giving him such a jolt. Curious now, she sat on the corner of her desk and waited. It didn't take long.

Gallagher slammed down the receiver and glared at Kate. His blue eyes sparked behind the horn-rimmed glasses. "Now they've done it!' He strained the words through clenched teeth. "They've finally done it. And, I, for one, say it serves them right!"

"Who are you talking about?" Kate asked, although she had a pretty good idea.

"You know damn well who I'm talking about. Don't give me that innocent act." Gallagher dropped into his chair and closed his eyes. "Those two old nun pals of yours have stepped into it this time. And this time they are in deep doo-doo."

Kate's mouth went dry. "Did something happen?" she asked, then felt silly. Something always "happened" when

Homicide received a call. "The nuns aren't hurt, are they?"

"Oh, no! Not them." Gallagher shot forward in his swivel chair. "We should be so lucky."

"Denny!" Kate tried to sound shocked. "You don't mean that."

"The hell I don't." Gallagher shook his finger at her. "And, if you were perfectly truthful, you'd admit that you feel the same way, too."

"I most certainly do not," Kate protested, her own temper beginning to fizz. She wasn't really sure if it was because Gallagher was shaking his fat finger at her, a mannerism of his that she hated; or if it was because he was telling her how she felt, another annoying trait he had; or because he had glazed the truth.

Not that she wished those two old dears any real evil. She didn't. Actually, she loved them both. Over the years, they had proved extremely helpful, both personally and in solving several murder cases. Even Gallagher admitted that. But they did have a tendency to become pesty. Maybe tedious was a better word. It might be nice to have a murder case without them underfoot. Kate, however, would rather die than admit it to her partner.

"Are you going to continue raving on, or are you going to tell me what happened?" she asked.

After drawing in a deep breath, Gallagher ran his hand over his bald crown and let out a long-suffering sigh. "You are not going to believe this one, Katie girl. The housekeeper at St. Agatha's rectory went to wake up the monsignor this morning and she found him on his bathroom floor 'asleep with the angels,' to quote her."

"Heart attack?" Kate asked, then realized what a stupid question that was. She really wasn't computing this morning. If they hadn't suspected something "unnatural" about the causes, their phone never would have rung.

Gallagher shrugged. "We'll know more when the lab boys get through. Right now, it looks like some kind of poison."

"And what exactly does the poisoning of the monsignor have to do with our nun friends?" She deliberately emphasized "our." Denny glared at her, as she knew he would.

"*Your* friends," he shot back, "were among the last people to see the good monsignor alive! They came to the rectory at about teatime with Irish soda bread."

He took off his glasses and slowly wiped the lens with the end of his green tie. "Why the hell weren't they in the convent where they belong, saying their prayers, instead of running around?"

"You can hardly call visiting a priest's rectory running around," Kate interjected, although she knew she was wasting her breath. "Any sign of forced entry?"

Gallagher shook his head. "It would be tough to blame this one on a wandering crazy breaking in to poison a perfect stranger."

Slowly, the magnitude of the case dawned on Kate. St. Agatha's, one of the most influential and affluent parishes in the city, was home to several ex-police chiefs and fire chiefs, two ex-governors, assorted other city and county officials, and a number of media types. Monsignor Higgins, although he was no male Mother Teresa, was their pastor and the pressure to find his murderer would be tremendous, especially if this murderer was someone they knew. Especially if two prominent nuns from Mount St. Francis College were among the last people to see the man alive.

In the car on their way to St. Agatha's, Dennis Gallagher filled Kate in on the details. "The paramedics that answered the call thought something looked fishy. Like I told you, we'll know more when the lab is finished. For reasons known only to God, and He ain't telling, the lieutenant gave us the case," Gallagher said.

"Do you have to tailgate?" Kate asked, bracing herself on the dashboard when Gallagher slammed on the brakes. "How do you know the nuns stopped by the rectory yesterday afternoon?"

"Because the housekeeper, one Eve Glynn, originally from the Old Sod, said so. According to the lieutenant, when the patrolman, John O'Reilly by name, responded to the call, she was rambling on about some evil meeting the monsignor held in the rectory yesterday afternoon.

"O'Reilly couldn't tell if she thought the meeting was evil or that holding it on the Sunday—which, by the way, is her evening off—was the problem. Anyway, it seems that she wrote down the name of everyone who attended, even before O'Reilly asked for them. She showed it to him, then insisted that she'd keep it to give to the man in charge. Anyway, according to O'Reilly, who should appear on the list but the SFPD's two favorite nuns."

"What do you suppose possessed the housekeeper to write a list of attendees?" Kate asked, relieved that the Sisters were not the only ones at the meeting.

"Five or six cop shows a week on the TV would be my guess." Gallagher snorted. "I'm beginning to think there are a lot of people in the city who know more about our job than we do from just watching that damn boob tube."

Inspector Gallagher pulled up the car in front of St. Agatha's rectory. A small crowd had gathered on the front walk and seemed to be holding a silent vigil. Several women had rosary beads in their hands.

"Who are they?" Gallagher asked the patrolman, who looked relieved to see them.

"The morning Mass group," O'Reilly said. "Seems when no one showed up to say the Mass, they got worried."

At the front door, a short, small-boned Filipino priest with an anxious look on his round face waited for them. "I'm Father Alex Calvo." He seemed unsure of whether or not to shake hands with Gallagher, then decided against it. Not to touch Kate was a forgone conclusion.

"I'm the assistant here," he said in a soft, breathy voice. "This is Father Cletus Greene." He turned to introduce a tall, painfully thin man with a bushy brown mustache covering his upper lip and the corners of his mouth.

Kate knew that she'd remember this priest's name because green was also the color of his face. "Are you all right, Father?" she asked, following him into the rectory's large foyer.

An elaborate chandelier hung from the ceiling and, if Kate wasn't mistaken, that was a genuine Persian carpet on the floor. Several doors led from the entry with all but one closed. Kate suspected that they probably led to individual conference rooms or to the priests' private quarters.

"Father Greene, are you all right?" she repeated.

Father Calvo answered for him. "Cletus is the one Eve, our housekeeper, called when she failed to raise the monsignor

37

this morning." He gave a sympathetic smile. "Poor Cletus forced the door open and went into the suite. Eve and he found him. May he rest in peace."

"The smell was awful," Father Greene said. His hand few up to his mustache and he gagged.

Kate Murphy knew the feeling. It was one you never quite get over. "Why don't you go for a little walk, get some fresh air, Father," she said, then glanced at the Filipino priest. Enormous beads of perspiration stood out on his forehead. "Both of you," she added quickly, "but don't stray too far. We'll need to talk to you in a few minutes."

The moment Kate and Gallagher were alone, a short, round woman in worn blue bedroom slippers appeared from behind one of the doors off the foyer.

"I'm Eveleen Glynn," she said in almost a whisper. "I was in my kitchen and I heard your voices." Kate noted a hint of a brogue.

"The monsignor's this way, Officers." Twisting one corner of her apron, she nodded toward the staircase at the far end of the foyer. "They call me Eve," she continued. "I am the housekeeper here at St. Agatha's. And that," she pointed to the open door where a weeping woman huddled miserably behind a desk, "is Charlotte Wixson. She's the parish secretary."

Mrs. Wixson's brunette head rose and she looked up long enough to give a perfunctory nod and blow her nose.

"I have no patience at all with women who fall apart at the slightest hint of anything wrong," Eve announced to no one in particular.

They began to climb the stairs. "I'd hardly call the sudden,

unaccounted-for death of Monsignor Higgins a 'slight hint,' "
Kate said.

Eve Glynn sniffed, but did not reply. Instead, looking annoyed, she pointed to an open door and folded her thick arms. The monsignor's suite was crowded with familiar faces from the coroner's office and the crime lab.

Shaking hands with a couple of the lab boys, Gallagher made his way toward the bathroom where most of the action and, presumably, the body seemed to be.

Kate hung back in the doorway with Eve. "The patrolman who responded to your call," she said, "mentioned that you'd made a list."

At first, Eve just stared at Kate though her smudged glasses. She acted as if she hadn't quite heard. Was she refusing to answer or did she not consider Kate the "man" in charge? Whichever the reason, Kate was having none of it!

"Your list?" she repeated in a firm voice.

Still without a word, Eve dug into her apron pockets. She pulled out a folded piece of paper torn from a lined yellow legal pad and handed it to Kate.

"I'm not one of those women who falls apart," Eve muttered, making her point. "My cousin, the sainted Monsignor Concannon, always told me, 'Keep a cool head and dry pants, Eve, and you'll be all right.' "

Struggling to keep a straight face, Kate unfolded the paper and studied it. Sure enough! O'Reilly had remembered correctly. Sister Mary Helen and Sister Eileen were listed last. First or last, it would be good to hear their version of this "evil meeting."

Quickly Kate Murphy made her way downstairs to Mrs. Wixson's office where she had seen the phone.

❦

The Sisters were still in chapel when Mary Helen heard quick footsteps coming down the side aisle, and felt a bony hand on her shoulder. They both belonged to Sister Therese.

"You are wanted on the telephone." Therese's dark eyes narrowed disapprovingly.

"Do you know who it is?" Mary Helen asked.

Sister Therese sniffed. "The woman didn't give her name, but if you ask me," she paused dramatically, "the voice sounds very much like that of Kate Murphy from the police department."

Sister Mary Helen picked up the receiver. "Good morning," she said and was surprised to hear the ice in Kate Murphy's voice. She must be using her official persona, Mary Helen thought, feeling a chill creep up her spine. But why on me?

Kate's next words made the reason abundantly clear. "I understand that you and Sister Eileen were among the last people to see Monsignor Higgins alive," she said. Before Mary Helen could answer, she went on. "Although we're waiting for lab reports to confirm it, we suspect that he was poisoned."

"The Irish soda bread." Mary Helen groaned, her mind jumping ahead of Kate's words, not really listening to what Kate said. That is, until she heard her ask, "Do you want Inspector Gallagher and me to come there, or will you be able to meet us at St. Agatha's?"

"We'll come to the rectory," Mary Helen blurted out. Visions of Sister Cecilia's solemn face, Sister Therese's sniff, Anne's wide grin, and old Donata's miss-nothing eyes danced like anything but sugar plums in her head. "We'll be right there," she repeated a little louder. She wanted to make very sure Kate and Gallagher didn't show up at Mount St. Francis College.

Fortunately, no one had signed out the convent Nova for this early hour. While Mary Helen saw to the transportation, Eileen gathered up some coffee and scones for the ride. Both nuns had worn their Aran sweaters to Mass.

"Even a condemned woman gets a last meal," Eileen said when she finally reached the car.

"Now is really not the time for convict humor," Mary Helen snapped. Something in Kate's manner had made her anxious and her mood gradually began to infect Eileen's.

Slowly the two nuns made their way across the city. They took the crowded Park Presidio Boulevard through Golden Gate Park. Then, despite all its signals, they decided on Nineteenth Avenue. "They say if you hit the signals just right, you never have to stop," Eileen said brightly, then sighed with relief when they hit the red. Apparently, neither one of them was very eager to get to St. Agatha's until they had time to sort things out.

For several minutes, they rode in silence. Small clutches of people huddled in kiosks on either side of the wide boulevard waiting for the Muni. Almost everyone wore something green.

On the Sunset side of Golden Gate Park some city designer with a real plan for the neighborhood had named the avenues in alphabetical order—Irving, Judah, Kirkham.

They counted off the blocks, getting closer and closer to St. Agatha's.

"Have you ever seen so many honorary Irishmen?" Eileen said, watching a group of Asian schoolgirls giggling on the corner. Their straight black hair was festooned with bright green ribbons. While the girls squealed and danced, the wind picked up the ribbons and twirled them above their heads like kite tails.

Eileen squirmed nervously in the front seat. "How in the world did we get into this mess?" she said finally.

Mary Helen didn't need to ask what mess she meant. "That blasted soda bread." She pulled around a pokey driver only to meet him again at the next stoplight.

Lawton. Moraga was next. On their right was the Shriners' Hospital for Crippled Children. Its wide front lawn was a playground of wooden leprechauns, complete with wild orange hair and top hats, pointing toward an enormous pot of gold.

They were getting close. "Tell me again, what exactly did Kate say?" Eileen asked.

"As I explained, I really was too shocked to listen as carefully as I should have," Mary Helen admitted. "If I remember correctly, she said that the police think that Monsignor Higgins, God rest him, was poisoned. And that housekeeper. What's her name?"

"Eve Glynn," Eileen supplied.

Mary Helen nodded. "She told the police that there was an awful meeting going in the rectory yesterday afternoon."

"She was right about that," Eileen said. "Anyone with eyes to see or ears to hear couldn't have missed the tension in that room." She shuddered at the memory and turned toward Mary Helen. "But we weren't involved in that," she said reasonably.

Mary Helen began a series of right-hand turns that would eventually bring her to the left side of the boulevard. Obviously, the city designers had not thought out the need for a left-hand turn as well as they had the street names.

"You're right," she said, waiting for yet another stoplight to change, "we did just walk into a very tense situation. Unfortunately, the man did not die of tension. He died of poison and we came with the soda bread."

Eileen stared at the rows of attached houses stretching up and down the avenues, then at Mary Helen. The dim light in the car darkened her gray eyes. "I'm sure that Kate can't for a minute think that we had anything to do with the monsignor's death," she said, more to herself than to Mary Helen. "Why would we want to kill the man? He was one of our benefactors. Besides, no one else is even sick, are they? You can't poison just one piece of a loaf, can you?"

No one else ate any of it, Mary Helen wanted to say, but at the moment her mouth was too dry to speak.

❧❧❧

From force of habit, Fred Davis, his heart thumping, grabbed his bedside telephone on the first ring. There was really no reason to be nervous. He knew that. There was no one else in the house, no one to wake up since Mildred had passed away. The thought of round, warm Mildred lying next to him, snoring softly, turned his insides into lumpy mush.

"Hello," he said, running his thumbnail under the waist-

43

band of his flannel pajamas. The damn things itched. One of these days I'll have to wash them, he thought, trying to remember how long it had been since he had. Then he realized that it might be better if he didn't remember. Mildred always took care of the wash.

"Mr. Davis?" the unfamiliar voice of a young woman asked.

"Yes, this is Fred Davis." He needed a cup of coffee. He hoped there was some. Yesterday morning he had scraped the bottom of the can. He couldn't remember whether or not there was another can on the shelf in the pantry. He'd meant to stop at the store on his way home from the rectory yesterday afternoon, but after that damn meeting he hadn't given coffee another thought.

Besides, Mildred always saw to the coffee. "That's in your column," he'd say, and good-natured Mildred would just laugh.

Typical of his accountant training, he always thought of things in columns, even their marriage. In Mildred's column were washing, coffee, shopping, meals, birthdays, Christmas, nursing the sick, making dentist appointments, the garden, PTA meetings, and driving their daughter, who was now an adult and driving herself. In his column were— at the moment, he couldn't think of exactly what was there, except to take care of the money and to take care of Mildred.

"Are you still there, Mr. Davis?" the voice on the phone asked.

"Yes." Fred's throat was swollen with longing for his wife.

"This is Inspector Kate Murphy," the voice informed him.

"Inspector of what?" Fred asked, leery that this voice was

going to try to sell him aluminum siding. What time was it, anyway? Fred's eyes burned and he squinted at the alarm clock. Seven-thirty! "What kind of an inspector gets to work at seven-thirty in the morning?" he asked.

"A Homicide inspector, sir," she said, all business. "I'm with the San Francisco Police Department."

Fred Davis slumped back on his pillow as if all his strength had suddenly been flushed, and waited for the bad news.

"This morning Monsignor Joseph Higgins was found dead," she began, her voice revealing no emotion.

"A heart attack?" Davis blurted out, then felt stupid. Homicide detectives don't call at seven-thirty in the morning about heart attacks. What must she think? Probably nothing. He forced himself to take a deep breath and let it out slowly. In her line of business, she must hear dozens of stupid questions, see all kinds of reactions.

As though he hadn't even spoken, Inspector Murphy continued. "Suspicious circumstances. . . . When we get the lab reports. . . ."

Fred was scarcely listening to her. His mind was scrambling. How should he react to the news? Devastated? Outraged? Shocked, but strong and faith-filled? The only way he knew that he shouldn't react was the way he really felt—elated. It was done! The scoundrel was dead. Now his Mildred would be saved.

" . . . The meeting at the rectory yesterday afternoon?" Fred heard the inspector ask, although he had no idea what the first part of her question had been.

His heart began to thump again, each beat echoing in his ears. "What is it you're saying about yesterday's meeting, Inspector? I'm afraid I'm not taking all this in as quickly as I might."

"Of course, Mr. Davis." Inspector Murphy sounded understanding.

He thought from her tone that she might even be feeling sorry for him. Maybe the shocked, loyal old parishioner stance was the one to assume. That would be easy. Six weeks ago, it would have been true. But that was before the trouble with the money and Mildred.

The betrayal he felt at his discovery *still* made his whole body burn. Perspiration formed under Fred's armpits and trickled down his ribs. He was clutching the telephone receiver so hard that his knuckles were eggshell white, yet it slipped in his wet palm.

"Do you think the meeting yesterday had something to do with our monsignor's death?" Fred stopped. He'd better not sound too naive. Once the inspector discovered the reason for the meeting, she couldn't help but suspect it as a possible motive. And someone was sure to tell her.

If he were a betting man, he'd lay odds on that big-mouth Tina Rodiman. He supposed Tina was a nice enough little thing, really. Pregnant half the time, as far as he could see, but she was the kind of woman Fred Davis detested.

She was what Fred referred to as someone "who could talk to a table leg and figure they both got something out of it!" He caught himself before he chuckled into the phone. How could he explain to the Homicide detective that he was laughing at an old joke when he was supposed to be a stunned and grieving parishioner? Actually, it had been Mildred's joke. She had read it in a book.

Fred was so preoccupied that he nearly missed the inspector's answer. All he heard was, " . . . St. Agatha's rectory in about half an hour?" It was a question.

"You want me at the rectory at about eight?" he asked. This should cement her impression that he was a shocked and aging parishioner. Perhaps the term *feeble* might even enter her mind. More's the better, he thought.

Fred Davis hung up, showered, and shaved quickly. *"I'll be loving you always . . ."* he hummed, studying his reflection in the bathroom mirror. Wrinkles, like small cuts, formed around the corners of his mouth.

"With a love that's true, always," he sang. That had been "their" song, his and Mildred's. He chose his dark wool "funeral" suit from his side of the closet. He hadn't worn it for over a year, not since Mildred was buried, actually. It seemed fitting for the occasion.

He checked his shoulders for dandruff and made sure that his wire-frame glasses were straight on his nose. Mildred would be proud. He practiced making a solemn face in the mirror until he thought he had it right. This morning, his perpetually red-rimmed eyes were to his advantage. They made him look as if he might have been crying.

Fred opened his front door onto a bright, crisp morning. Across the street his neighbor had unfurled a large Irish flag in honor of St. Patrick's Day. The flag was on a pole jutting out from a living room window. Its bottom edge hung nearly to the top of the garage door.

Watching the gold and green and white snap smartly in the ocean breeze, Fred felt like an Irish patriot off to his destiny. Maybe James Connelly before the Easter Rising! "We

47

are going out to be slaughtered," Connelly had declared. Or some such thing.

Not me, Fred thought, checking his front door to make sure it was locked. I'm off to play the role of my life. When he arrived at St. Agatha's, he knew he must act as if he were sad about Monsignor Higgins's death when, truthfully, the only thing that could make him happier was to know that Joe Higgins had suffered, as Fred himself had suffered, as his Mildred might be suffering right now.

Taking care of the money and Mildred were the only things that had been in Fred's column during their long marriage. He had done all right with the money. That had never been a problem. But, he admitted, he had not done too well taking care of Mildred while she was alive. Now that she was dead, he sure as hell was going to do everything in his power to make up for it, Monsignor Joseph Higgins be damned!

❧❦❧❦

Surprisingly, Sister Noreen didn't notice the commotion next door at the rectory until after breakfast when she was on the second floor of the convent. More precisely, until she was standing over the small sink in the corner of her bedroom brushing her teeth.

Pulling back the edge of the curtain far enough to peek out, she saw the cause of it. Several police cars, their red and blue light bars flashing, were parked in front of the rectory.

Her stomach knotted as she rinsed out her mouth. Automatically, she reached into her pocket for her roll of Tums, but they weren't there. I must have left them somewhere, she thought, finding a new roll inside her nightstand.

She hadn't expected the police so soon. She wondered who'd called them. Probably Eve. That Eve never missed a thing. And she must have made quite a fuss to have them send more than one car. Was it really necessary to flash their lights?

Cautiously flipping back the curtain edge again, Sister Noreen took a second look. Sure enough! There was Eve, still in her blue bedroom slippers, standing as important as you please, next to a red-headed woman who looked like an official of some kind.

Noreen had watched enough police shows on the television to know that the woman could be the officer in charge.

Why don't they all go inside? Noreen thought, her stomach churning. Can't they get out of the way before the parents and the children start arriving for school? Bad enough that every busybody on the block—and their number was legion—had seen the squad cars. What can be gained from continuing to stand in the street?

Don't they know I have enough to do just running the place, Sister Noreen stewed, without having to answer a million questions about Monsignor's business? She rinsed off her oversize bifocals.

And there would be a zillion questions, not only from the parents and children, but from the teachers and the old-time parishioners, not to mention the other nuns!

Tightening her lower lip, Noreen set the glasses on her short nose and studied her reflection in the mirror of her medicine cabinet. She couldn't imagine why she'd allowed the optometrist to talk her into those glasses. She looked exactly like one of those white-faced owls—down to the freckles scattered around her eyes—that some oil company or other was trying to save from extinction.

She pinched her cheeks in an attempt to raise a little color, but it was no use. For one long moment, Sister Noreen toyed with the idea of pretending she had the flu. Not that she'd need to pretend very much. Her stomach was upset. Her head ached and she felt weak all over. Surely her face was pale enough.

But she knew it would do no good. Someone was sure to come to her room and knock on her door. The only real way to avoid the issue was to be dead. That was difficult to fake.

Sister Noreen checked her wristwatch. Her teachers would be arriving any minute, concerned and curious. Although she knew that she should be on her way, Noreen sank down into her easy chair and closed her eyes. Taking several long, deliberate breaths, she tried to gather her wits. Shock and sadness would be the best ways to handle the news.

How, she wondered, had the cat got out of the bag so quickly? "A whisper in the ear is louder than a shout from the highest hill," her mother used to say. What had happened was no mere whispered indiscretion.

Noreen's stomach burned. She needed another antacid. She had just popped one in her mouth when the inevitable knock sounded on the bedroom door.

"Noreen?" a soft voice called. "Are you still here?"

Noreen was tempted not to answer.

"Noreen?" The knocking persisted.

Small mercies! At least, it was Sister Bernice who had come to get her. Nothing seemed to faze Bernice, who could be as silent as the stars when the circumstances called for it.

"Come in." Noreen, hoping that she sounded calm and in control, pushed herself up from her easy chair.

Cautiously, Bernice cracked open the door. Her eyes were wide and her usually ruddy face had lost some of its color. "It's the monsignor," she said quietly.

Noreen steeled herself for the announcement.

Bernice cleared her throat. "He's dead!" she blurted out.

Her words hit Noreen's stomach like punches.

"Dead?" she asked, suddenly light-headed. That was not at all what she expected Bernice to say. "Monsignor is dead?"

"A police detective, an Inspector Kate Murphy." Bernice's words sounded far away. "She wants you to go over to the rectory as soon as possible."

Woodenly, Noreen followed Bernice down the convent front steps. He's dead. The monsignor's dead. She repeated to herself, trying to get used to the idea. Pompous, high and mighty, above the law, J. P. Higgins is dead! The very notion of it made Noreen a little giddy.

God is good! she thought, stopping just inside the convent front door to gather her wits and straighten the collar of her suit jacket. Death is far easier to explain than that awful business of yesterday's meeting.

May he rest in peace! Noreen prayed, slipping another antacid pill into her mouth. She pulled open the front door. And may he take any breath of that awful scandal to the graveyard with him.

Head down, Sister Noreen walked toward the rectory, scarcely noticing the gathering crowd. Her mind was too full of all the bits of business she'd need to see to in order to give the pastor of St. Agatha's a fitting funeral.

George Jenkin jerked at his feet, trying to free them from his bed clothes. He was breathless now, chasing the man down the long, narrow church aisle. The music from the huge pipe organ rang in his ears. Ignoring it, George reached out, then lunged, missing again the tail of the black serge jacket by inches.

Relentless, George pushed ahead, his legs tangled and numb now, and heavy with the effort of running. The stained-glass windows cast an eerie glow across the pews and striped his fingers and his lower arms with puce and chartreuse and pale pink.

The pipe organ was deafening. The little twerp of an organist who demanded a bloody fortune for his service seemed stuck on one note. Over and over it blared until George thought his head might split open like an overripe pumpkin and his brains spew out in every direction.

Again, he dove forward. He'd catch him yet. And when he did, watch out! But like the silver fox that he was, Monsignor Higgins shifted clear of George's grasp, turning back just long enough to sneer.

Groaning, George put his hands over his ears. "Stop!" he shouted, then realized that the blast he heard was not St. Agatha's pipe organ, but the ringing of his own telephone. He reached for it, knocking the receiver off the hook.

"Hello," he croaked once he had recovered it. His eyelids were glued together. He must have really tied one on. His head throbbed. His throat felt dry and sandy, and his mouth tasted as if it were full of dirty socks.

That's the trouble with Jim Beam, George thought, trying to raise his head from the pillow. It is smooth going down, then it hits you with a sledge hammer. His neck felt as stiff and unbending as an iron pipe.

"George Jenkin?" a businesslike female voice inquired.

"Yes." He tried to sound civil although he had no idea if it was necessary. What time was it, anyway?

"This is Inspector Kate Murphy, San Francisco Police Department." Her words acted like a dash of ice-cold water.

George sat up quickly, too quickly. A wave of nausea swept over him. He covered the phone, hoping she had not heard him dry heave.

Perspiration broke out on his forehead and on the palms of his hands. What had he done? He had no memory of anything after he poured his fourth drink. Or was it his fifth? The blackouts had been worse since Stella left him.

After twenty-eight years of marriage and raising three kids, she had left him. The thought of it still made him burn all over again. And that scum of a monsignor had not only encouraged her, but suggested that she try to get a church annulment.

When Stella had told him, George had really gone on a bender. "I'll show you *annulment*," he had shouted and swung at her in his drunken rage.

George's stomach was jumping. He began to shiver. "Get me out of this one, God," he prayed, waiting for Inspector Murphy to continue, "and I swear, this time I'll take the pledge." He stopped, fully expecting to hear God give a gigantic belly laugh.

"Mr. Jenkin, this morning Monsignor Higgins was found

dead," the inspector explained briskly, as if finding dead bodies was an everyday occurrence.

I guess for her it is, George thought.

"We understand that you attended a meeting yesterday afternoon. . . ." Her words went on, but George had stopped listening.

Monsignor Higgins was dead! George's lips stuck on his dry teeth. Finally, someone had killed him! Someone had actually made George's recurring dream a reality.

After agreeing to be at St. Agatha's rectory as soon as possible, George Jenkin stumbled into the shower. Someone had finally put the slimy so-and-so out of his misery before he could do any more harm to anyone, he thought, turning on the faucets. As the hot water beat on his back, he prayed harder than he'd ever prayed before that that someone wasn't he.

⚜⚜⚜

Tina Rodiman had decided to walk to the rectory. After her phone call from Inspector Kate Murphy, she was shaking all over. She lived close by and, if the truth be told, with the state her nerves were in, she didn't trust herself to drive.

As she walked along the avenue, nibbling one waxy red lip, she wondered if she'd remembered to give the kids their lunches. Actually, she wasn't too sure they all had on both shoes. It was that kind of a morning. She was tying Mary Rose's oxfords when the inspector's call came. Tina remembered that much. At least, her daughter was shod. She remembered the boys searching for their school shoes, but as hard as she tried, she couldn't remember if they'd found them. What she did remember was Mike whining and Mark pouting and Kevin spilling his milk before she slapped each of them harder than she had intended. In chorus they began to wail, the sound making her cringe.

Her husband would be upset when the boys told him. And they surely would, his boys. They knew Tony disapproved of her hitting the children, no matter what the provocation. Well, he could be as disapproving as he pleased. Tina felt tears sting her eyes at the unfairness of it all. These breakfast battles never seemed to break out while he was at the table. He was always long gone when they did.

Many a morning, after the dishes and housework were over, she had walked down this same avenue searching for an adult. Someone, anyone, she could talk to without using baby talk or cutting up pancakes.

Throwing back her shoulders, Tina took a deep breath and tried to enjoy the crisp morning air. A sharp breeze ran like fingers through her brown curly hair. Shading her eyes, she gazed down the avenue. It was clear all the way to Ocean Beach where whitecaps sparkled in the sunlight.

Not that she didn't love her babies and her husband. She did. And Tony was not a bad husband. He was really a very good husband and a good father. He works hard and provides well, Tina thought, struggling to be fair. He is upbeat most of the time and involved with his kids and his parish. That's why he started coaching soccer, which seems to consume most of his free time. That is, before he got involved in this parish bingo business to raise money for St. Agatha's School. Not only was he involved, he insisted that Tina get involved, too.

"It will be good for you to get out of the house, honey," he had said.

To Tina, "getting out of the house" meant something more like going out to dinner and a show or taking an evening course at City College.

But Tony had been so enthusiastic. He was enthusiastic about everything. Tina kicked at a loose stone on the sidewalk. Even about having more children. Her husband didn't believe in birth control of any kind, even though Tina had had several miscarriages.

"We'll take what God sends," he'd said last week when she told him she thought she was pregnant again. In the morning, he'd given her a pleased little smile on his way out the front door, as if he had done something wonderful. Why not? He was not the one with morning sickness and swelling feet and backaches and labor pains.

He was not the one who changed diapers and wiped runny noses and cleaned up after sick stomachs. He's not the one who gets blamed for not getting the kid's soccer uniforms washed on time and for losing those blasted school shoes. He is just "Daddy" who comes home and hugs you and plays with you.

Tina wiped an angry tear from her cheek. Why would Tony believe in birth control? she asked herself reasonably. To be honest, on that subject, he was more Catholic than Holy Mother Church, Herself. One of these days, Tina feared she would blow her top and tell him so in no uncertain terms.

She could just see that insufferable, forbearing expression on his face as she ranted on. Just like the expression he'd

56

worn last night when she'd told him about the meeting at the rectory.

The meeting at the rectory! The very thought of it . . . she felt her face flush with anger. She covered her burning cheeks with her hands. After all the time she'd spent setting up those heavy tables and those blasted chairs for bingo! After all the hot dogs she'd boiled and served. And all the pull tabs she'd hawked for a dollar apiece because she thought the money was helping the school. Only to find out. . . .

When she'd told Tony, she was so angry that even her ears felt as if they were on fire. She had slammed down her fists on the kitchen table and kicked her high-heeled shoes across the food-spotted linoleum. She felt a little ashamed when the boys ran for their bedrooms and even little Mary Rose scurried off after them.

It seemed as if the harder Tony tried to calm her down with his pious platitudes, the more angry she became.

"No one is perfect," he had said, "and we are all sinners."

"What are you going to do about it?" she had glared accusingly at him. Then the words came tumbling out. "I, for one, could kill the man!"

Her husband, looking shocked, had said, "Let's sleep on it, honey."

Well, they had slept on it, as far apart as two people could get in one bed. This morning she was even more upset than she had been last night, if such a thing was possible—so upset that she'd forgotten to put on her jewelry.

Something about wearing jewelry always seemed to cheer

Tina. On days when she felt especially trapped, she'd wear a ring on every finger, except, of course, her thumbs. She'd put on a stack of bracelets and long dangling earrings. She felt better when she watched the stones in her rings sparkle in the light, or heard the soft, delicate clink of bracelets. The sensual brush of silver or gold along the sides of her neck soothed her.

Tina was glad that ankle bracelets were back in style. She'd had a half dozen stashed away, just in case. Most mornings she fastened one around her left ankle.

This morning she'd fully intended to wear her good bangle bracelets and the jade green shamrock earrings. Tony had given the earrings to her years ago as a surprise in honor of St. Patrick's Day. To his credit, he still remembered to bring home thoughtful little surprises sometimes. She wondered for a moment if she should go back to the house and get her jewelry, at least the earrings.

No. She was too close to the rectory. Eve Glynn had undoubtedly seen her from some upstairs window. The housekeeper never missed a thing. Besides, Inspector Murphy was waiting for her. Tina felt weak in the knees. In a matter of minutes, she would be walking into a situation that no amount of jewelry would be able to help.

❧❧❧

For the first time in months, Debbie Stevens parked her car in the spot behind the rectory. My spot, she thought. That secluded space where the overhang from the hydrangea bushes and the rhododendron trees hid it from the prying eyes of the parishioners. As if they were dumb enough not to know that something was going on unless they saw her car parked at the rectory.

Debbie switched off the ignition and rested her head against the back of the car seat. She closed her eyes. The lids felt sandy from lack of sleep.

Being so secretive had been Joe's idea. Actually, the whole thing had been Joe's idea. Now, she was left to face the music. The police were inside waiting for some answers.

Forcing herself to sit up, Debbie checked her lipstick in the rearview mirror. The lipstick was fine, but she noticed that several new wrinkles had formed at the corners of her mouth.

She examined her short hair, admiring her new cut. It accented her high cheekbones. That's what Rene, her new hairdresser, had said. She tended to agree with him. Why not? The cut-styling, as he called it, had cost her a small fortune.

But it was worth every cent if it improved her self-esteem. That was what her psychoanalyst had assured her at their last session. God knew, at seventy-five dollars an hour, Debbie chose to believe her.

Luckily, Debbie had received an excellent education while she was in the convent. With her credentials, her experience, and Joe's connections, she had been able to get a good job. That was the only thing that had gone right for her since she first met Joe Higgins.

She was young and naive. Actually, much as she hated to admit it, when she met him, she'd been more naive than young. Sister Mary Deborah, as she was known, was on a sabbatical.

Her order's Superior had urged her to take one. "It will be a good experience for you," Sister Superior had said. "You've worked hard and you deserve some time to refuel."

The superior had shown Deborah several brochures for sabbatical programs and had encouraged her to choose some place as different from their Wisconsin motherhouse as possible.

"A new experience will be broadening," Sister Superior had insisted.

At the time, neither Sister Superior nor she had the faintest idea of just how new and broadening the experience would prove to be.

Debbie had decided on a program which claimed that it would "liberate your creative power."

When she arrived, Joe Higgins, sophisticated and suave, was already there, seemingly having no trouble with his liberation.

For Deborah, the attraction had been immediate, but she had fought against it, never dreaming how hard she would fall. It had taken Joe a little longer.

That should have been my first clue, Debbie thought, forcing herself to get out of the car.

A small crowd had gathered on either side of the front walk leading to St. Agatha's rectory. Many of them stared at her with open curiosity. Their expressions weren't too different from the one on Sister Superior's face when Debbie had marched into her office one crisp October day not long after she had returned from her sabbatical.

"Sister, there is something I want to tell you," Debbie began gently. Then, realizing that the only good way to tell bad news is fast, she blurted out, "I'm leaving the convent. I want to get married."

When the color returned to Sister Superior's face, she had asked Debbie all the right questions. Although Debbie felt that the Superior had dwelt a little too long on, "Are you sure you're not jumping into this without thinking it through?"

Sister Superior had blanched again when Debbie told her that her intended was a priest. "He's from the Archdiocese of San Francisco," Debbie had added quickly, hoping that Joe Higgins ministering half a continent away from the mother-house would make Sister Superior feel better.

"This week he intends to tell the archbishop that he wants a dispensation, and I'm flying out to meet him. . . ." The puzzled frown on the Superior's face stopped Debbie mid-sentence.

"All the bishops are at a meeting in Baltimore this week," Sister Superior said, a bit distracted. "Are you sure, Sister Mary Deborah, that this is what you both want?" Sister Superior's ponderous blue eyes studied her with—of all things—compassion.

Debbie was furious. She didn't want this old woman's sympathy. Let her save it for those who needed it.

"You just don't know what it's like to be in love, Sister," Debbie said hotly. Without waiting for the Superior to respond, she fled in tears from the office and down the long, deserted motherhouse hallway.

Once outside, Debbie made her way through the mother-house grounds. Gold and red and brilliant amber trees stood out against a denim blue sky as she wound her way down the path to the clearing where the old incinerator burned fiercely.

Standing back from its heat, she reread Joe's letter. "I love you, my sweetest Debbie, my gift from God," he'd written. "I want to spend my every waking—and sleeping—minute with you." She skimmed a few more lines of *love talk*, there would be plenty of time to savor it later, and skipped to the last paragraph. "This week I'm going straight to the Arch's office and asking him for my dispensation. You take care of things on your end. Then, finally, we can be together." Well, today she'd definitely taken care of "her end."

Pulling open the incinerator's heavy door, Debbie had flinched and cowered back from the heat and the roaring of the flames. Removing the thin gold band from the ring finger on her left hand, she studied it.

Old Bishop Armstrong, a saint if there ever was one, had blessed this ring on the day Debbie made her final vows. He had slipped it onto her finger saying reverently, "May this ring be a sign of your profession of the vows of poverty, chastity, and obedience in this congregation. With the help of God's holy grace, may you keep them faithfully all the days of your life."

Deliberately, before she had time for doubts, Debbie had pulled back her arm and flung her ring as far as she could into the roaring, leaping bank of flame. Instantly, the ring was swallowed up. Debbie's stomach pitched, and with a vicious push she slammed the metal door shut.

A thin white strip of flesh where the ring once had been was all that was left to remind her. The memory awoke a deep rage which, like the fire in that old motherhouse incinerator, roared and burned and snapped in Debbie Stevens. It licked at her mind whenever she thought of the things that had happened to her since that cold autumn day at the order's motherhouse.

"Ms. Stevens?" A woman's voice interrupted her reverie. Debbie nodded.

"Thanks for coming. I'm Inspector Kate Murphy. Homicide. If you would just follow me this way."

❧❧❧

Professor Nicholas Komsky clutched the steering wheel of his aging Ford until the veins in his hands stood out like cords. The memory of yesterday's meeting at the rectory continued to fill him with a sickening sense of shock.

If he were perfectly candid, what had shocked Komsky most was the fact that he was shocked. He'd thought he knew Monsignor Joe Higgins too well for anything to throw him. Yet, the flagrant greed and cupidity of the situation appalled and disgusted him. And the arrogance of the man!

Not that Komsky expected priests, especially Monsignor Higgins, to be perfect. They were human, just like anyone else, with the same weaknesses. Komsky knew that. Anybody even slightly familiar with the history of the Church, he reasoned, was aware of the blatant examples of priests with "feet of clay." Although intellectually he knew better, idealistically he never stopped hoping that such wickedness had died with the Richelieus and the Rasputins of yesteryear.

As a professor of history, keenly aware of the depth of evil that humanity can perpetrate, Komsky had considered himself a man impossible to scandalize. Yet, to come face-to-face with such hypocrisy and avarice in a professed man of God *had* shocked him. "A hard and obdurate sinner" were the words the old catechism would have used to describe the monsignor.

Komsky stuck his arm out the car window and signaled for a right turn. The blasted signal indicator was on the blink again. He'd have to get it fixed before he drove on the freeway.

His neck felt stiff and one shoulder was sore. He hadn't slept well. Instead, he'd restlessly let his distaste and disgust, coupled with the dislike he already felt for the monsignor, jell into a cold rage.

Nicholas Komsky made a hard right on Ulloa Street. On either side of the block, girls in green plaid uniform skirts and boys in Kelly green sweaters, like clusters of grasshoppers, laughed and jumped and tagged one another on their way to St. Agatha's School. The sight of their open innocence only hardened Komsky's fury. Monsignor Higgins was supposed to be their pastor, for God's sake!

Komsky could kick himself for ever getting involved with the man in the first place. Why in the world had he allowed his kids to talk him into joining the parish council and then becoming chairman of the liturgy committee?

"Sunday Mass is dead and the homilies, when you bother to listen, are either pure heresy or pure pap!" his son, Jim, had railed. "I can hardly drag the kids and they're only eight and nine years old. What about when they're teenagers?"

Komsky had listened with a mixture of sympathy and amusement. How quickly they forget, he reflected, remembering his own struggles with Jim when his son was himself a teenager.

His daughter, Sarah, always practical, had said, "People are leaving St. Agatha's in droves, Dad. You're a wonderful teacher. Why not teach those priests how to give a decent sermon? Besides, Dad, it would be good for you, too."

Sarah had not elaborated, but Komsky knew what she was getting at. Since Marie's death, he had felt as if he were walking around lost in a low, thick fog.

For nearly fifty years Marie had been his life. They had planned to travel when he retired. But a fast-spreading cancer had taken both Marie and most of their savings in just nine short, painful months.

Now, every day he woke to an empty house and went to bed with empty dreams. Although it was almost two years since Marie's death, Komsky never got used to it.

His eyes filled until the blacktop in front of him was a blur. At the arterial stop, he wiped his face, blew his nose, and took a deep breath, trying to calm himself before he arrived at the rectory.

An impatient toot reminded him to move. Actually, his daughter, Sarah, had been right, Komsky conceded, stepping on the gas. The liturgy committee had taken up some of his empty hours. He enjoyed meeting with the youth minister and with Sister Noreen.

Poor Noreen—afraid to try anything innovative for fear of criticism. What a painful way to live, he thought, wondering how much yesterday's meeting had disturbed her. He wouldn't be surprised if she'd broken out in a painful rash.

Monsignor Higgins, as Komsky should have figured out, would have none of his help.

"Thanks, Nick," he'd said in that arrogant, complacent

tone of his, "but you can't teach an old dog new tricks. Besides, no one's complained to me."

Perhaps no one dares, Komsky had thought at the time. Rumor was strong that the monsignor had his little ways of getting back, all innocent and understandable. Anyone can forget to ask the janitor to open the church door for the florist on a wedding day, can't they? Or change the date of a baptism at the last minute, for an urgent reason, of course. Or not realize that the grieving family wants an organist hired for the funeral services.

So, except for insisting on a few liturgical regulations, Komsky had left the monsignor pretty much alone. Their one running battle had been women as Eucharistic ministers. The monsignor opposed them. Komsky favored them. With the backing of the chancery office, Komsky had seemingly prevailed.

On the other hand, the curates at the parish—now they were called associate pastors—had proven to be willing pupils, eager to engage Komsky's help in making the liturgy "more meaningful for the people," to quote them.

Secretly Komsky didn't give much credence to that approach. In many ways, most ways actually, he was a traditionalist. In fact, Marie used to say that he'd be just as happy if the Mass were still in Latin and if the priest said it with his back to the people.

Much as he hated to admit it, his wife had had a point, especially with some of these grinning, clown-faced fellows improvising on the sacred words.

To him, the ever ancient, ever new Liturgies of the Word and of the Eucharist held meaning for any thinking human being, which probably made him a fossil or, if the truth be told, a bit of a snob.

That's what he knew practical Sarah would say. Komsky conceded that she might have an edge on the truth.

Sarah! The thought of his lovely daughter filled him with pride and a touch of sadness. When she'd graduated from the University of California at Berkeley, Sarah had married Todd, a young man she'd met there during their senior year.

Neither Marie nor he had cared too much for the fellow. They both sensed something was not quite right with him, nothing either of them was ever able to put a finger on. And, since Sarah seemed to be so much in love with Todd, they said nothing.

At first, when Sarah had come by the house with bruises on her arms, they thought nothing of it. When Marie and she went to lunch and Marie noticed her daughter's swollen, bruised jaw, she had asked about it.

"The dentist," Sarah had answered too quickly.

Finally, when Sarah arrived alone at her brother Jim's birthday party with a black eye, the story came out amid tears and protestations. The sad and violent truth was that Todd was an abuser.

The Komskys helped Sarah take quick action. Within a matter of months, she was divorced and Todd was slapped with a restraining order.

Several months ago Sarah had met Ian. Although she was not yet ready to consider remarriage, it seemed to Komsky as though Ian and she were heading that way. They spent a great deal of time together.

Komsky was delighted for her. Since there was no Marie

with whom to share his joy, impetuously he had confided in the pastor.

"I think Sarah might even be living in sin," he had said jokingly, referring to the couple's habit of taking weekend trips together to Ian's family cabin on the Russian River, about sixty miles north of San Francisco.

Monsignor Higgins had said nothing, but smiled indulgently. Actually, Komsky had forgotten all about his remark until that terrible Sunday.

Komsky pulled into the diagonal parking place in front of St. Agatha's rectory. Several police cars with their blue and red light bars flashing were parked in front of the doorway. Komsky recognized George Jenkin's car. And there was Debbie Stevens hurrying around from a parking space behind the building.

Pulling down the visor, Komsky tried to recall whether or not he'd combed his hair before he left home this morning. Not that it made much difference. His hair stood out from his head like thick, white cotton candy and he had eyebrows that matched.

"The eccentric Einstein look," Marie used to tease, and threaten to give him a Mohawk while he slept. The hair was an affectation he knew, but it was a poor family, indeed, that couldn't afford one affectation.

Professor Komsky raked his fingers through his hair, flipped the visor back into position, and took a deep breath. The police inspector who called him had implied that Monsignor Higgins was murdered. That should surprise no one. With lingering anger, he remembered that Sunday when he could have killed the guy with his own bare hands.

The day would have been Marie's and his wedding anniversary. Ian and Sarah had picked him up for Mass. Until that Sunday, Komsky had no idea of Monsignor Higgins's cruelty nor his resentment over the women as Eucharistic ministers issue.

At Communion time, Sarah had approached the altar. Nick was right behind her. She had crossed the palm of her hands, carefully raising them to receive the host.

The choir had been singing a chant from Taize. Nick would never forget it. "Eat this Bread, drink this Cup. Come to Me and you shall not hunger. . . ."

Looking as pious as Lucifer before the fall, Joe Higgins had raised the small, white host. For a moment, his cold eyes met Sarah's. Deliberately he shook his head refusing to give her Communion, then shot Komsky a quick, knowing glance.

"Living in sin. . . ." Nicholas Komsky's own words flashed back to haunt him. He could feel his face flush with fury.

In front of him, he heard Sarah gasp, then watched her turn from the altar. Quick tears wet her cheeks.

The monsignor, a righteous expression twisting his mouth, held up the same host for Nick to receive.

Fighting down the impulse to punch the priest in his self-satisfied face, Nicholas Komsky rushed from the altar to comfort his daughter.

Practical Sarah had recovered sooner than he had. "Monsignor's wrong," Sarah had declared while Ian, Nick, and she were having a fancy brunch at the Cliff House.

Still spouting threats to leave the Church, Nick had tried to calm himself by listening to the rhythmic crash of the waves against Seal Rock while sipping his second Ramos Fizz.

69

Sarah spoke quietly. "He's an unhappy man, Dad. And quite an ignorant one, to be so far off the mark both theologically and pastorally. You can't just walk away. He needs a man like you, Dad, to help him see truth. There's no sense any of us holding a grudge. Grudges only hurt the people who hold them."

Where did we get her? Nick had wondered as he tried as hard as he could to forgive and forget. Despite his efforts, Nicholas Komsky never quite got that Sunday Mass out of his craw. He had forgiven the monsignor the only way he knew how—intellectually. He was unable to do more than that. He was sure that God did not expect any more.

Nick thought he was managing to live pretty well with the uneasy peace, that is, until yesterday. Yesterday, at last, like the whited sepulcher that he was, the dead bones of lies and greed had spewed out of Joseph P. Higgins for all to see.

At the sight, all the rage Nick had felt on that awful Sunday morning came flooding back, threatening to drown him in its depth.

❦❧

They are all here, and in record time, too, Sister Mary Helen thought, checking her wristwatch as Professor Nicholas Komsky strode purposefully into the dining room of St. Agatha's rectory. The parish council members whom she'd met yesterday afternoon were now all reassembled. And if her memory served her correctly, each had taken the same seat around the large mahogany table. At its head, Monsignor Higgins's vacant chair stood as a grim reminder of the reason they had been summoned.

Sister Noreen and Debbie Stevens, sitting across the table from each other, made a hushed attempt at conversation that quickly petered out. To Debbie's left, Fred Davis morosely studied the thumbnails of his large, folded hands, while to her right, Tina Rodiman's bright, penny-colored eyes darted around the room, settling on no one.

George Jenkin, his face the color of dead cigarette ash, didn't seem to hear Nick Komsky's greeting as the professor settled on the chair next to him.

The strain in the room, like a giant boulder, had successfully crushed all normal conversation. Even Sister Eileen sat beside Mary Helen in strained silence.

The pantry door swung open with a bump, startling them all. Eveleen Glynn, the housekeeper, her eyes cold but amused behind her finger-smudged glasses, led in a small procession, each carrying a kitchen chair. Without a word, the parish council members shifted to make room at the table. Eve, Charlotte Wixson, the parish secretary, and the two associate pastors, Father Calvo and Father Greene, managed to wedge their chairs around the table.

"Ten Little Indians," Eileen whispered, scooting her chair closer to Mary Helen's.

Sister Mary Helen rolled her eyes. "Twelve, if they're counting us," she said, "and from the looks of it, they undoubtedly are."

The group was scarcely settled when Inspector Kate Murphy appeared at the entry to the dining room. Kate was wearing dangling shamrock earrings. Behind her loomed Inspector Dennis Gallagher with a bright Kelly green tie, sure reminders that it was, after all, still St. Patrick's Day.

And what a way to spend it, Mary Helen thought, then wondered idly what the two inspectors were thinking. The frown on Gallagher's red face suggested that she wouldn't have to wait long to find out.

Kate stood behind the monsignor's empty chair gripping its back. "We have asked you all to come here this morning," she began, her freckled face serious, "because, as far as we know, you were the last people to see Monsignor Higgins alive."

"Except, of course, the murderer," Nicholas Komsky said with a touch of arrogance.

"Not necessarily." Kate's eyes turned sharply toward him.

"What do you mean?" There was a slight edge on Komsky's voice.

Mary Helen tightened her jaw. This is not the time nor the place to challenge Kate Murphy, she warned the professor silently.

As though he'd heard her, Komsky's face softened. "Ah, ha! Do you mean that he was given something, something that caused his death later? Something like poison?" he asked, any touch of self-importance gone.

"That is exactly what I mean." Kate studied her notebook, apparently looking for his name. "Professor Nicholas Komsky?" she asked.

The professor nodded his bushy white head, but said nothing. Mary Helen watched the corners of his mouth turn down as he sank into what could only be described as a brown study.

"Are you saying that you think one of us poisoned him?" Tina Rodiman asked in a high-pitched voice. All the color had drained from her face leaving her lips looking more than ever like those waxy red mouths that novelty stores sell around Halloween.

George Jenkin stood up so quickly that his chair tumbled backward, clattering to the ground. Sister Noreen squealed.

"I need to use the can," George rumbled. "I think I'm going to be sick."

Kate and Gallagher exchanged quick glances. "Come with me, sir," Gallagher said, leading a wobbly Jenkin from the room.

"Do you think I should open a window?" Noreen dithered softly, attempting to rise.

Kate shot her a look that put the round-faced nun right back into her chair. The room fell silent. The sounds of children laughing and balls bouncing floated in from the school yard. Their innocent gaiety formed a striking contrast to the fear dominating the room.

The minutes dragged by until finally George Jenkin reappeared with Inspector Gallagher right behind him. Fred Davis's red-rimmed eyes followed Jenkin to his seat.

"Fathers, Sisters, ladies and gentlemen," Kate began again. This time she sounded as if she were giving a commencement speech. "Thank you all for coming here this morning. We have asked you to assemble because Monsignor Higgins died last night of what we suspect was poison. The medical examiner, of course, will confirm that suspicion and tell us exactly what kind of poison was used. From what we have been told, you were all with the monsignor yesterday afternoon, just hours before his death."

"You *do* think one of us did it, don't you?" Tina Rodiman's voice was edging toward hysteria.

"Can't you ever keep that tongue of yours in your jaw, woman?" Eve Glynn's voice filled the room. The priests on either side of the housekeeper stared at her in open disbelief.

Kate Murphy shifted her attention toward Eve who, apparently unwilling to make eye contact, was now studying the toes of her blue bedroom slippers.

After what seemed like hours, but was probably only twenty seconds, Kate continued. "As I was saying, my partner and I would like to speak with each of you, take a statement about what you remember from yesterday afternoon's meeting. . . ."

"How long do you intend to keep us?" Fred Davis raised his long narrow face toward Kate.

"Shall I make some coffee?" the parish secretary, whose mind was obviously somewhere else, asked cheerfully.

"If there is coffee to be made, I'll make it," Eve snapped and watched Charlotte Wixson sink back into her chair.

"You!" Debbie Stevens's high nasal voice rang out. "You! Can we trust you to make us anything?"

Eve Glynn's face twisted in rage. "I'm not the one who can't be trusted," she snarled.

"Let's listen to what Inspector Murphy is trying to tell us, shall we?" Mary Helen said in her best schoolmarm voice. Amazingly, it seemed to settle the group.

After assuring them that they were free to move around the first floor of the rectory and that they'd probably be finished by noon, Kate sent the housekeeper to make coffee and to put out some snacks.

"My partner and I will talk to you, one at a time," she said, "across the hall in Mrs. Wixson's office."

She opened her notebook. "We'd like to start with . . ." She paused.

As the group waited expectantly, all the air seemed to be sucked out of the room. Mary Helen gathered up her pocketbook. She knew, as sure as she knew that the sun would rise, that hers would be the first name called.

❧≈≈❧

"What in heaven's name were you doing here, Sister?" Kate Murphy asked before Mary Helen even had time to sit down.

Carefully, Inspector Gallagher moved a small picture from the edge of the secretary's desk. Mary Helen noticed the words *I love you. Grandma* surrounding a snapshot of an adorable baby. He propped one hip where the frame had been and openly glowered at her.

Mary Helen could feel herself begin to bristle. It's a free country, she wanted to say, and I'm an adult. But she bit back the words. Her friends were only concerned. She smiled, giving them the benefit of the doubt.

"To tell you the truth, I'm more than a little surprised to see you here, too," she said pleasantly. When neither Kate nor Gallagher commented, she decided against any more pleasantries.

"Sister Eileen and I just dropped by the rectory to deliver some Irish soda bread. Monsignor Higgins, may he rest in peace, was one of our benefactors. We usually give our benefactors cookies for Christmas, but this past Christmas was somewhat unusual. . . ."

75

As soon as the words were out of her mouth, she regretted them.

Inspector Gallagher lowered his head like a bull ready to charge. "We know about your unusual Christmas only too well, which is why we are wondering what in the hell—"

Kate Murphy touched her partner's leg. "That's history, Denny," she said softly.

"If you ask me, there is way too much *history*," Gallagher growled.

"I can hardly be held responsible for stumbling on to people who murder other people," Mary Helen said with all the dignity she could muster. She moved on the hard visitor's chair. It certainly wasn't designed for people who wanted to stay any length of time, not that she did.

"Doesn't it strike you that you *stumble*, your word not mine, over an awful lot of people who murder other people?"

"And just what word would you use to describe the situation?" Refusing to be bullied, Mary Helen's eyes met Gallagher's.

"More like *deliberately look for*." He strained every word through clenched teeth.

"Even you, Inspector Gallagher, can't believe that!" Mary Helen was indignant.

"Enough, you two." Kate put up both hands. "This isn't getting us anywhere."

Gallagher moved off the secretary's desk. The edge of a desk must be even more uncomfortable than this chair, Mary Helen thought and, despite herself, smiled.

Inspector Gallagher must have interpreted her grin as an

attempt at reconciliation because he smiled back. A little sheepishly, Mary Helen was glad to see.

"That's better," Kate said, completely misreading the situation. "We are, after all, all on the same side."

When neither Mary Helen nor Gallagher objected, Kate Murphy continued. "Will you please tell us again, Sister, what you were doing here?"

Quickly Mary Helen reiterated the reason Sister Eileen and she happened to be at St. Agatha's rectory on that particular Sunday afternoon.

"The moment we entered the dining room, we knew something was going on."

"What do you mean *something*?"

"You could cut the tension with a knife, to use a cliché," Mary Helen said. "The only one who was really pleased to see us was the monsignor. He greeted us with the same relief that I suspect a drowning man greets the lifeguard."

"Do you have any idea what was causing so much tension? In other words, do you know who was meeting and what they were meeting about?"

"Monsignor Higgins told us that the parish council was meeting, which is unusual. Meeting on a Sunday, I mean. I assumed it was an emergency of some sort."

"Do you have any idea what the emergency was?"

Mary Helen shook her head. She wished she did know. Give me a few minutes with the group and I'll find out, she wanted to add, but knew better.

"And don't go nosing around trying to find out," Inspector Gallagher blurted.

Is he reading my mind? Mary Helen wondered, straightening her shoulders. "I am not in the business of *nosing around* anything, Inspector," she said with dignity. "If you like, I could make a few discreet inquiries."

Sister Mary Helen watched with satisfaction as Dennis Gallagher's face and neck turned a deep shade of red.

"That's all right, Sister," Kate answered quickly. "What we really want from you is to tell us everything you can remember about yesterday's meeting."

"I'll do my best," Mary Helen said. Breathing deeply to regain her composure, she began. With as much detail as possible, she told Kate about a very alive, if gray-faced, Monsignor Joseph P. Higgins bursting into the rectory kitchen, ordering tea and Irish soda bread to be served.

She recalled the others in the room, their faces turning toward Eileen and herself, some angry, some nervous and upset, some with a look of shock or disbelief.

She told about Eve Glynn arriving with the tea tray and the way in which the nuns' perfect cake of soda bread had been hacked and the sticky honey bear. The animosity that seemed to exist between the housekeeper and Debbie Stevens. She included every detail she could remember.

"Frankly, Sister Eileen and I could scarcely wait to get out of there," Mary Helen said, her eyes meeting Kate's. I'm beginning to feel the same way about this room, she thought, shifting on the hard chair.

"To quote Eve the housekeeper when we left, she said that she'd seen a happier scene at a deathbed! And honestly, Kate, she was right."

Throughout Mary Helen's entire recital, Kate Murphy had

said very little. "Have you any idea at all what the meeting was about?" she asked now.

"No, I really don't, although I must admit I was curious." She paused, then threw caution to the wind. "I'm sure I could find out from one of the participants, if that would be helpful," she said, deliberately not looking Inspector Gallagher's way.

"No thank you, Sister," Kate said, disappointingly fast. "That's our job." She checked her watch. "I'll talk to Sister Eileen next, and when I'm done, the two of you are free to head back to Mount St. Francis College, if you want to. I know how to reach you."

"And by the way, don't be thinking about taking any trips for a while," Gallagher said. "In case we find anything fishy in your Irish bread."

"What do you mean *fishy?* What could possibly be wrong with our bread?" Mary Helen asked, pebbles of fear forming in her chest.

Inspector Gallagher studied her over his horn-rimmed glasses. "The man was poisoned," he said. "We're not sure yet how the poison was administered. Irish bread wouldn't be a bad idea, especially on the day before St. Patrick's Day."

He is only trying to scare me, Mary Helen thought, rising stiffly from her chair. And the worst part of it is, he's succeeding!

❧❧❧

"That was just plain mean," Kate Murphy said when she was sure that Sister Mary Helen was well out of earshot.

Her partner stared at her, his big watery blue eyes full of innocence. "Mean?" His voice rang with feigned disbelief. "Mean? What? Just 'cause I want the lady to keep the law?"

"Not even you can imagine that those two old nuns killed the monsignor with poisoned Irish soda bread! The idea sounds like a skit on the old *Carol Burnett Show*."

"I can imagine it," Gallagher blustered. "With those two, nothing is beyond my imagination."

"For heaven's sake, Denny, what possible motive would they have for killing the man?"

"Maybe life at their college was getting a little dull. After all, it's almost," he stopped to count on his broad fingers, "three months since their last brush with murder."

And what an awfully long three months they've been, Kate mused, twisting a piece of her short red hair into a curl. Especially for her husband, Jack. She'd almost lost him when he and his partner, Bill Jordon, were shot trying to apprehend the perp whom the press had dubbed the Sea Cliff rapist. Jack's partner had died. The memory awoke in Kate a deep pang of sympathy for Bill's wife and his child.

Kate didn't even want to think about the long days and seemingly endless nights when Jack was in a coma. The whole ordeal still seemed like a nightmare.

Distracted, she stared out the rectory window, scarcely seeing the rhododendrons and the azaleas forming a blazing hedge along the side wall of St. Agatha's. Calla lilies stood at stiff green attention, with velvety white leaves surrounding golden spikes.

Good can come out of anything, she'd always believed. She was just now beginning to recognize anything positive about all that pain. For instance, the small things that had annoyed her about her husband had become just that, small things. The long hours Kate and her mother-in-law had spent together had drawn the two women into a kind of mutual respect.

"Are you with me?" Gallagher's voice startled her.

"Of course, I'm with you." Kate blinked. What had her partner said that started her reliving those painful days and weeks which were still not over?

Although Jack had recovered more quickly than even he had expected, he was still impatient to feel like himself again. His best distraction during recovery had been the baby. Thank God for little John, Kate thought. It is nearly impossible to feel depressed for too long when you are surrounded by the unconditional love and the irrepressible antics of an outgoing three-year-old.

"Shall we see what the second partner in the gruesome twosome has to say?" Gallagher asked.

"Can't you just call her Sister Eileen?" Kate snapped, dragging her mind back to St. Agatha's and the murder of Monsignor Higgins.

"Funny, you knew exactly who I meant." Gallagher hitched up his trousers. "While I get the good Sister, why don't you call Jack. Maybe then you'll be able to concentrate on this case."

Kate wanted to shout something, but she knew that her partner was right. Jack had just returned to work, to a desk job. Although he had been told it was temporary, Kate was anxious about his adjustment, more anxious than he was probably.

Quickly, she pulled Mrs. Wixson's telephone toward her. Picking up the receiver, she dialed the unfamiliar number, hoping she'd remembered it correctly.

"Recruiting Unit," a friendly, female voice answered. Kate's stomach dropped. It wasn't Jack. He always answered. Was something wrong? Had he quit already? Not that she blamed him. It was a stupid place to put an officer who'd just been shot, Kate thought angrily. Doesn't anyone upstairs have even half a brain?

"Recruiting. Can I help you?" the voice asked.

Kate shook herself. She'd have to get out of this habit of always expecting the worst.

"May I speak to Jack Bassetti, please," Kate asked tentatively. "This is Kate Murphy, Homicide. I'm his wife."

There was silence on the line. With Kate using her maiden name at work, it almost always took the uninitiated a few seconds to unravel the relationship.

"I'm sorry, Inspector Murphy," the voice said finally.

Despite herself, Kate waited in dread for the rest of the sentence.

"Jack's gone out for a coffee break. He should be back in ten minutes or so."

"A coffee break?" Kate tried to control her growing fear. "It's only nine o'clock in the morning. Is he feeling all right?"

The woman on the other end of the line began to laugh. "He's feeling great, as far as I can tell, Inspector. A couple of his buddies from Sexual Assault stopped by and he's gone with them. Actually, he has a lunch date, too, with some guys from Vice, if you're worried about his appetite. Shall I tell him you called?"

"No, thanks," Kate said, feeling as if a bowling ball had been lifted from her chest.

She was replacing the receiver when Inspector Dennis Gallagher opened the office door. Stepping aside, he let small, round, Sister Eileen enter the room first.

❧❧❧

From across the hall Sister Mary Helen heard the door click shut. Eileen was in with Kate Murphy and Inspector Gallagher. Although the priests' dining room was warm, Mary Helen felt an unexpected chill. Suppose their Irish soda bread *had* been used to poison the monsignor? Not that either Eileen or she had known anything about it. But, much as she hated to admit it, Inspector Gallagher was right. It would be a fitting, if a bit bizarre, way to kill an Irishman on the eve of St. Patrick's Day.

Would they be able to prove their innocence? They had no motive, of course, but think of what the *Chronicle* and the television news could make of the speculation!

Suddenly, Mary Helen felt light-headed. The image of Sister Cecilia's long, thin face flashed before her. The college president's tight mouth formed only one word: *How?*

Don't ask me *how?*! Mary Helen wanted to shout. I don't know *how* we ended up in this mess! But I'd sure as blazes better figure *how* to get out of it.

Moving her chair toward the window, she tried to get a grip on herself. Patches of blue sky rounded the tops of the clouds. A sparrow, unaware that she was watching, bounced on a branch of a rhododendron bush, then dropped to the lawn to peck among the blades of grass.

Mary Helen drew in a long, deep breath. As she slowly let it out, Robert Browning's words skittered across her mind.

> The year's at the spring
> And day's at the morn; . . .
> God's in his heaven—
> All's right with the world.

Not quite, she thought realistically, but with your help, Lord, we'll put it that way!

Resolutely, she turned from the window to survey the priests' dining room. Half of the group had taken up Kate Murphy on her invitation to wander freely around the first floor of the rectory. Not that there were many places to wander.

In the distance, a toilet flushed. Eve Glynn, or at least Mary Helen assumed it was she, was banging cupboard doors in the kitchen. Only three others remained in the room.

Sister Noreen didn't seem to have moved at all. She sat owl-eyed, looking as if she was having trouble breathing. Across from her, Tina Rodiman slouched in her chair, staring down at her swollen ankles. Although no sound came from her, her lips moved as though she were having a heated argument with someone.

With red-rimmed eyes, Fred Davis searched the room, settling on no one in particular. When his eyes did meet Mary Helen's, he smiled meekly, then, cracking his knuckles, rose from his chair and went out the door.

With Fred gone, maybe, Mary Helen thought, I can get the two ladies talking. She stood up and moved her chair next to Noreen's. She felt rather than saw the nun flinch.

Reaching over, Mary Helen patted one of Noreen's plump hands. When the woman didn't pull away, she asked gently, "Are you all right, Sister?"

"How can I be all right?" Noreen's hazel eyes fastened on Mary Helen and her heavy shoulders sagged. "Have you any idea what this will start?" She narrowed her eyes. "Talk," she said with as much horror as some might say "the bubonic plague."

"And the police have put up that stupid yellow tape which is supposed to keep people away. If you ask me, it attracts more people than it repels!" She pushed a strand of gray hair off her forehead.

"You might be right," Mary Helen said, feeling that some response was called for.

"And how am I going to answer all the questions?" Noreen was picking up steam. "What will I say? What am I going to tell the other nuns and the parishioners, and the teachers, and the children. The poor children!" A sob caught in her throat and her eyes filled. "To think I was almost glad when Sister Bernice told me he'd died."

"You were glad?" Mary Helen tried not to show her surprise.

"Yes. Almost." Noreen qualified her answer. "It is easier to explain a sudden death than to explain why he did what he did."

"Did what he did?" Mary Helen parroted, scarcely able to contain her curiosity.

"Yesterday's meeting!" Noreen's hazel eyes were sparking

behind her heavy glasses now. "The one you and Sister Eileen walked in on. Don't tell me you couldn't feel the tension."

Only a corpse could have missed it, Mary Helen thought morbidly.

"The good monsignor had just been discovered embezzling funds! I thought our pastor's sudden death would be easier to explain than his being a common crook. Wouldn't you know, he'd go and get himself murdered."

Mary Helen's stomach fell like a stone and she grunted with surprise. This must be some sort of bad dream. Had she heard correctly?

"Embezzling parish funds?" Her throat was tight. "This is what yesterday's meeting was about?" she asked, feeling as if someone had tilted the room. She grabbed the edge of the table to steady herself.

Noreen, tight-lipped, nodded her head. "How could he?" she asked no one in particular.

How could he, indeed? Mary Helen thought. She felt suddenly sick, trying to absorb the monsignor, the college benefactor, as a thief. In the uneasy silence, she didn't hear Tina Rodiman move to the chair beside her.

Tears ran down Tina's cheeks. "Last night I could have killed him myself. I told Tony—that's my husband, Sister," she explained unnecessarily to Mary Helen, "that I could kill the man. I thought the school was getting the money, Sister Noreen."

Tina fumbled in her pocket for a tissue, wiped her eyes, and blew her nose. "All those hours! All those hot dogs!" Her words were muffled by the tissue. "All those pull tabs!"

Mary Helen must have looked as puzzled as she was.

"Bingo," Sister Noreen explained. "You remember. Tina and her husband run our bingo."

"And to think that all that money went into his private . . . coffers," Tina's voice was strained. "I can see how someone could kill him," she said.

"Better keep that to yourself, Tina." Fred Davis let the door to the dining room swing shut behind him. "The police will take you for a suspect."

All the color drained from Tina's face. "What about you, Fred? Yesterday afternoon you were as mad as I was." Her words petered out as if she was afraid she'd gone too far.

"You're right about that," Fred said in a clear, strong voice that surprised Mary Helen in someone his age—until she realized that his age was about her age, too.

Fred turned toward her. "I was mad. I still am!" His eyes blazed making the skin on his face seem fairer, more paper-thin. "That bastard!" he said without apology. "He stole all the money I left to have Masses said for my wife, Mildred."

With the economy of words you'd expect from an accountant, he continued. "He lolls at his cabin in Clear Lake while Mildred languishes in purgatory. My first item of business, now that he's gone, is to make sure that some priest gets my Masses said."

"You can't believe that God would detain Mildred's entrance into eternal happiness because. . . ." Mary Helen began, but the annoyed frown on Fred's face warned her to quit while she was ahead.

"Don't tell me that a woman of your age is into those modern theologians who don't believe in purgatory?" he growled in a tone that made it clear that this was not the time to try to tell him anything. Mary Helen imagined poor Mildred had had any purgatory she was going to have by simply living with Fred.

"You are the head of the finance committee, Fred?" Changing the subject, Mary Helen tried to remember how Monsignor Higgins had introduced the man yesterday afternoon.

"And I wish to God I'd never heard of the finance committee or this parish either, for whatever that's worth." Fred adjusted his wire-rimmed glasses and fixed his eyes on Mary Helen. "Whoever said 'ignorance is bliss' must have been thinking of me.

"Before Mildred died, I never came near this place, except on Sundays. All the 'churchy' stuff was in her column. But after she was gone, I thought she'd be pleased if I offered my services. I had the time. Too much time, to tell the truth. So much time that I discovered this . . . this . . ." His eyes blazed. "This *abomination!*" The word pierced the room like a scream.

With a bang, Eve Glynn threw open the door from the pantry. Apparently oblivious of any tension, she shuffled into the dining room, her blue bedroom slippers scraping along the carpet.

"I suppose you need more coffee," she said, then scowled at the pot on the sideboard which was hardly touched. "What's wrong with my coffee?" she asked in a low flat voice. "No one's had any."

Her pale blue eyes swept the room like a searchlight. "Are you all afraid I poisoned the pompous peacock? Not that I wouldn't have liked to, and not that I didn't have the opportunity."

She began to rearrange the cups on the sideboard. "Some thought that because the man was a monsignor, he must be a good man, but I say, you don't know a man until you pick up after him."

Leaving the group in baffled silence, Eve made great work of checking the sugar bowl and the cream pitcher. "As my dear cousin Monsignor Concannon, God rest him, often said, 'What can you expect from a pig but a grunt?' "

Only Sister Noreen's face showed any shock at the remark and the housekeeper didn't miss it. "So, Sister Goody-Two-Shoes." Eve's face twisted into a sneer. "You don't like to hear the truth, now do you? You are so almighty perfect, with your 'Yes, Monsignor' and your 'No, Monsignor.' It seems to me that if anyone knew the man was a thief, it would have to be yourself."

She squared her body to face Noreen. "Or, didn't you ever look at the school's books? Did you just accept the monsignor's numbers? I suspect that not even you are that big a horse's hind end. As they say, 'A lie looks better for having a witness.' "

Sister Noreen's hand flew to her throat and her cheeks reddened as though she'd been slapped. "How dare you!" Noreen hissed.

"How dare I?" the housekeeper mimicked savagely. "How dare I? How dare you look down your stubby nose with those big, innocent eyes. I'm only speaking the truth."

Eve's thick hands rummaged through her apron pockets

and she drew out a roll of antacid tablets. "You'll need these by now, I'm sure."

She slammed down the roll on the mahogany table. "I found them after you left," she said menacingly. "You should be more careful where you leave things."

A flat silence filled the dining room. The half-full package of tablets rolled toward Noreen. Mary Helen was relieved to hear familiar footsteps in the hallway. Sister Eileen's interview must be over.

♏❧♏

Sister Eileen swung back the dining room door. "Next," she called. Seeming not to notice the brick wall of silence in the room, she smiled and nodded toward the housekeeper. "Inspector Murphy would like to speak with you next, Eve," she said, "in Charlotte Wixson's office."

Grumbling to herself, Eve shuffled from the room. As the door shut behind her, the tension evaporated like air from a balloon.

Tina, Sister Noreen, and Fred all began to jabber at once, with no one listening. Nor were they paying any attention to the nuns.

What in heaven's name was going on? the expression on Eileen's face asked.

Mary Helen winked. "We had better ring the college and let Sister Cecilia know where we are." She spoke loudly and distinctly for the benefit of the group. Fred Davis was the only one who stopped talking long enough to acknowledge that he'd even heard her.

"Intersecting monologues," Mary Helen muttered, as the

two nuns hurried from the room. They discovered a small cubbyhole off the foyer with a telephone in it. Actually it looked as if someone had converted an unused closet into a makeshift phone booth.

"We can talk here," Mary Helen said, motioning Eileen in first. "This is about as alone as we are going to get." She wedged herself in, nudging Eileen's shoulder. "Why do I feel like Superman?" she asked.

"Don't you wish?" Eileen whispered, then perched on the small stool. "Quick now, tell me what I walked into in the priests' dining room?"

Not wasting any words, Mary Helen filled in her friend on the revelations and heated accusations which she had just heard.

Eileen's bushy eyebrows rose and the color left her face. "No wonder I could practically taste the tension," she whispered, struggling, no doubt, as Mary Helen had, to absorb what she had just heard.

"Three people, three motives," Mary Helen mumbled, "and who's to say that if we talk to three others, we won't find three more?"

"Don't forget Eve Glynn," Eileen added, pushing back the closet door for a little air.

A fresh breeze, rushing into the foyer from the open front door, made Mary Helen realize just how clammy the booth had become.

"You had better call the college," Mary Helen said. Stepping out, she waited while Eileen dialed and spoke briefly to Gloria at the college switchboard.

"We're home free!" Eileen said when she replaced the receiver. "Sister Cecilia is in a meeting which, Gloria says, should last for the rest of the day. She left instructions not to be disturbed—except in case of dire emergency."

"This is hardly what anyone would call a dire emergency," Mary Helen said.

"Right! With any luck at all, we won't have to face her until supper tonight. Not that anyone, even Cecilia, can blame us for getting involved in this mess." Eileen's gray eyes were wide. "After all, old dear, all we did was deliver the Irish soda bread which, after all, was her idea!"

Mary Helen's stomach pitched. "We are not sure that our bread wasn't the culprit," she whispered, but Eileen was not listening.

"What now?" she asked, eagerly.

Mary Helen adjusted her bifocals on the bridge of her nose. Seeing more clearly helped her to think more clearly, or at least she thought it did. "Now, we try to find Deborah Stevens, Professor Komsky, or George Jenkin. Strike up a conversation. See where it leads."

"Shall we go together or shall we, in the interest of time, divide and conquer?" Sister Eileen's question was answered by the unexpected appearance of Deborah Stevens.

"Oh!" Debbie seemed startled to see the two nuns. "I was paged on my beeper." She pointed to the small square box clipped to the waistband of her skirt. "I'm looking for a phone," she said in her high nasal voice. "I need to call my office right away. Are you finished?"

"We just hung up," Mary Helen gave Debbie her most pleasant smile. "It's all yours."

"The two of us were just saying that we could use a good, hot cup of coffee," Eileen announced. "Weren't we, Sister?"

Although it was news to her, Mary Helen nodded in agreement. "Would you like to join us, Debbie? You look as if you could use one, too."

Debbie's dark eyes jumped nervously from the nuns to the phone.

"After you've made your call, of course," Eileen added quickly.

"That would be great," Debbie agreed in a tone that sounded as if she thought the idea was anything but. "Anything, I guess, but tea."

Even though the door to the phone booth was shut and the two nuns had moved away to give her privacy, they could still hear Debbie punching in a series of buttons. After a few minutes in which she said only "yes," "no," and "thank you," Debbie Stevens emerged from the phone booth, her angular face burning.

"Are you all right, dear?" Eileen asked, a frown making a horseshoe just above her short nose.

"As all right as I can be when I'm being held for questioning in a murder case and I should be at my office taking care of clients." Debbie clipped her words in frustration.

Like a well-trained border collie, Sister Eileen shepherded Mary Helen and Debbie across the foyer and into the enormous rectory kitchen. They crossed the gleaming stainless steel room walking through ladders of light spread by the crisp morning sun across the Navaho white linoleum floor.

They settled at a cozy round table placed against the triptych of windows. On the tabletop a full-blown pink rhododendron flower was flanked by the sugar bowl and the creamer.

Quickly, Eileen found a cupboard, produced three cups, and filled them with dark, thick coffee. All three women decided to take their coffee black.

"It hits the spot," Mary Helen said, trying not to make a face. Actually, the coffee reminded her of axle grease, not that she'd ever tasted any. "I think I will have a dollop of cream, after all," she said, pouring a generous helping into her cup.

"So, then, Debbie." Eileen, who seemed to have no trouble swallowing the stuff, took the lead. "Do I remember correctly? Are you the chairperson of the parish outreach committee?"

Debbie nodded. "Yes, I am. Or, should I say, 'I was'? There will be changes, I'm sure, now that Joe is dead." Her face blanched.

"I suppose." Mary Helen's breath was back. "But, a good outreach person is hard to replace," she said, knowing from experience how difficult it can be to convince the affluent and even kind-hearted people that they have a duty to help those less fortunate.

"I'd imagine the new pastor, whoever he is, will be glad to have you."

Debbie shrugged. "You never know about priests," she said.

Mary Helen watched the struggle on the woman's face. Was there something, a secret perhaps, that she wanted to tell? Mary Helen waited expectantly. She sipped her coffee. The moment passed.

Debbie Stevens shifted noiselessly in her chair. She gazed out the window and fixed her eyes on something in the blooming hedge. The hum of the refrigerator snapped off, leaving the kitchen so still that Mary Helen heard the hollow tick, tick of the daisy clock on the far wall. Outside, the automatic sprinklers threw water against the side of the rectory, then rhythmically moved their spray toward the lawn.

"Who do you think did it?" Debbie asked, almost as if she were talking to herself.

When neither nun spoke, Debbie asked teasingly, "Do you think it was one of us at the meeting?"

Without warning, she turned toward Mary Helen, a strange light in her eyes. "You're the nun I read about in the *Chronicle*, aren't you? The one who keeps stumbling onto killers." She gave a short, mocking laugh. "Do you know who you stumbled on this time?"

Though the kitchen was warm and sunny, Mary Helen felt as if a cold cloud was passing overhead. "Don't believe everything you read in the papers," she said, hoping she hadn't sounded too flippant.

"How long have you been in the convent?" Debbie asked. The question seemed to come out of nowhere.

Mary Helen didn't ever remember the exact number of years, nor did she have the patience right now to figure it out. "Well over fifty years," she said.

"You, too?" Debbie's Hershey's kisses eyes shifted toward Eileen.

"Me, too," Eileen answered.

"I was in the convent," Debbie said, "for almost twenty

years. That's where I met Joe." As soon as the words left her mouth, the woman looked as if she wished she could scoop them back inside.

"Did you work in the same parish?" Eileen asked, ready for a chat.

Debbie shook her head so slightly that not a lock of her short, stylishly cut hair seemed to move. "I'm from the Midwest. Wisconsin, to be exact. Joe and I were on a sabbatical together," she said. "That's how we met."

From the pained expression on Debbie's face, Mary Helen suspected that she had been more depleted by her sabbatical experience than enriched.

"But enough about me." Debbie's bravado returned. "Like I asked before, do you think Joe's killer is one of us at the meeting?"

The suddenness and the callousness of the question hit Mary Helen like a splash of icy water. "You'd have a better insight into that than I," she said, wondering what her face showed. Was Debbie Stevens always this blunt and outspoken? If so, she'd be a more likely victim than the monsignor. Was the wrong person poisoned?

"Maybe you can tell me," she prodded. "Do you think any of your fellow parish council members had a motive for killing their pastor?"

The secret Debbie Stevens longed to tell them twisted on her face again. Just as it seemed that she might reveal it, the beeper at her waistband sounded.

"Excuse me," Debbie said, standing to squint at the numbers on the display. "It's my office, again. I need to use that phone."

"What do you think she's hiding?" Eileen asked when she was sure that Debbie was no longer able to overhear.

"Plenty would be my guess," Mary Helen said, "but what exactly? I have no idea."

"Odd woman, isn't she?" Eileen stirred two teaspoons of sugar into her coffee. "This stuff," she frowned at her cup, "is strong enough to make a mouse trot."

Mary Helen was just about to say, "For a while there, I thought your tongue was anesthetized," when Eileen put her finger to her lips.

She pointed toward the pantry door. "Someone is out there," she mouthed.

The door cracked open just wide enough for Mary Helen to see one liquidy brown eye, thoroughly bloodshot.

"Mr. Jenkin," she called out without hesitation. "If you're looking for coffee, you've come to the right place."

The door inched forward slowly revealing long-legged George Jenkin, his face fish-white. "Did you say coffee?" he asked in a throaty growl. His shoulders hunched, and he kept his neck and his head so still that Mary Helen was sure it must be agony for him to move either of them.

"Are you all right?" she asked, while Eileen went to find a clean coffee mug.

"Who said, 'The wages of sin are death?' " he asked, closing his eyes. "Who cares?" he added before Mary Helen had the chance to say, Wages of sin *is* death, and St. Paul to the Romans 6:23.

Like a man in agony, Jenkin eased himself into the

wooden chair just vacated by Debbie Stevens. "Still warm." He sighed. It took Mary Helen several seconds to realize he meant the seat.

The two nuns sat in fascinated silence watching George Jenkin slurp down his coffee. The color in his face actually seemed to improve with each long, noisy swallow. Finally he set his mug on the table. "More, please," he mumbled without looking up.

Eileen poured and the aroma of the coffee blended with a slightly sour odor that Mary Helen assumed was coming from Mr. Jenkin's clothes.

"You'll have to excuse me, Sisters." He shivered. His eyes did not meet theirs. Actually, what he seemed to be studying was his own enormous feet and the scuffed brown loafers that covered them.

"Are you all right?" Mary Helen asked again. This time, she was fairly certain of what caused Jenkin's sickness. "The Irish flu," some wag used to call it.

"I'm all right," he said, then stopped while a coughing spell racked his body. "If you can call a man 'all right' who feels like death warmed over, then I'm all right."

"I can't imagine why anyone in his right mind would have another drink if he knew it made him feel like this in the morning." Eileen put down two pieces of dried toast in front of the man.

"Have you never heard it said, 'It's the first drop that destroys me, there's no harm at all in the last'?" He held his head in both hands.

"Too many times," Eileen muttered, settling back in her chair.

Sister Mary Helen broke the awkward silence. "Are you up to talking about yesterday's meeting?" She smiled brightly. Jenkin stared at her with rheumy eyes as if yesterday might have been a lifetime ago.

"Yesterday's meeting? Ah, yes! That, I do remember. The monsignor," he pronounced the word as if it were an epithet, "finally got his just desserts."

Mary Helen watched Jenkin warm to his subject. His sallow cheeks gained still more color. "He was finally named for the scoundrel he was, for the whited sepulcher, for the pious Pharisee who was all preach and no practice."

He poked one long, skinny finger at her. "Do you know that that man—the monsignor—thought nothing of interfering with the relationship between a man and his wife? He thought nothing of telling a man's wife—any man's wife—my wife, in fact, to leave because of something as trivial as a man needing a few drinks at the end of the day to unwind. After three kids and nearly thirty years of living together, the bitch took his advice."

Jenkin stopped, trying to focus his eyes, hoping, no doubt, to read the nuns' reactions to his outburst.

"But Mr. Jenkin, if your wife left you on Monsignor Higgins's recommendation, why in heaven's name would you volunteer to be on his parish council?" Eileen asked with maddening logic.

Jenkin perked up. "What better way to get at a man's Achilles' heel?"

Mary Helen wasn't sure that she'd heard correctly. "Pardon me?" she said.

For a moment Jenkin looked almost embarrassed. "Despite what you'd like to believe, Sister, everyone's motivation isn't as noble and pure as you'd like to think it is."

At my age, only an old fool wouldn't know that every human being's motives are mixed, saints as well as sinners. Mary Helen chewed on the thought, but to take on a good work to find another person's weak points? That's stretching it.

"No, Sisters." This time he included Eileen. "We can't all be as righteous and upstanding as you'd like to hope we poor lay folks are—"

"And did you find his Achilles' heel?" Eileen cut in mid-sentence.

Mary Helen noticed an uncharacteristic edge on her friend's voice. Obviously, he had stepped on Eileen's Achilles' heel, which, Mary Helen knew well, was being patronized.

Jenkin's watery brown eyes studied Sister Eileen who, with her chin out and her short nose turned up, left no doubt about her feelings.

"Indeed, I did find it!" he said, seemingly unaware that he had offended anyone.

Poor Mrs. Jenkin must have been a saint, Mary Helen thought, waiting for the man to continue.

"I was with the *Chron* for years, you know. Tough job. Odd hours. Hard on family life. And old habits die hard. When you smell something bad, you sniff out the source."

"And?" Mary Helen steeled herself, almost sure where this was leading.

"And, he was a common thief! Nothing but a common thief!"

The words hit like explosions. Although this was the second time she had heard them, they still sent shock waves through her body.

Strange, she thought, watching the dust motes twirl in the beam of sun touching the top of the kitchen table. Moments ago I was offended that this man insinuated that I was naive enough to be shocked by a fellow human being's failings, yet I do naively hope—no, expect—that a priest will be different. I presume that he will realize his responsibility to lead a life of personal holiness and selfless service and I should know better. She shifted on her chair. Even Jesus had one of His twelve apostles betray him.

In the distance, Mary Helen heard the high-pitched laughter and shouts of children playing. It must be morning recess for St. Agatha's primary grades. She wondered how these children would react to the murder of their pastor and the scandal surrounding it. Maybe Sister Noreen was right about "talk," as she called it. Even Jesus was unforgiving about someone who scandalized little children. "It is better for him," Jesus said, "that a millstone were hung about his neck, and he cast into the sea."

"So, Sisters, what do you think of that?" George Jenkin's gravelly voice brought Mary Helen back. "Our pastor is— was—a thief!"

"I don't know what to think," Mary Helen said, suddenly cold. "How did you discover it?"

Jenkin took several deep breaths and let them out slowly, almost as if he were pumping up to speak. "Like I said, I was a reporter for the *Chron*. When I took on this parish council job, I became privy to lots of 'insider' information. And some of it didn't add up. For example, the number of people who play bingo versus the revenue; and, the monsignor's little cabin in Clear Lake versus his monthly salary. Actually, looking at the sets of diamond and onyx cuff links is what started me sniffing. Nobody buys those on eight hundred dollars a month."

"They could have been gifts," Eileen offered.

"Could have been," Jenkin agreed, "so I put Fred Davis on the job. Suggested that Higgins was embezzling. Now, Fred's a guy who never would have believed the monsignor was capable of such a thing. As a matter of fact, I think he began to look just to prove me wrong. But once he got onto a discrepancy, he was like a bloodhound on a scent. And, sure enough, 'Eureka!'—or should I say 'Bingo!'—he found it.

"When the poor guy discovered that the money he'd given the monsignor to say monthly Masses for his dead wife was all spent, with no proof of any Masses ever being said, he was furious. I can't remember ever seeing anyone in such a rage."

"Was he angry enough to kill someone?" Eileen asked.

"In my opinion, yes," Jenkin answered slowly. "So I guess that makes two of us, at least, who could have killed the man."

"You and Fred Davis?" Mary Helen wanted to make sure that she'd understood him correctly.

Jenkin nodded.

Sister Mary Helen shoved her bifocals up the bridge of her nose and looked directly at George Jenkin. "And did you?" she asked, feeling a cold shiver run down her spine.

"Did I kill Joe Higgins?" Jenkin's face was ashen again. He put his elbows on the kitchen table and rested his head in his open hands. Swaying slightly from side to side, he groaned.

"Did I kill Joe Higgins? Did I kill Joe Higgins?" he chanted again and again.

Without warning, he looked up. Tears ran down his pasty cheeks. His dark eyes were as vacant as someone in a stupor. "I don't know, Sister," he said miserably. "I honestly cannot remember."

The awkward silence spread over the sunny kitchen table like spilled water. Mary Helen was relieved to hear a faint tap, tap at the swinging door and see the face of Professor Nicholas Komsky.

"May I come in?" he asked. The blue eyes below wild white brows were wary. "Am I disturbing something? I just want a cup of coffee. I could take it and go somewhere else."

Jumping up, George Jenkin must have seen his opportunity to escape. "Come in! Sit down, Nick," he called. "I was just about to leave anyway." And without any further comment, he did.

Professor Komsky studied the nuns through his horn-rimmed glasses. "You two look as if you've been hit by a Mack truck. Are there still such things as Mack trucks?" he wondered aloud. "By the way, did I come in at a bad moment?"

"Not at all," Eileen answered quickly.

Mary Helen noticed that a hint of the brogue had crept into her friend's speech. That was a sure sign that Eileen was anxious. And why wouldn't she be? Hadn't George Jenkin just admitted that he couldn't remember whether or not he'd killed Monsignor Higgins? To Mary Helen's way of thinking, that was quite a bit to forget!

She moved Jenkin's empty coffee mug while Eileen went in search of another for the professor.

"I never expected to meet you here, Nicholas," Sister Mary Helen said, which was true. What she had expected was that a retired professor would have had enough committee meetings to last him a lifetime. The farthest thing from her mind when she really retired was to join another committee of any kind.

With a gracious nod, Komsky accepted the coffee from Eileen. "And I never should have come," he said, with a pinch of bitterness. "But after Marie's death, I was really in a funk. The kids, especially Sarah, thought it would be good for me to get involved. And it was, up to a point. Poor Sarah."

His open face with its halo of wild white hair looked over at her earnestly. Mary Helen knew the man well enough to know that something was bothering him; something he wanted to get off his chest; something he wanted Eileen and her to understand.

"Sarah?" Mary Helen probed. "Is something wrong with your daughter?"

The small opening was all Nicholas Komsky needed. The mention of his daughter's name seemed to awake the fury which lay just below the surface.

"Dear Sarah." He swallowed, gaining control of the emotion in his voice. Succinctly and simply—for like all brilliant people, he was simple—the professor related his story. He told them why he had joined the liturgy committee; the resistance he met from the monsignor; his daughter's unhappy marriage and divorce; her dating a fine young fellow named Ian; since his wife was gone, his confiding the whole story to the pastor. Finally, he told of that terrible Sunday at Mass when the pastor had refused to give his Sarah Communion.

"Refused, plain refused to give her the host," he repeated, tears welling up in his eyes. "Can you believe that, Sisters?"

"No," Mary Helen said, her throat nearly closed by the utter meanness of the act. She felt Eileen stiffen beside her.

"The wisdom of the Church has always been to give Communion rather than publicly reveal a person's sin." Eileen seemed to be talking to no one in particular. "It is hard to imagine that Monsignor Higgins could be so ignorant or so lacking in compassion."

"Cruelty! That's what he wasn't lacking in!" The malice in Nicholas Komsky's usually placid voice startled Mary Helen.

Obviously he was not only angry, but deeply hurt by the monsignor's humiliation of his cherished daughter. What father wouldn't be? Did that mean that Nicholas Komsky killed the priest?

As though he had heard her question, the professor looked up. His white caterpillar eyebrows undulated as he spoke. This time his voice was soft. "I can't tell you how many times I daydreamed about torturing and killing that scoundrel. And getting away with it, of course. Intellectually, I know as Christians we are supposed to forgive, to turn the other check, but, somehow, I could never do it emotionally.

"Every time I thought I'd forgiven the man, risen above his cruelty to my child. Every time I thought I'd put the incident behind me, he'd do something else to stir up the embers."

Sister Mary Helen didn't need to ask for examples. It was as if the painful boil of Komsky's rage had burst and the pus ran freely.

"He was absolutely insensitive to Sister Noreen," Komsky said with a cold smile. "Poor, good-hearted Noreen. She was always trying to cover for him, to keep the parish gossip to a minimum. Why, I don't know since he seemed to delight in ridiculing her genuine concern."

Sister Eileen poured some hot coffee into the professor's mug. He took a quick swallow, almost as if he were refueling.

"And our monsignor had no pity at all on tall, old drink of water, George Jenkin." He studied the nuns through his horn-rimmed glasses like a teacher making sure the pupils are still with him.

"Everyone in town who knows George knows he has a bit of a problem with the sauce. His wife, long-suffering soul that she was, finally left him. Every chance he got, the monsignor rubbed George's nose in it. Almost as if the monsignor had had something to do with it. At most of our meetings, you could almost see George writhing with pain and anger."

Mary Helen listened attentively, searching for some sort of clue as the professor made his way though the members of the parish council.

"Then there's Tina Rodiman," he said, pushing his back against the hard kitchen chair. "For the most part, our monsignor treated the woman as if she was an idiot. Although he didn't mind how much work he asked her to do, he dismissed her ideas and suggestions willy-nilly."

"How did Tina take that?" Eileen asked.

Professor Komsky thought for a moment, then shrugged. "Actually, the woman hardly seemed to notice. Her husband, Tony, treats her about the same way, so maybe she's used to it."

Or maybe she's seething inside and is enraged enough to murder someone, Mary Helen thought, sad that some women still allowed themselves to be degraded.

"What about Debbie Stevens?" Eileen asked. "Now there's a woman who acts as if she would hold her own."

Professor Komsky shrugged again. "The relationship between Ms. Stevens and the monsignor is difficult to put one's finger on," he said. "Clearly, he doesn't—didn't—like her too much. Under the pretense of teasing—he was good at that—he made short, cutting remarks about her hair, or her clothes, even her angular body. And you're right. She never did let him get away with any of it. To put it simply, theirs was a love/hate relationship, with hate winning in my opinion.

"But the showstopper came at yesterday's meeting. Just before you two arrived!" It was evident from the sparkle in his blue eyes that Komsky had enjoyed whatever had happened.

"The monsignor always treated Fred Davis as if he was a senile old fool. Even belittled his belief in purgatory and the urgency Fred felt to help his wife, Mildred, whom he thinks might be there."

Eileen sucked in her breath. "Well, I never!" she said, appalled, no doubt, at the priest's callousness.

"Not in so many words, Sister," Komsky assured her. "Just a jab here and an off-handed jibe there. Jolly an old fool along."

Professor Komsky gave a scornful laugh. "But was our monsignor wrong! Davis is as sharp with numbers as any man can be. Once he found a slight discrepancy in the parish books, he held onto it with the tenacity of a bulldog with his teeth sunk into the seat of Monsignor's pants.

" 'Creative bookkeeping,' Fred called it at first. I think he, like the rest of us, found it difficult to believe that any priest, even Joseph P. Higgins, would do such a thing.

" 'Nothing but cold, calculated embezzlement' is what Fred called it at yesterday's emergency meeting, and he had the hard facts to prove it.

"The monsignor tried to treat the problem as if it was a joke, but even he wasn't laughing. The rest of us were first shocked, then enraged at his betrayal of the parish trust."

"Do you think any of the council members were angry enough to have killed Monsignor Higgins?" Mary Helen asked bluntly, but she could tell that the idea had already entered the professor's mind.

He toyed with the teaspoon, bouncing it up and down on the tabletop while he formulated his reply. The old professor habit of acting as if you're formulating a learned answer dies hard, Mary Helen thought, watching him.

"The police say that the monsignor was poisoned. Since poison is usually administered in food, I don't think that we can rule out the cook, nor, as you say, anyone who ate with us in the dining room."

Including Eileen and me, Mary Helen thought and felt a feather of fear tickle her spine.

"Speak of the devil," Eileen whispered, as Eveleen Glynn pushed open the swinging door into the kitchen. Her pale blue rabbit eyes bore into Professor Nicholas Komsky.

"The lady policeman wants you in Charlotte Wixson's office," Eve announced in a flat voice. "Now!"

Without a reply, the professor stood, ran his fingers half-heartedly through his wild white hair. Then, looking like a frightened Einstein, he left the warmth of the kitchen.

"I suppose that you two are playing at detective again," Eve snapped from the doorway. "As if there weren't enough of them in the house."

Sister Eileen met her stare. "We were just having a cup of coffee," she said with more politeness than Mary Helen thought the remark deserved.

"I'd have to be blind, now wouldn't I, not to see that." Eve scooped up the coffee mugs and made a great show of clearing off the tabletop. With one broad hand, she swept the crumbs from George Jenkin's dry toast into an empty cup.

"May we help?" Eileen offered.

Crossing the kitchen noisily, Eve put the few dishes in the sink and turned on the faucet. "You'd probably be more trouble than you're worth," she mumbled, making sure that they overheard.

Piqued, Sister Mary Helen studied the housekeeper's broad back. Her slightly stooped shoulders were topped with a tiny tent of dull brown hair fringed with gray that Lady Clairol had failed to conceal.

Now there's an unhappy woman, she thought, watching Eve splash drops of water on the floor and on the toes of her bedroom slippers.

"Beef to the heel like a Mullingar heifer!" At the sight of the woman's legs that old quip of Eileen's popped into Mary Helen's mind. She could scarcely believe it. It was always Eileen who had a saying "from back home" to fit nearly every occasion, not herself. In fact, Mary Helen often accused her of making them up. Maybe it was contagious!

As abruptly as Eve had turned on the water, she shut it off then wheeled to face the nuns. "Are you waiting to talk to me?" She stared at them through finger-smeared glasses.

The unexpectedness of the question left Mary Helen fumbling for an answer, but she shouldn't have worried. Eve wasn't waiting for one.

"Because if you are," she said curtly, "you'll need to follow me outside into the back garden. The bushes and plants haven't been properly watered in days. The automatic sprinkler is no good at all, if you ask me. And, with all this hubbub, I'll wager no one will see to them if I don't. I only keep it up, you know, because my sainted cousin loved it so."

Stopping, she snatched a tan sweater out of the broom closet and slipped it on over her apron. The elbows of each sleeve and the ribbing around the waistband were stretched from wear. The rest of the sweater fit every bump on her body as if it had been knitted to order.

Eve pulled a red plaid kerchief from one sagging pocket. Covering her head with it, she tied the ends under her chin like a babushka. "It can get bloody cold when you're watering," she said, starting toward the back door, "especially if the fog comes in."

Wondering if they should follow her, Mary Helen caught Eileen's eye, who shrugged a quick "why not?" The two nuns, trailing the housekeeper, found themselves in the backyard of St. Agatha's rectory.

Despite Eve's warning about the cold, Mary Helen found the fresh air a treat after spending so many hours in the excessively warm rectory. The morning sun shone clear and crisp, shifting the shadows toward the house and turning the blades of grass in the small lawn a brilliant emerald green.

While the housekeeper unwound the coiled snake of hose,

Mary Helen moved to stand in a patch of direct sun. She felt its warmth through her black shoes onto her toes. With a little stretching, she could almost see the ocean, and so far no hint of fog had rolled onto the horizon.

She was aware that Eileen had sidled up next to her to enjoy, she suspected, the same spot. In the distance she heard the hum of the Sunset Scavenger's garbage truck.

"Have you any questions in mind to ask?" Eileen whispered, bringing Mary Helen back to their reason for being here.

"You two will have to speak up," Eve shouted above the sound of water hitting against the glossy rhododendron leaves, "if you want the answers to your questions." The bell-like blossoms glistened in the sun.

Next to the rhododendrons, magenta-colored azaleas bobbed under the pressure from the hose. Mary Helen moved closer to the housekeeper. "Honestly, I don't know exactly what to ask you," she said, watching the steady stream of water batter the cobalt blue balls on the hydrangea bush. Mud splattered on the creamy white calla lilies.

"There's plenty went on in this place." Eve turned toward Mary Helen, her blue eyes glinting with meanness. "Enough to write a book about, if you ask me. But it's all over now!" She nodded and a slight breeze ruffled the small piece of her hair sticking out from the kerchief. "Someone finally killed the man, and I'm not surprised."

She shot a stream of water at a camellia bush heavy with peppermint pink-striped blossoms. "Myself, I never did like the man, though I did for him for twelve years. Not from the first moment I saw him did I like him. A pompous kind of fellow, he was. You could tell by the look of him." She gave Mary Helen a knowing glance, then nodded her head, agreeing with herself. "What with that 'glad fellow, well met' voice, his mane of white hair, and that sunlamp tan. But there's no way to disguise the cold in a man's eyes.

"And the way he treated the assistant priests!" She wiped one hand against the front of her apron. "Like he was the king and they were his peasants. I wouldn't blame either one of them if they did poison him, not that either of them would. Both of them are too good to have done it, but what I'm saying is I wouldn't have blamed them."

"Did he treat you badly, too?" Mary Helen hoped her question didn't sound too pointed.

Eve Glynn stared at Mary Helen. Her blue eyes were wary now. "He treated me as bad as he thought he could get away with." She shrugged and moved the stream of water. "He was a little careful of me, was our J. P. Higgins. You know, I still have a few friends left. Actually, friends of my cousin, Monsignor Paddy Concannon. God rest him, it's nearly a sin to mention Higgins and that decent man in the same day." Eve crossed herself.

"Paddy's friends still take care of old cousin Eve. And well they might, with all the dinners I cooked them lads over the years. So, yes and no. He treated me as bad as he dared. But not nearly as bad as he treated others."

Watching the water drench the golden daffodils, Mary Helen was hoping the housekeeper would elucidate on her last remark. Instead Eve stared into the middle ground, apparently finished for the moment.

From the other side of the garden wall, they heard a car

door slam, then an engine turn over. "That one for instance," Eve pointed in the direction of the noise.

"Who is that one?" Eileen spoke up for the first time.

Eve twirled toward her, spraying water against the stone wall. "So you do have a tongue after all," she said sarcastically. "I was beginning to wonder if the cat had got it!"

Monsignor Higgins and Eve Glynn must have been some match, Mary Helen thought, watching Eileen's face flush. She was in awe of her friend's self-control.

Tires squealed. "That's Ms. Debbie," Eve said, mockingly. "Showing off again. You'd have to be deaf, dumb, and blind not to notice what was going on between them two."

Mary Helen must have looked puzzled. "Between his nibs, the monsignor, and Ms. Debbie, Sister." Eve pronounced each word distinctly, as though she were talking to a slow child. "What with the sly looks they were passing and the silly giggles, and those late-night, one-ring phone calls, and the creaking around on the floor above me."

Sister Mary Helen felt her stomach somersault. She hoped she wasn't right about what Eve was getting at, although it did make sense of what the professor had just told them. And, of course, there was Debbie's own attitude.

"And what exactly do you think was going on?"

Eve stared at her, full faced. There was a gleam of malice in her pale eyes. "That's for me to know and you to wonder." She clamped her lips together and stubbornly stuck out her chin.

I'm surprised someone hasn't murdered you, Mary Helen was thinking when the back door of the rectory swung open, and Inspector Kate Murphy stood on the top step.

"Sisters, may I see you for a moment?" Kate called out from the kitchen door, sounding as pleasant as she could. There was no sense getting those two loaded cannons pointing at you until you had to, she thought, smiling at them. She knew from many past encounters that the gentle approach was the best approach when dealing with any nuns, but especially with Sisters Mary Helen and Eileen.

"Yes, dear, of course," Sister Eileen agreed cheerfully. Sister Mary Helen followed her across the yard, looking a little preoccupied.

This is not a good sign, Kate thought, stepping back into the kitchen out of earshot of the housekeeper, she hoped. Watching the nuns wipe the dampness and mud from their feet, Kate rehearsed just how she was going to phrase her message for optimum success.

"What can we do for you?" Eileen asked, her round, wrinkled face open.

Not a good beginning, Kate thought, wondering how best to turn the question around into "what you can't do for me."

Crossing the kitchen floor, Mary Helen sat down heavily in the wooden chair and absently toyed with a teaspoon left behind from their coffee.

"What is it? What is bothering you?" Kate asked, unnecessarily. She could have bet money that Sister Mary Helen had discovered the same thing that Gallagher and she had from every one they questioned—the purpose of the emergency council meeting. Hard as it was to swallow, the good monsignor was nothing more than a smooth embezzler, and someone had murdered him because of it.

At first, Mary Helen acted as if she hadn't heard. Kate repeated her question. "What's bothering you, Sister?"

Looking up, Mary Helen smiled. "Nothing is bothering me really, Kate. I was just trying to make some sense out of the things I've heard this morning."

Reaching over, Kate patted the old nun's shoulder. "Not even someone as used to seeing evil as I am wants to see it in a priest," she said sympathetically. "Or to suspect that his murderer may be a pillar of the parish."

Mary Helen wagged her head. "What I need is a little time to think."

Kate was just about to say, "Let me know what you come up with," but she caught herself. She'd promised her partner that she'd discourage the two nuns from getting involved.

"You don't need to bother with it, Sister," she said, hoping her tone wasn't too patronizing. "Denny and I will take over from here. I have a hunch that one of the people who was at yesterday's meeting is our perp. Apparently, they were the last ones to see him alive. They all had opportunity and, from what I've gleaned, most of them had motives."

"But which one could it possibly be?" Eileen asked candidly. "They are all really good people."

Kate shrugged. "Even good people come to the end of their ropes," she said. "When the lab work is complete, we'll be able to narrow it down possibly to who had the means. As I said, Denny and I will take it from here."

Sister Mary Helen stood up abruptly. Her shoulders stiffened. "What you're trying to tell us, then, is that you don't need our help?"

Kate felt her face flush and, momentarily, she hesitated to meet the old nun's gaze. Put that bluntly, it sounded harsh, but that was her point exactly.

"For your own safety, Sisters," Kate mumbled.

"You're quite right," Mary Helen said, pushing her chair into its place under the kitchen table. "I take it then, Kate, that we are free to go." Her mouth had a tight little smile.

Kate nodded, feeling suddenly apprehensive about her quick success. For Mary Helen to acquiesce that easily was certainly out of character. Had she been extremely convincing, or did the old nun have something up her sleeve? Kate didn't want to even imagine what it could be.

Kate nodded. "You're free to go, for the time being," she said, "and have a happy St. Patrick's Day." With an inexplicable sense of foreboding, she watched the two nuns leave the rectory kitchen.

❧❧❧❧

"How did it go?" Gallagher asked when Kate rejoined him in Charlotte Wixson's office.

"Pretty well, I guess." Her stomach growled. She remembered that she'd left the house this morning without eating any breakfast. She'd intended to duck out of St. Agatha's rectory and grab a bagel on Noriega, but there hadn't been time.

"It looks as if we're about done here for the day," Kate said, slipping her notepad into her purse. "Can we grab a bite to eat before we get back to the hall? I'm starved."

Gallagher grunted. "If everything went so well, why do you look like your dog just died?"

"I don't even have a dog," Kate said. "And everything did go well. If anything, it went too well." She knew better than to share her uneasiness with her partner. "I guess I'm just feeling a bit ungrateful about being so short with them."

"Ungrateful!" Gallagher roared. "What do you mean ungrateful?"

"They have helped us several times," Kate reminded him.

"And how many times have they gotten in our way?" He loosened his Kelly green tie and undid the collar button of his shirt. "You know as well as I do that there must be an extra set of guardian angels assigned to keep those two from getting themselves killed."

"But they *have* been helpful," she needled, just for the fun of it. "Even you have to admit that."

Kate watched Gallagher's face turn red and swell up like a blowfish. Quickly, she opened the door of the secretary's office hoping that her partner wouldn't want everyone hearing him shout. Fortunately, he didn't.

❧❧❧

Back at the Hall of Justice, Inspectors Kate Murphy and Dennis Gallagher spent a long afternoon fielding phone calls and doing paperwork. Kate hated the pressure and paperwork parts of her job. From the tight scowl on her partner's face, she wasn't the only one.

She was just about to go for another cup of tired coffee to keep herself awake until quitting time when the phone on Gallagher's desk rang, again.

"It's the lab," he said, covering the mouthpiece.

Kate watched over Gallagher's shoulder as he scribbled down some of the facts.

"Carbohydrate andromedotoxin," he printed clearly. "Toxicity six."

Supertoxic, whatever it is, Kate thought. Six or seven drops of it are fatal.

"Death about six hours after ingestion," Gallagher wrote.

That figures.

After listening for several more seconds, Gallagher put down the receiver. "They'll send over the entire written report in the morning," he said. "Mike just wanted us to know that the monsignor was poisoned. Seems to have been dissolved in the tea. Looks like honey was the culprit. Although there was no new evident in the container we found in the kitchen." He wagged his head. "I've a good mind to say it was in the Irish bread. Although my better judgment says to say nothing and hope the perp slips."

Kate nodded. "Where do you find carbohydrate andromedotoxin, anyway?" she asked. "Any place we know?"

"You're not going to believe it." Gallagher ran his hand over his bald pate.

"Try me," Kate snapped, checking her watch. She was anxious to go home and talk to her husband, to see how his day had been.

"Flowers," Gallagher said.

"Any particular kind?"

"Those big rhododendrons. You know, Katie girl, the ones that bloom every spring in Golden Gate Park. And those pretty little plants people give for presents. Pink and white buds. Harmless looking things. Azaleas. They're both deadly!"

Gallagher cleared his throat. "So that narrows down our suspect list to everybody in San Francisco with a grudge against the good monsignor and who has a rhododendron or an azalea bush in their yard. Hell, my missus loves those things. Our backyard is full of them."

So is the backyard of St. Agatha's rectory. Kate's mind pulled up a needle-sharp picture of Eve Glynn, green hose in hand, watering the glossy bushes with showy blossoms of pink and white and purple. She saw the azaleas bobbing under the pressure of the water and the big rhododendron blossom on the kitchen table.

Gallagher's voice trailed on. "Or our murderer could also be anyone who walked through the park recently and picked a blossom." He scratched his head. "Or . . ."

Kate remembered the enormous blossom on the kitchen table. "I don't think we have to go any farther than the rectory itself," she said. "First thing tomorrow morning, we need to get serious about who had the opportunity."

❧❧

"How about a walk along Ocean Beach before we go back to the college?" Sister Eileen asked, once Mary Helen had successfully started the convent's Nova. "It may do us good to clear our heads before we get home."

"Great idea," Mary Helen said, heading straight down Ulloa Street to the Pacific.

Without much trouble, they turned onto the Great Highway and found a parking spot. They crossed over to the wide concrete strand which runs along the beach from Sloat Boulevard to the Cliff House. Even taking a part of the three-mile walk should clear the cotton, Mary Helen thought, pulling in a deep salty breath.

Leaning against the chest-high wall separating the strand from the beach, Mary Helen felt the awe she always felt at the ocean. She stood transfixed as the giant waves crested, then crashed against the wet hard sand. In the sudden silence that followed, she watched a family of tiny sandpipers chase the receding water through a mantle of lacy white foam.

"What do you say we walk twenty minutes up, then twenty minutes back?" Eileen suggested, pulling up the collar of her Aran sweater and stuffing her hands into its pockets.

Mary Helen nodded her agreement and followed suit with her collar and hands.

Although the day was clear, the wind was brisk. It hurled small grains of sand against the two nuns as they walked, tugging at the tails of their heavy sweaters and ruffling their hair.

A colorful hang glider hovered over the Pacific dangerously far, Mary Helen thought, from the cliffs of Fort Funston, where he must have taken off.

"What shall we do?" Eileen asked, ignoring the gray-and-white gull perched on the wall studying them with one piercing black eye.

"About which thing?" Mary Helen asked. Her head was crowded with potential problems.

"First things first," Eileen said, as if anyone should know

exactly which thing that was. "What shall we do about Sister Cecilia?"

Mary Helen gulped. Cecilia had been the least of her worries. But Eileen was right. They'd have to give the college president some explanation when they arrived home.

"What do you suggest we tell her?" Mary Helen asked, hoping that Eileen had formulated a plan.

"I say, we march straight into her office. Tell her that Monsignor Higgins has been murdered. Although someone probably heard it on the noon news and has told her already. Then we tell her that he was poisoned, we think, and that we are possibly under suspicion because we were there just before it happened with that blasted Irish soda bread."

Mary Helen stopped to catch her breath. "With that approach at least, she can't accuse us of not being forthright. Put that bluntly, however, poor Cecilia could be bowled over."

"We've a saying back home . . ."

Mary Helen groaned. Here it comes.

" 'The first sip of broth is always the hottest.' "

"Meaning?"

"Let's give her the worst scenario first. After that, anything she hears will seem not such bad news. Besides, I'll wager that if we sound as if the Mount's soda bread is in danger of being blamed, she'll be so preoccupied with having the college come out smelling sweet that she'll forget all about us."

"Possibly." Mary Helen gazed out across the Pacific. On the horizon, a lone freighter looked as tiny as a toy.

"What about us?" She was glad Eileen had brought up the

subject. The Homicide inspectors' accusations that Eileen and she might be involved worried her. Even though they both knew they were innocent, and she suspected that the inspectors did, too, she also knew that you don't have to throw much mud on the wall to make some stick. If the media picked up even the hint, the esteem in which the college was held could be permanently damaged.

"What do you mean, what about us?" Apparently Eileen hadn't considered this a real problem.

Mary Helen moved aside for a jogger. "I think it would be to everyone's benefit if we proved to Kate and Inspector Gallagher, once and for all, that we are innocent bystanders," she said.

"And how do you propose to do that?"

"By proving who is guilty."

Sister Eileen's round face grew serious. "You know full well that both Kate Murphy and Inspector Gallagher were adamant about our not getting involved."

"When has that ever stopped us?"

"This time it's different. This time, we could be suspects." Eileen's speech was beginning to have a telltale brogue.

"Exactly my point," Mary Helen said. "We owe it to the college. No! No! We owe it to religious life! No! Above all, we owe it to ourselves to find the real murderer."

"Not meaning to repeat myself, but how do you propose we do that?"

Fortunately, Mary Helen remembered a line from a Hercule Poirot mystery she'd recently watched on the PBS channel. "This affair must all be unraveled from within," the fussy Belgian detective had declared.

Mary Helen pulled her hand from her sweater pocket long enough to tap her forehead in perfect imitation. "These little gray cells. It's up to them."

"All well and good," Eileen was obviously unimpressed, "but who can it be? Today we talked to everyone who was there. Let's think . . . Tina." She shrugged. "Her big complaint seemed to be that the monsignor took the bingo money. Would she kill a man over bingo?"

"Don't forget her low-burning rage at being generally held of no account by the significant males in her life," Mary Helen countered, playing the devil's advocate.

"Sister Noreen seemed innocent enough. She genuinely acted as if she didn't know the monsignor was dead until this morning when the police called."

"But what about the roll of antacid tablets that Eve found?"

The two nuns skirted a homeless man rummaging through a garbage can for aluminum cans. He gazed at them with dark unfocused eyes.

"My heart goes out to Fred Davis," Eileen said. "That poor old fellow seems to have lost everything. We certainly can't suspect him."

"But what more has he to lose?" Mary Helen asked.

"Eve Glynn, of course, seems the obvious suspect." Eileen checked her wristwatch. "It's almost time to start back to the car," she said. "Do you want to sit for a minute?"

The two nuns found an empty wooden bench bordering the walkway and sat down. "Eve Glynn is too obvious," Mary Helen said. Watching the wind twirl some loose sand on the sidewalk into a miniature tornado, she asked, "Debbie Stevens is hiding something, don't you think?"

"Absolutely," Eileen agreed. "And then there's George Jenkin. He admits he could have killed Monsignor Higgins gladly. Yet, he can't seem to remember whether or not he did. Odd, isn't it? And Nicholas Komsky even daydreaming of torturing and killing the monsignor!"

From the beach beyond the low wall, they heard two dogs yelping playfully, totally unaware of the leash law. "After what he told us, I can scarcely blame him." Mary Helen pulled her sweater tightly around her. The sun was sinking fast in the lavender and pink sky. A band of gray fog hovered far out on the horizon, waiting to roll in and cover the Golden Gate.

Eileen shook her head. "We've known Professor Komsky too long and too well to believe him capable of murder. I wish we'd paid more attention to who passed what to whom while we were there on Sunday," she said.

"Then you agree with me that someone in the room was responsible for the monsignor's death?"

Eileen nodded. "It's a typical locked-room mystery, if you ask me."

"And you and I, old friend, will just have to discover the right key to unlock it," Mary Helen said, without thinking to apologize for the dreadful play on words.

❧❧❧

The moment Inspector Kate Murphy picked up her son, John, at the baby-sitter's, she knew that something was bothering him. When he scampered off to collect his things, she whispered to Sheila Atkins, "What happened?"

Sheila, who had cared for John since Kate returned to

work nearly three years ago, shrugged. "I don't really know. Jordie Holmes and he were playing trucks after their naps. Everything seemed fine, but by snacktime, I knew something had upset John. I asked him if everything was all right and, in typical John fashion, he looked at me with those big brown eyes and asked, 'Why?'

" 'Because you look like something is the matter,' I said, sure I had made my point." Sheila pushed a lock of auburn hair off her forehead. "By now, I should know better than to try to match wits with a three-year-old. He just looked some more, then ran off to feed Ernie the guinea pig."

On their way home in the car, Kate tried several times to make conversation. John sat quietly in his car seat in the backseat. "Are you feeling all right?" she asked at a stoplight. Half turning, she studied his round face which looked neither flushed nor pale. "Does your tummy hurt?"

John studied her with "those big brown eyes of his." "No," he said firmly.

"How was Ernie today?" Kate asked, knowing that John loved that little guinea pig.

"You know how a guinea pig eats?" he asked.

Ah, conversation at last, Kate thought. "No," she said. "How?"

John puckered up his mouth, wrinkled his pug nose, and did a perfect imitation. He looked surprised when his mother laughed. Spurred on, he tried his "guinea pig eating" imitation on several passing motorists, none of whom thought it as funny as his mother did.

When Kate pulled up in front of their yellow house on Geary Boulevard, she was glad to see her husband's car. Jack had beat them home. Today was her turn to pick up at the sitter and Jack's turn to cook. She felt suddenly famished and hoped that he had started dinner.

Rather, she hoped he remembered. Their smooth routine had suffered several bumpy months during Jack's recovery. Kate yearned to return to some kind of normalcy.

Unbuckling the belts of little John's car seat, she wondered if Jack's returning to work was what had upset the baby. He was so young, he probably didn't remember what their normal routine had been.

As soon as she helped him down to the curb, John dashed across the sidewalk and, using both hands and feet, scrambled up the front steps into his father's waiting arms.

"What's up, buddy?" Jack asked, scooping up his tiny son and covering his face with loud kisses.

Unexpected tears filled Kate's eyes when she thought of how close they'd both come to losing him. Reaching up, she drew her husband's face to hers and kissed him hard.

"What's that for?" Jack sounded surprised.

"It's St. Patrick's Day," Kate answered, moving past him to hang her coat in the hall closet. "You know how carried away I can get on St. Patrick's Day." Carefully, she stored her gun next to Jack's on the top shelf of the closet.

The delicious aroma of frying hamburger and onions filled the house. Kate's mouth began to water. "What are you fixing?" she asked.

"Tacos." Jack set little John down, free to run.

"Tacos on St. Patrick's Day?" As soon as the words were out, Kate regretted them. How many husbands, she wondered, actually take a turn cooking dinner? Jack grinned.

"O'Tacos with green chili," he said, playfully. "My mother offered to bring over corned beef and cabbage, but then we'd have my mother." He shrugged.

After Jack was shot, actually even before, his mother, Loretta Bassetti, was a frequent visitor to the Murphy-Bassetti household. A well-meaning, generous woman with an opinion about everything, she had proven overbearing on several occasions. Still, throughout Jack's ordeal, Kate had come to admire her mother-in-law's strength and courage. Neither she nor Jack could ever doubt her sincerity or her tremendous love for them and for her grandson.

It was, however, good to be alone, even if it meant eating Jack's tacos.

"Did you notice how quiet the baby was at dinner?" Jack asked while he and Kate were cleaning up. Their son was watching his favorite television program, *Wheel of Fortune*. Kate thought it was the spinning wheel that fascinated him. Jack thought he recognized the letters and, of course, Mama Bassetti was convinced that her grandson, the three-year-old genius, could read!

"Something is on his mind, that's for sure," Jack said. He fished out the last of the hamburger meat left in the frying pan.

"He was that way when I picked him up today," Kate said. "I asked Sheila if anything had happened."

She bent over to load the dishes into the dishwasher. "Sheila told me that, whatever it was—and she had no idea—happened between naps and snacks when he and Jordie Holmes were playing 'trucks.' "

"Who's this Jordie Holmes, Kate?" Jack asked, sounding like a Vice detective.

"I don't think he's dealing dope," Kate teased, "if that's what's worrying you."

"Is he new?" Jack asked, not put off. "I never heard you mention his name before."

"He's been at Sheila's for a month or so. From what I can see, he's a cute little three-year-old with straight dark hair and enormous blue eyes whose mother just had a baby. He must have been there when you picked up John. I'm surprised you didn't notice."

Jack thought for a minute. "Skinny little kid with freckles?"

"That's the one."

"John seems to like him."

"I think he does. Sheila didn't say that they fought or anything."

The sudden jab at the front doorbell startled Kate. "Who the heck can that be?" she wondered aloud. "I've paid the paperboy."

Two quick jabs following the first left no doubt in anyone's mind, "Nonie," little John squealed, running to the front door.

Jack Bassetti stifled a groan. "What's my mother doing here?" He ran his fingers through his thick dark hair. "I told her we didn't need anything."

"She can't help herself," Kate whispered, wiping her damp hands on her apron. Planting a smile on her face, she swung open the front door.

"Thank God you're home," Mama Bassetti said without waiting for a hello. Her soft cheeks were flushed. She handed Kate a large shopping bag and stepped into the house. Bending over, she hugged her grandson and covered his face with noisy kisses.

"When my Jackie told me that he was making tacos for St. Patrick's Day, I couldn't believe it." She looked up at Kate. Her brown eyes were full of sympathy. Shedding her wool coat, she strode toward the kitchen still talking. Little John and Kate followed her. Jack seemed rooted to the hall carpet.

"What kind of a son did you raise, Loretta? I asked myself. What kind of an unfeeling lout did you produce that he would give his Irish wife Mexican food on St. Patrick's Day?"

"What did you bring?" Kate asked, used to her mother-in-law's tirades. Setting the heavy bag on the kitchen table, Kate peeked in. Little John clambered up on the chair to see.

"What my own son should have thought of. Shame on you!" Clicking her tongue, she stared accusingly at Jack, who now stood in the doorway looking more amused than ashamed.

"Let me guess, Ma," he teased, getting down the glass cups from the cupboard. "Can it be my mother's favorite after-dinner drink? Can it be the makings of Irish coffee?"

With mock surprise, he removed the contents from the bag, including a small paper cup from Baskin-Robbins. "And can this be some mint chip ice cream for John?"

The baby squealed with delight. Mama Bassetti reached over and squeezed his chubby cheeks. "I don't suppose I'll have to make it, too. Do you, John?" she asked her grandson. "I hope your father can at least do that much."

"Why don't the queen mother and the crown prince go

129

watch *Wheel* while your humble servants whip this up?" Jack bowed ceremoniously.

His mother simply sniffed and led her grandchild into the living room.

"She's a classic," Kate said softly, hoping her mother-in-law was out of earshot. She measured the coffee for a fresh pot.

"Like you said, she can't help herself." Jack poured the whiskey into each cup, then began to whip the chilled cream. "She thinks that butting in is the divine right of mothers."

They heard whispers and giggles coming from the living room. "At least somebody is having a good time," Jack said over the sound of the beater.

"Maybe she'll be able to find out what's wrong with John." Kate couldn't seem to shake her concern.

Jack grunted in agreement.

"Time for me to get back home," Mrs. Bassetti announced as soon as she'd drained her drink. Little John, who had eaten all his ice cream, cuddled up next to his father on the couch and, almost immediately, the two of them had dropped off to sleep.

"Let me wash off his fingers and mouth," Mama Bassetti said, pointing to John. "He's all sticky."

Carrying her cup, Mama Bassetti went into the kitchen for a wet cloth. Kate followed her to the sink.

"Loretta," she asked, "did you think the baby was unusually quiet tonight?"

"At first." Mrs. Bassetti wet the edge of a dish towel.

"At first?"

"Until I found out what was bothering him."

Kate waited, her temper rising. What *was* bothering him? she wanted to shout. Instead, she decided to wait it out. "Did it have something to do with Jordie Holmes?" she asked when she thought she could stand it no longer.

Mama Bassetti nodded and rinsed her cup.

The woman is maddening, Kate thought. "I see," she said. "Is it something Jack and I should be concerned about?" She tried to sound calm.

Mama Bassetti let out a hoot. "If not Jack and you, then who else? Not me, that's for sure." Laughing at her own private joke, she patted Kate's shoulder. "Kate, John's little friend Jordie just got a brand-new baby sister. Every day at the baby-sitter's . . ." She rolled her dark eyes heavenward. "I knew I should have taken care of him. . . . Anyway, this Jordie tells John about the baby. How she goos and grabs his finger and smiles at him—although we both know it's probably gas. He tells John he's a big brother. I notice he never says how the new baby cries or how she dirties her diapers. So, of course, your son wants to be a big brother, too. He wants a baby at his house. That's all."

That's all! Kate felt her heart thudding like a tennis ball. She took a deep breath struggling to still it.

"Just like his father." Loretta shook her head. "When my Jackie was little, BoBo Spencer down the street—you remember, I told you about BoBo Spencer and the BB gun. Anyway, BoBo's mother had a baby. Nothing would do. My Jackie had to have one, too." She rolled her eyes again. "He nearly drove his poor papa and me crazy with the whining and the crying and the begging. Not that I think your having another baby is a bad idea. I don't. Now would be the perfect time, too. When John really wants one. Three is a good age to have a little brother or sister. A few more years and who knows? You and Jackie might have spoiled him, although it would be hard to spoil that little angel. . . . "

Loretta Bassetti's words flowed on like water down a drain, but Kate didn't hear. She was too shook up with the thought of having a brand-new baby!

❧❧❧

Jack Bassetti had turned off Jay Leno and set the alarm clock while Kate was still brushing her teeth. "Are you coming, hon?" he called eagerly from their bed.

"Coming, pal," she called back, hoping she didn't sound too distracted.

Jack was hard to fool. He watched her thoughtfully as she climbed into her side of the bed.

"Okay," he whispered, wrapping his strong arms around her. "What did my mother say?"

"Nothing," Kate hedged.

"Nothing much." Jack playfully planted kisses on her ear and down her neck. "You've been on another planet since she left. Do you know I asked you if I should carry the baby upstairs and put him to bed in the bathtub and you said, 'Great, pal'?"

"I did not," Kate protested, although she wasn't really sure she hadn't.

"Come clean, hon. What did my mother say, now?"

Kate hesitated. Was she up to the discussion she knew would follow? It had been a long day, but knowing her husband, it promised to be an even longer night if she didn't tell him. Kate rolled out of Jack's grasp.

"It can't be that bad. Or can it?" Jack propped himself up on one elbow so he could study her face. Playfully, he ran his index finger down her short freckled nose.

"You can tell me, hon. Nothing my mother would say can surprise me."

"It's about John." Next to her, Kate felt her husband's body tense. Quickly she told him about Jordie Holmes's baby sister and about their son wanting one, too.

Jack chuckled and said exactly what Kate was afraid he'd say. "That kid is full of great ideas."

"But, Jack." Kate dreaded starting this discussion. Not that they'd ever had it. Actually, they had deliberately skirted it on several occasions. "Do you think it's fair to have another child?"

"Fair?" Jack looked hurt. "What's unfair? We are good parents. At least, we try to be. And you've got to admit, we make beautiful kids."

Kate had to smile. "It's not that simple, pal," she said. "Do we want to bring another innocent child into this crime-filled world?"

"Who better than police parents?" Jack asked, undaunted.

"That's another problem. We are both in law enforcement. Something could happen to either one of us or to both of us." Her stomach felt queasy at the mere remembrance of Jack's close brush with death.

"Should we leave one kid all alone? Wouldn't it be better to give him a sibling?" Kate could tell by his tone of voice that Jack was serious.

"Do we have the time it takes to raise two kids?"

"For God's sake, Kate, Dennis Gallagher, a police person, raised six!"

"But Mrs. G. did not work." An uneasy quiet filled the darkened room bedroom. Kate couldn't believe she'd said that. She watched the street lamps and the headlights from Thirty-fourth Avenue combine into long moving shadows across their bedroom ceiling. In the distance, a helicopter whirred, probably hunting some felon.

"You don't have to work," Jack said quietly. "It was your decision."

"Can we afford two kids on one salary?"

"I repeat, Gallagher raised six."

"Those were different times."

"Just different priorities," Jack said softly.

"I'm bushed," Kate said. "Can we talk about this later, pal?"

"Sure," Jack agreed quickly. "I'm beat, too."

As they rolled away from each other, Kate thought wryly, I guess that tonight there will be absolutely no danger of bringing another child into the world. She was surprised that she felt a little sad.

❧❧❧

The scene with Sister Cecilia played out much better than Sister Mary Helen ever expected it would.

"If you have a next life, you should probably be an actress," she whispered to Sister Eileen when the two nuns finally left the college president's office.

"One life will be quite enough for me," Eileen snapped,

"and you should talk, old dear. For a few minutes there, you were smearing it on with a trowel."

"What do you mean?" Mary Helen asked, hoping she looked offended rather than pleased.

"When you went into that business about the college being implicated by those members of the press who might harbor anti-Catholic bias because of the poisoning potential of our soda bread, I thought the poor woman was going to faint."

Mary Helen felt her face flush. "Do you think I overdid it?" she asked.

"Not at all, Hazy Helen. Or do I mean Helen Hayes? Not at all," Eileen said, "although I was glad you stopped while I could still keep a straight face."

"Don't tell me about faces. Yours was so solemn when you told her that we, too, are suspects, that you even had me scared."

Sister Eileen let out a breath. "Never mind scaring you. I scared myself, as well," she admitted.

The rest of the evening had gone very smoothly, largely because it was so apparent to all the other nuns that Sister Cecilia was upset by the events at St. Agatha's. None of them referred to the murder. Instead, to a woman, they put their best efforts into making the annual St. Patrick's Day party fun.

Their laughter and good spirits, of course, made the corned beef and cabbage taste better than usual. Even the soda bread, which Mary Helen only tasted for politeness, seemed lighter.

Sister Maureen's rendition of "Danny Boy" sounded more poignant than ever. When Sister Anne and a few of the younger nuns did as much of an Irish step dance as they could remember, the nuns applauded as if they were right from the company of *Riverdance*. There was a round of Irish jokes. Everyone laughed even if they had heard them before.

The only glitch in the otherwise delightful evening came when old Sister Donata, her brown eyes sparkling, complained loudly that Sister Therese was a little stingy with the Jameson's whiskey in the Irish coffee.

"I made it according to the recipe," Therese pursed her lips. With an offended air, she poured a healthy shot into Donata's glass.

"Yuck!" Donata squealed when she took a taste. "What are you trying to do? Poison me?"

An uneasy quiet descended on the room until Sister Petronilla, who apparently was unaware of any tension, pulled out her squeeze box for a chorus of "The Rose of Tralee."

Despite the events of the long day, when Mary Helen finally climbed into her bed after a long hot soak in the bathtub, she felt that she was relaxed enough to drop right off to sleep. That is, until she snapped off her bedside lamp. Almost immediately, her mind snapped on. Wide awake, she lay in the darkness.

The events of the day played nonstop across her mind: Father Adams solemnly announcing the death of Monsignor Higgins; Kate's early-morning summons; sitting around the mahogany table in the dining room of St. Agatha's rectory with the other suspects.

In the darkness of her bedroom, Mary Helen heard the whir of a helicopter. Probably a police helicopter, she thought. Crazily, the sound brought back the same uneasiness she'd experienced this morning being considered one of the suspects.

She thought of the many conversations she'd had during the long day at the rectory. And of the many cups of coffee which accompanied them. Maybe that's why I can't sleep, she thought, readjusting her pillows. I'm chucked full of caffeine. But she knew that caffeine wasn't the real reason.

How she wished that she'd paid more attention on Sunday afternoon to who passed what to whom at that fateful table! The identity of the murderer was just beyond her grasp, like an itch that can't be reached. In her mind's eye, she saw six people around the table, staring with needle-sharp eyes at the monsignor.

In the darkness, she visualized the scene. The monsignor introduced them to Fred Davis. The old man clenched his fists until his knuckles were white. Next to him sat Debbie Stevens, her eyes glinting with anger. Tina Rodiman nervously nibbled at her waxy red bottom lip. George Jenkin's face was the color of whitefish. Next to him sat Sister Noreen, who looked as if she might be sick at any moment. Finally, their old friend, Professor Komsky, was there. His blue eyes were hard as glass.

Her memory replayed Eve Glynn arriving with the tea and the sliced bread. She saw the butter and jam, the honey bear with its sticky green plastic top. She remembered Sister Eileen and Sister Noreen serving the monsignor first, of course. The passing of the plate around the table, followed by the sugar and the cream. She certainly remembered Eileen trying desperately to make conversation.

The last thing that stuck in Mary Helen's mind was the housekeeper's remark: "I've seen a happier scene at a deathbed."

Did Eve Glynn know that Monsignor Higgins was literally on his deathbed? Wouldn't that be a very incriminating statement to make if you intended to murder the man?

Sister Mary Helen's mind rewound the reel. It began to play again. This could go on all night. Better if I sleep on it. Perhaps it will be clearer with a fresh eye, she thought.

Deliberately, she pulled her mind away from the rectory dining room. Slowly she tried to fill it with other things. She reflected on St. Patrick, whose feast day the nuns had celebrated with such style. He was not a man of learning, but a man of action and of rocklike faith. His mission to convert pagan Ireland had come to him in a dream.

Maybe the solution to the problem of Monsignor's murderer will come to me in a dream, she thought, that is, if I ever get to sleep! She rolled over on her other side, but not before she noticed that the large luminous numbers on her clock read 12:30. The low wail of a foghorn floated in from the Gate.

If I don't get to sleep soon, I'll be as limp as a dishcloth in the morning, Mary Helen thought, feeling under her pillow for her rosary beads. Fingering the worn beads, she reflected on St. Patrick, the priest. His holiness is known only by the tremendous fruits of his work.

Unexpectedly, she felt a pang of sadness for the monsignor. The fruits of his works had been his own painful murder.

Sadly, she touched each bead, praying over and over again the familiar comforting prayer. "Holy Mary, Mother of God, pray for us sinners, now and at the hour of our death." As she did, she felt sure that God in His infinite mercy would show compassion to Joseph P. Higgins, His all too human, and all too greedy, priest.

Tuesday, March 18

❦❦❦

Feast of St. Cyril of Jerusalem, Bishop and Doctor

Sister Mary Helen awoke with the beginning of a sick headache. Now is no time to get delicate, old girl, she thought, splashing her face with very cold water and swallowing two aspirins.

The pills plus a cup of good hot coffee should fix things up, she reckoned, slipping quickly into her clothes.

At the coffee pot in the small convent kitchenette, she ran across young Sister Anne. "You look terrible," Anne said kindly, adding a dollop of cream to her own cup.

That surely does a lot to make me feel better, Mary Helen was tempted to say, but she knew that Anne meant no harm.

"But compared to Cecilia, you look wonderful," Anne continued.

Mary Helen stared into middle space. "What's wrong with Cecilia?" she asked, knowing full well.

"She looks as if she's been up all night worrying. Her bags are packed under both eyes. You know how she gets."

Mary Helen did. With a twinge of guilt, she swallowed the rest of her coffee. Hoping to avoid Cecilia, she hurried off to the chapel and slipped into a pew beside her friend Sister Eileen, as morning Mass was about to begin.

Father Adams, the college chaplain, had just finished his homily when the message came. Mary Helen was still pondering what he'd said about St. Cyril in the fourth century attending the second ecumenical council, the Council of Constantinople. The saint had helped to promulgate the Nicene Creed which was still said at Mass today. Father Adams made the point that sometimes we have no idea of the outcome of our decisions.

Mary Helen was absorbed in applying his premise to the events of Sunday afternoon when Sister Therese arrived at the end of her pew. In a stage whisper, Therese announced that Inspector Murphy had called and that the inspector wanted both Eileen and "you, Sister" at St. Agatha's rectory A.S.A.P. "Whatever that means," Therese sniffed.

Although Sister Cecilia was two pews in front of her, Mary Helen saw the college president's back stiffen. Poor dear, she thought. For her sake alone, let's hope this mess is solved today.

As the final hymn began, the two nuns slipped out of the chapel. They paused just long enough to call their respective offices and report that they'd be out for the day. While Mary Helen went for the keys to the convent Nova, Eileen gathered up two Danish rolls and two Styrofoam cups of coffee to tide them over.

Overnight, the dry, cold polar air had swept into the city from the bay bringing with it sparkling clear weather. Not a shred of fog appeared in a cold blue sky and the crisp sunshine gave everything in its path a hard true edge.

The laughter and shouts coming from St. Agatha's schoolyard seemed exceptionally loud and clear as the two nuns approached the wood-paneled door of the rectory. Even the melodious chimes of the doorbell sounded sharper.

Glad that her headache was gone, Sister Mary Helen stomped her feet to keep warm, much as she had done on Sunday when they innocently arrived with their Irish soda bread. Father Adams was right when he said that one never knows where the simplest decision might lead. It is somehow all in God's providence. On that subject, Mary Helen had a number of questions to ask God when they finally met face-to-face. For instance, why had so many of her simple decisions led her into such complications? And God had better have some decent answers!

"We'll be nothing but icicles if they don't hurry and let us in," Eileen said, her breath coming out in little white puffs.

Charlotte Wixson swung open the door. The secretary's round face was an unnatural red and her dark eyes jumped nervously from Sister to Sister. "Come in," she said in a breathy voice. "You're the last ones here."

Without another word, Charlotte led them into the priests' dining room. The six members of the parish council sat around the mahogany table in the same seats they had occupied on Sunday and again on Monday. Mary Helen's heart turned over as the six pairs of eyes, sharp as needles, pinned her as they had Joe Higgins at the pastor's last council meeting.

❧❧❧❧

Fred Davis felt his eyes burn as he stared across the rectory dining room at Sister Mary Helen and Sister Eileen. "Come in here, for God's sake, and sit down," he wanted to shout at them. "The group has been waiting for you two for. . . . " Davis pulled back the sleeve of his dark wool jacket. He checked his wristwatch. To be precise, they had been waiting for two minutes and thirty-seven seconds.

Why in God's name can't people be on time? That had been one of Mildred's faults, God love her. She was never very late, just a minute or two, which made Fred even more angry with her. "If you're only that late, there is really no excuse at all for not being on time!" he'd shouted too often. It had driven him to distraction.

Tears filled his eyes. What he wouldn't do to have his Mildred back with all her maddening faults. He dug in his suit pocket for his handkerchief. It was lumpy and hard. He guessed it had been in his pocket since Mildred died. Fred felt his throat begin to swell with the familiar longing for her. He touched the roof of his mouth with the tip of his tongue to push it down, yet it wouldn't go. He shut his eyes. Pull yourself together, he warned himself. You're a concerned senior member of this parish, dismayed by the death of your beloved pastor. To break into sobs would be overdoing it.

With great effort Fred pulled his face into a welcoming smile. Not too happy a smile, he hoped. It would never do to

144

let anyone really know the satisfaction he felt now that that despicable Joe Higgins was dead. It couldn't have happened to a more deserving chap, he thought, hoping that his loathing of the man wouldn't creep into his voice when he spoke. And he knew he'd have to speak before the morning was finished.

Fred Davis studied the two nuns as they stood in an awkward silence at the head of the mahogany table, all eyes on them. Yesterday, if you asked him, the two of them never stopped talking. Like Mildred. His dear Mildred was a woman who woke up talking. She used to drive him crazy with all her questions and inane comments before he'd even drunk his first cup of coffee.

That is, until he'd hit upon a solution. He made it his habit to go right from their bed into the shower so that he could wake up in peace. Mildred didn't seem to mind. At first, she'd try to shout over the noise of the water. Then, one morning, much to his relief, she'd given up and he was able to wake up in peace and quiet.

Fred spread his large hands on the tabletop, pretending to study them. What he wouldn't give now to hear just one of Mildred's questions, one of her comments.

He hoped Mildred knew how sorry he was that he hadn't listened to her. Souls in purgatory must know what their loved ones on earth are feeling and thinking.

A strong, deep anger stirred within him. His Mildred might still be in purgatory when he wanted so badly for her to be in heaven. She might be suffering because of the greed and avarice of a priest, a priest who thought he was above the law. Well, no one is above the law!

Fred glanced up again at the two nuns. The taller of the two, although they were both short, Sister Mary Helen, was looking right at him. What did she see? Fred felt the sweat trickle down from his armpits over his ribs.

He wondered if his good shirt stank. Mildred had always made sure that his shirts were fresh. He could see her still. As soon as he'd take off his shirt, she would snatch it up. Her short stubby nose sniffing at each of the armholes. Her mouth turned down.

He hated to watch her. It made him feel like spoiled meat. He had made such a fuss that Mildred had finally taken his dirty shirts out to the laundry porch where he couldn't see her sniffing, unaware that he could still hear her.

Fred let his face relax, surprised that he was still smiling. Enough of that, he thought, holding Sister Mary Helen's gaze. Her short nose reminded him a little bit of Mildred's. Would she be sniffing around like some bloodhound, poking her nose into places it didn't belong, pontificating on things she could never understand, like sin and punishment?

Yesterday, if he had heard her correctly, the woman had practically denied the Church doctrine of purgatory, hadn't she? Insisting that a good God would not judge harshly. Well, Sister, he thought, God's judgments are different from man's and if Mildred's faults drove me crazy, what must an infinitely perfect God feel?

Fred adjusted his wire-rimmed glasses. At her age, and a religious, too! She should have better sense. For all he knew, she probably didn't believe in capital punishment either. All that liberal, fuzzy, bleeding-heart thinking usually went together like mixing debits and credits until you can't tell which is which.

Well, no matter what these New Age theologians are teaching, Fred Davis would go to his grave believing right is right. And that no one, not even a priest of the Church, is above punishment for his sins. Sometimes good people must take the punishment into their own hands. Nothing any nun could say would ever change his mind.

He stared at Sister Mary Helen until his burning eyes began to water. He had to admit that he felt a certain sense of relief when the nun finally shifted her gaze down the table to Tina Rodiman.

❧❧❧

Why is she looking at me? Tina Rodiman wondered. Her whole body felt warm under Sister Mary Helen's gaze. Maybe she did see us at the beach yesterday afternoon.

The gold bangle bracelets jingled on her quaking arms. To still them, Tina squeezed her fingers together until her rings cut into her flesh. Even though her fingers stung, looking down at the sparkling gold and gems made her feel better. Thank goodness, she thought. I need something to cheer me up.

Yesterday Tony and she had had the worst fight of their married life. Although this morning her husband was all sweetness and light, she could still get angry when she thought about it.

By the time she'd arrived home from the rectory in the afternoon, her kids were already there. They sat huddled together on the front steps, their tear-streaked faces telling her that they were terrified.

"Where were you, Mommy?" Mary Rose wailed accusingly. "We rang the bell and you didn't come. We thought something bad happened to you," she sobbed.

Tina's heart did a somersault. "My poor babies," she crooned, gathering the four of them in her arms. She had not thought of giving them a key, never imagined that they would arrive home first.

Before she was able to open the front door, a car screeched to a stop by the curb. A car door slammed.

"Daddy!" Kevin cried.

"Daddy?" Tina's stomach fell.

"Mikey went back to school and called him because we were scared," Mark explained.

Tony had taken the front steps two at a time. Before Tina could struggle to her feet, Tony loomed over them. His face was white with fear and his lips as tight as if they were sutured.

"What happened to you?" he asked in a voice rising from the deep freeze. His eyes blazed.

Before she could answer, he unlocked the front door. "Inside, kids," he commanded.

The children, sensing the tension, melted into the house and began to play quietly in the family room.

"We need to talk," Tony said, sounding too much like Tina's own father. "Get in the car. Mikey can watch the other three for an hour. He seems to have enough sense."

"As much as I do, is what you're saying?" Tina asked, but her husband did not answer. He had gone to the family room to talk to the kids.

The couple rode to the beach in silence. Tony parked along the Great Highway facing the Pacific Ocean. Without even a glance at its vast magnificence, he turned toward her. "What were you thinking of?" he asked above the crashing of the waves. Without waiting for her answer, he unloaded all his anger and frustration, leaving Tina feeling like a child who had been soundly scolded.

At first, tears of hurt welled up in her eyes. She bowed her head, not wanting to meet her husband's accusing glare, much as she had done her whole life whenever she was scolded. Her insides felt like the kids' Jell-O wigglers as she tried to hold down the anger. Shows of temper had never gotten her anything but more trouble.

How could he say such things to me? Her bottom lip quivered. How could he make such untrue accusations? How could he?

Wheeling over the beach, a seagull screeched. The sea spray was sharp with salt. "Please, Tony," she began, her words as choppy as the ocean.

He stared straight ahead.

"Tony," she repeated, meaning to sound penitent. Without warning, something inside her burst. Tina felt a hot stream jet down through her body, then bounce up from the soles of her feet back to her head. Her temples throbbed. Her face and ears burned. Everything—the car seat, the steering wheel, even Tony—had a red edge.

Her tears were no longer tears of hurt, but tears of rage. "Just who the hell do you think you're talking to?" she shouted in a voice she didn't recognize. Her "naughty" word surprised even herself.

Tony looked in shock. For once in their married life, he was speechless. His face paled, except for his cheeks, which were blazing as if she'd slapped him hard. At the moment she wanted to slap him over and over again until the palms of her hands stung.

Instead, like blows, she hit him with what she thought of his attitude toward her, his demeaning manner, his total disregard for her feelings and opinions. Her anger still unspent, she went on to how she felt about his insistence that they participate in parish activities, including soccer and bingo. Especially bingo. Still unable to control the rage, she threw in her opinion of his views on birth control.

"Shh," he pleaded, pointing through the steamy car windshield toward the strand. "Those nuns might hear you."

Looking up, Tina recognized Sister Mary Helen and Sister Eileen walking along the strand. Totally engrossed in their own conversation, they didn't seem to notice Tony and herself, not that she cared if they did.

When she had finally run out of words, Tina leaned back against the headrest, unable to believe what she had just done. Tony had never witnessed one of her full-blown temper tantrums before. Seated beside her, he looked shaken. Without a word, he turned on the ignition and they drove home.

"Mommy's had a tough day," he announced to the kids when they arrived home. "Let's take her out for dinner."

The children, still wary, quickly turned off the television, put on their jackets, and lined up by the front door. With big eyes, they studied their parents' unusual behavior. Not one of them, not even Mary Rose, begged to go to McDonald's for a Happy Meal.

To Tina's amazement, Tony drove to Joe's of Westlake and insisted that they order a bottle of red wine with dinner. He's either repentant, or he thinks I'm the monsignor's murderer, Tina thought, feeling guilty. Watching him pour her a second glass of wine, she wondered how long she could keep him guessing.

Last night, when the couple finally went to bed, Tony had made sure that he wasn't on her side. Tina had spread out, luxuriantly enjoying her entire half and even putting one foot over on his.

"May I?" he had asked putting his arm around her. Reluctantly, she had snuggled against her husband.

His gentleness had brought fresh tears to her eyes. "I'm so scared about the monsignor's murder, Tony. What if the police think I did it?" she had whispered.

"No one would believe that," her husband had said, but she felt his body stiffen. She knew exactly what he was thinking. No one would believe it unless he'd seen your act at the beach.

Today, under Sister Mary Helen's steady gaze, Tina Rodiman felt the perspiration break out on her forehead. She was relieved when Sister Noreen spoke.

❧❧❧

"Welcome, Sisters," Sister Noreen said brightly. She smiled up at the newcomers, hoping that she sounded sincere. Actually, she wished the whole lot of them would go home and let her run her school in peace. Not that there was much possibility of doing that until the monsignor had been buried and his murderer caught.

Noreen folded her plump hands and noticed with surprise a new sprinkling of liver spots on their backs. The pastor's murder was enough to cause anybody to age in a hurry, she thought. And it was just like him, too, to cause such a furor. He couldn't die of a heart attack or anything simple like that. No, not Joe Higgins!

Her esophagus burned and she dug into the pocket of her navy blue suit jacket for a roll of Tums. As inconspicuously as possible, she thumbed the top one from the pack and popped it into her mouth.

Things could be worse. They probably would be worse, too, when it came out in the media that not only was the monsignor murdered, but that the reason was related most likely to his embezzlement of parish funds.

Sweet relief, Noreen thought, biting into the chalky tablet. Her shoulders tightened. Worst of all, I'll have to act sorry about his death and shocked about his greed.

It would never do to admit to anyone that—priest or no— she had absolutely no use for the man. Never had. Not even on their first meeting when she was about to take over St. Agatha's School. What was it now? Six years ago? Even then she had thought that he was a pompous, self-important fraud. Over the years, he had done nothing to change her mind.

Rather than wow her, his startling white hair, sharp blue eyes, booming voice, and movie-star tan had put her off. Toward the end, even the spicy aroma of the man's aftershave made her gag.

Noreen suspected that it had something to do with her realization that he was fooling with the funds. Her face felt hot when she remembered the sheer arrogance of the man to think that he was fooling her about the deficit in the school's books. Jollying her along with his talk of capital outlay and depreciation funds. Did he think she was a simpleton? She wondered in retrospect if he ever suspected that she knew what he was up to. Probably not. He was conceited enough to think that he had fooled her. Gray hair doesn't mean that the gray cells aren't working, she'd wanted to shout. What was the use? He would have pretended not to understand.

Making room for Sister Mary Helen and Sister Eileen to take their places at the large table, Noreen shifted her chair. She was getting very weary of sitting on the hard chair. The room held an unhealthy silence. What time was this meeting going to start, anyway? She had a million things to do. She'd heard the voices of the two homicide inspectors coming from Charlotte Wixson's office. So—

Surreptitiously, Sister Noreen slipped another antacid tablet into her mouth and wondered just how much she should tell the police detectives. Should she tell them that, foolishly, she had thought that she could talk sense to the monsignor. That after the council meeting on Sunday, she'd followed him up to his suite. Should she tell them how she'd begged him to make restitution, and how he had dismissed her with a wave of his soft hand, his diamond cuff links gleaming in the light from his desk lamp. He dismissed her as one dismisses a usually pleasant child who has awakened grumpy from a nap.

Noreen felt warm all over. There seemed to be no air in the dining room. Or was it the thought of her final confrontation with Monsignor Higgins making her angry all over again. The unmitigated gall of the man! She shouldn't let her feelings distract her. Right now she had to make some decisions. She felt light-headed. Concentrate, Noreen!

What should she tell the two officers? Should she tell them of the loathing she felt for the man? Should she explain that during their last brief conversation, she must have dropped her roll of antacids? That the monsignor had been alive and strutting when she left him? Would they be interested in knowing that the man was not sorry at all about how he had abused the parish funds and the parishioners' trust? Not a bit repentant about his betrayal of his sacred calling. Or should she let them find out for themselves?

Sister Noreen removed her large bifocals and rubbed an imaginary spot on the lens. She wondered if the room was beginning to feel like a sauna to anyone else. She pushed back a strand of hair from her damp forehead.

Noreen checked her wristwatch. The Archdiocese was sending the chancellor over in less than an hour to meet with her. He would surely have a list of all the details that needed to be covered in the burial of a pastor.

Her stomach felt queasy. Surely, she could count on Sister Bernice to prepare the children's choir. Most likely there'd be an honor guard of the youngsters in their school uniforms. Sister Jane was good at managing large groups. Maybe she'd ask Sister Jane to take charge of the honor guard.

When, she wondered, would the body be released? Nothing was going to be simple. What was that old saying? "As you live, so shall you die?" It was unrealistic to expect that anyone who lived as devious a life as Joseph P. Higgins would ever have a straightforward death and burial. She might just as well resign herself to that.

Embroiled in her own thought, Sister Noreen was startled, then relieved, when the dining room door swung open. It was that tall, slim, young, red-headed homicide inspector. What was her name? Murphy? There was about to be some action, at last.

❧❦❧

Inspector Kate Murphy's mind was only half on the murder of Monsignor Higgins when she swung back the door. The other half of it was still back in Charlotte Wixson's office, gazing transfixed at the picture of the secretary's adorable granddaughter.

The picture was precious. The baby was precious. No wonder her son, John, wanted one. Kate felt a pang in her heart. All babies are precious, she thought reasonably, but they grow up and need shoes and food and their parents' attention.

Having a baby was a very serious decision, a serious responsibility. She wondered when Jack and she would talk about it again. This morning had not been the time. They were both rushing around getting ready for work, getting their son ready to take to the sitter's. Besides, her husband seemed a little distant.

When she asked him about it, he'd denied it. "I'm just tired, that's all," he'd said. "I didn't sleep too well."

Who had? Kate thought, stepping close to the mirror on her dressing table to examine the darkness under her eyes. She never slept well when things weren't absolutely all right between them. She'd liked to have told him that one of the times she was awake, he'd been snoring!

Now is not the time to worry about home problems, she reminded herself, stepping into the rectory dining room. Now I need to put my whole attention on finding a murderer.

Inspector Dennis Gallagher followed her into the spacious room. He gave a little cough. "Good morning, ladies and gentlemen. May I have your attention, please?" he asked unnecessarily. The room was deadly still. All eyes were riveted on them.

He checked his notepad. Kate knew he had nothing on it. It was just Gallagher's way of making a group feel ill at ease. After a quick sweep of those present, Gallagher turned to Charlotte Wixson, who was hovering in the entryway.

"Will you get Miss Glynn and the two of you join us, please?" he grumbled.

Eve Glynn must have been eavesdropping at the pantry door because it opened immediately. "Nobody needs to go looking for me," she said, shuffling into the room still in her blue bedroom slippers. "I'm right on call as always."

With the shifting of chairs and a few grunts, all the suspects were seated at the large mahogany table. Their faces, though for the most part pale, were composed.

I'm positive one of you is our murderer, Kate thought, although I have no idea which one. Studying each innocent-seeming upturned face, she hoped one of them would make a mistake and show his or her hand soon. The chief, the commissioner, His Honor "Da Mayor," the chancery's office, assorted supervisors, and even the governor's office were already on the police's tail to come up with the perp as quickly as possible.

She cleared her throat. "Thank you all for getting here so

promptly," she began. "Now that we know for sure what killed the monsignor, my partner and I would like to ask each of you a few more questions."

"What killed him?" Eve blurted out.

"Poison," Kate replied flatly. A tense silence filled the room.

"Do you know what kind of poison?" Debbie Stevens asked in her high nasal voice. "Or how it was ingested?"

Kate nodded. "Forensics tells us," she said, "that the monsignor was poisoned by carbohydrate andromedotoxin."

"Whatever is that?" Sister Noreen's eyes were large behind her owl glasses.

"That's a toxic poison found in several common plants," Kate said.

"Such as?" Debbie Stevens snapped.

"Such as rhododendron and azaleas." Kate watched Eve Glynn's face darken.

"How was it ingested?" Sister Mary Helen asked, sounding unusually timid.

Kate was tempted to say, "on Irish soda bread," but resisted. "Most likely with the tea," she answered honestly.

Debbie Stevens snorted. "It couldn't have been the tea we drank at the meeting. We're not poisoned. "Joe drank tea constantly. Maybe he had a cup with someone else." She searched the room for support.

"If anyone would know how much tea he drank, you would, girly girl," Eve said, almost under her breath.

"And exactly what does that mean?" Debbie half rose from her chair, her angry eyes piercing the housekeeper.

"A body doesn't have to be a genius or even a detective to

know how much time you've spent with himself," Eve said meanly. "Working on parish business, so I'm told."

Debbie's face tightened like a fist. "You old busybody!" she snarled. "I suppose you didn't notice that I hadn't seen much of him recently."

With a cunning smile, Eve twisted one corner of her apron. She bowed her head so Kate could see her crown where the gray roots were just beginning to push out from the dull brown hair. "To tell you the God's honest truth, Miss Debbie, it leaves me wondering. Is it that you had been seeing less of each other, or is it just that you were getting more cagey about it?"

"Enough, ladies," Kate interrupted, afraid that Debbie Stevens was going to make a lunge for the housekeeper. "Maybe we should talk to you first, Miss Glynn. You seem to know a great deal about the workings of the rectory."

Eve's round flat face reddened. Straightening her heavy shoulders, she stared at Kate through smudged glasses. Kate could almost feel the heat coming from those pale blue eyes.

"A housekeeper is supposed to know what goes on in the house she keeps," Eve said in a surprisingly obsequious tone of voice. "And I'll be very happy to share whatever I know with you." Her eyes covered the room. "This whole thing is a scandal, a blot on the good name of the Holy Catholic and Apostolic Church." She blessed herself. "A stop should be put to it as soon as is humanly possible."

Puzzled, Kate Murphy nodded amicably. What whole thing? Murder? Monsignor's embezzling parish funds? What went on in the rectory? She would have to talk to Eve Glynn to find out exactly what the housekeeper meant.

This should be some trip, Kate thought, following the shuffling woman out of the dining room. With a soft click, Kate shut the door behind them.

❦❦❦

"Poisoned with rhododendrons," Professor Nicholas Komsky muttered to himself, "just like Xenophon's army."

"What was that you said, Professor?" Sister Mary Helen seemed to be the only person in the room who had heard him.

"Nothing really, Sister. I was just thinking aloud," he said, wishing he had bitten his tongue.

"Something about Xenophon?" Her hazel eyes sparked with interest, too much interest for him to ignore the question.

"You're familiar, Sister, I'm sure, with the Greek general and historian. His entire army was poisoned with the nectar, or was it the honey, made from the rhododendron." He tried to act addled. "I just saw the similarities, that's all." He shrugged and gave a rough laugh. "Occupational hazard, I guess."

Sister Mary Helen smiled. His explanation seemed to satisfy her. Komsky felt damp all over with relief. He pulled a white linen handkerchief from the pocket of his tweed jacket and mopped his forehead. Nervously, he smoothed down his caterpillar eyebrows.

Why can't you resist the urge to show off? he berated himself. His wife, Marie, was always after him for that. And Marie was right. That was what had propelled him into this mess in the first place.

If I hadn't been such a showboater with the liturgical reform and homiletics, I never would have incurred the monsignor's envy and anger in the first place. It would never have spilled over on unsuspecting, undeserving Sarah. Poor Sarah!

Nick's heart hurt remembering the expression on her face when the monsignor refused to give her Communion. He could have killed the man on the very steps of the sanctuary! Trying not to meet the eyes of anyone else in the room, Komsky sank deeper into his chair. Only the nun, however, had seemed to take any notice of what he'd said. Good. Bad luck that she'd heard it. She's too sharp for her own good, he thought. His heart thudding, he took a deep breath and let it out slowly.

Just because I know what poison was used to kill Xenophon's army doesn't mean I am the murderer, does it? No one would think that, would they? I am, after all, an educated man, a history professor. That's what you'd expect from a history professor, isn't it? To know some history?

His knees felt like liquid. He'd like to get a cup of coffee from the kitchen, but he didn't trust himself to stand.

"How about you, Nick?" George Jenkin's throaty growl broke into his thoughts. "Coffee?" Jenkin said. "I'm getting myself a cup. Two's just as easy to carry."

Komsky nodded gratefully. Coffee, hot and black, was just what the doctor ordered. He watched Jenkin's long legs take the room in a few strides.

When he returned, Nick took the cup in both hands and savored his first delicious swallow. Removing his horn-rimmed glasses, he closed his eyes.

Sister Mary Helen is an educated woman, too, Komsky reasoned. Also, an historian, if I remember correctly. No wonder she was interested in Xenophon. That's the only reason she asked.

He took another sip. *She's known me far too long and far too well to ever suspect that I'd be responsible for causing anyone such a painful death. And it was very painful, too, if* Komsky remembered his ancient Greek history. *The poison reacts slowly. About six hours is what it takes to do its work. The victim's death begins with a touch of nausea, then some drooling.* Komsky tried not to enjoy the picture of the pompous Monsignor Joseph Higgins drooling on his fresh silk shirt. He tried not to gloat at the idea of the monsignor's eyes filling with tears like the tears of hurt he'd caused Sarah to shed.

If Komsky remembered his history correctly, *as the poison takes hold of its unsuspecting victims, the vomiting starts, then diarrhea, then paralysis. Finally come the seizures. How frightening it must be to feel your entire body losing control, shaking violently, and to be unable to restrain even the smallest muscle.*

Another renowned Greek, Anaxagoras, if Komsky's memory served him, had said that "the descent to Hades is the same from every place." *Not so,* thought Komsky. *The descent from those final moments of unspeakable agony must have been hell itself. And, it couldn't have happened to a more deserving guy,* Komsky thought cruelly.

He admired those wonderfully intelligent Greeks who had discovered that honey made from the bees which fed on certain blossoms is poisonous.

In his mind's eye, Komsky saw himself among the ancient warriors. . . . He walks up to the monsignor wearing his chlamys and carrying a golden platter in his hand, pauses, and asks cordially, "Would you care for a honey cake, Monsignor?"

Komsky opened his eyes to find Sister Mary Helen studying him. Quickly, her eyes darted away, leaving him to wonder what the woman was looking at. Was he, without realizing it, talking aloud? Certainly not! If that were the case, others would be studying him, too.

Did the expression on his face give away his sinister thought? Surely not! If anything, he probably looked pleasant. Can she read minds? Absurd, he assured himself. She's clever, but no mind reader. None the less, her eyeing made him uncomfortable.

"Ashamed" was probably a more accurate description of what he felt. Ashamed that he had been such a coward, that he had never told the monsignor how deeply enraged he was, that he had never told the man how roundly he hated him for what he had done to his Sarah. Instead, he had allowed that hatred to grow in him and nourished it until it was almost a person itself.

He was deeply ashamed of the pleasure he now felt in contemplating the tiniest detail of another human being's torturous death. He would never want the nuns to know what a truly cold, merciless, vindictive man he had allowed himself to become. Above all, he would never want his Sarah to know.

❧❧❧

What's wrong with old Nick? George Jenkins wondered. He studied the professor, eyes closed, gulping down the coffee that George had just handed him. It took him a moment to think of what Komsky reminded him of—Einstein with a headache!

Good line, George, he congratulated himself and wished he could share it with the others in the room. Their faces looked as if they could use a laugh. He knew some good "dead" jokes, but now didn't seem to be the time.

Geez, he felt great this morning! He swept his hand across his receding hairline. No throbbing head. No queasy stomach. No stiff neck. Not even a cottony mouth. And on the morning after St. Patty's Day, too, a day on which he traditionally tied one on! Stella, his wife, ex-wife, he reminded himself—annulled wife, to be completely accurate—would be proud. Actually, Stella would have a tough time believing it. But fear not, he'd make up for it today. Already he'd had a little bourbon juice for breakfast.

George studied the scuffed toes of his shoes. One of these days he'd have to get those big clodhoppers shined. Maybe for Monsignor Joe's funeral. It would never do for a member of the parish council to arrive looking anything but spiffy. He might as well keep up appearances in honor of Joe Higgins, who was big on appearances.

The miserable old hypocrite! George Jenkin felt his face flush with anger. Someone had put him out of his misery! He wondered who.

George dug into his jacket pocket for his ever-present pencil and reporter's pad. He set them in front of him on the dining room table. Almost immediately, he began to bounce the rubber eraser on the pad.

"Shave and a haircut, two bits," he tapped over and over.

The rhythm helped him to think, and he needed to think about the events of Sunday evening—those he could remember.

How much of what had happened was his fault? He couldn't duck all the blame. After all, he was the one who had put that old tight ass, Fred Davis, on the scent of the monsignor's transgressions. Sure enough, despite his initial disbelief, Fred discovered that the revered monsignor had a bad case of sticky fingers.

Jenkin wondered just what else might have come to light if he'd continued on the monsignor's case. Was there something else, or were all the council members as mad as they seemed about the money? He couldn't remember seeing so many angry people in one room since the last meeting of the San Francisco Board of Supervisors. Another good line, George!

"Will you please stop that!" Debbie Stevens's high nasal voice filled the room.

At first, George had no idea what she was referring to. He looked up innocently.

Her Hershey's kisses eyes flashing, Debbie pointed to his eraser.

"Sorry, sweetheart," George said in his best Humphrey Bogart imitation. He was reasonably sure what reaction he would get and was not disappointed.

The muscles in Debbie's square jaw moved furiously. "I am not your sweetheart!" she snapped, "nor do I appreciate being patronized."

George held up the palms of his hands as if to ward off her blows. "Sorry, Ms. Stevens. God knows, I wouldn't want to patronize you." George winked. "You're upset enough already." He brought his fist up to his chest. "Mea culpa. I should have realized how deeply the monsignor's death would affect you."

"What exactly does that mean?" Debbie asked with an acid twist of her mouth.

"It just means that I know that you and the monsignor were such good friends." He stuffed as much meaning as he could into the word *good*.

Silence filled the dining room. He'd struck pay dirt. Up to now, he'd only suspected that the monsignor and Debbie had something going on the side. He hadn't been sure until Debbie's reaction just confirmed it.

Outside, a garbage truck hummed. A dog barked and another answered. Tires swished and a horn honked on the boulevard. Suddenly, the shouts and laughter of children burst in upon the room. It must be recess.

"I am sure we are all deeply affected by the monsignor's passing," Mary Helen said. Her tone let him know that, if he continued, he was dicing with death.

Jenkin's first impulse was to chance it, lash back at the old bag, but he caught himself. Just as well to stop the banter. What he really needed to do now was to think.

Putting his pencil back into his pocket, he picked up his coffee cup and took a sip. Lukewarm! Yuck! That wouldn't help him concentrate. He tilted his head back.

Sunday night? Sunday night was a blur. He must have passed out. The only thing he remembered was the dream he was having just before the phone call came from the police.

Odd! He rarely remembered his dreams anymore. This

one was especially vivid. He had been chasing the priest, lunging at him. Fortunately for George, the priest had been poisoned, not bludgeoned.

He did feel a small twinge of guilt, Catholic guilt, the worst kind—almost impossible to blot out, even when you were three sheets to the wind. He'd spent his share of time with enough other maudlin Catholic drunks to know that for a fact.

George took another swallow of coffee. Too bad there wasn't a little stick to go in it. He felt for the flask in his pocket. The moment he was alone, he'd remedy that.

After all, he thought, ignoring the nagging blame, I only wanted to find the guy's Achilles' heel. Have a little "payback" time. And, sure enough, after a little prodding from him, Fred had found it. Had found at least one "heel," that is. George couldn't help chuckling at his unintended pun. Once a writer, always a writer!

On the serious side, how responsible was he for what had happened? I set him up for the fall, George conceded, his stomach jumping. Fred brought him down. But all of us had the opportunity to poison the bastard.

Who was it? Was it good old straight-arrow Fred? Not likely. We all had the opportunity, or did we? George strained to re-enact the end of the meeting: the passing of the cups, the tea, the bread, the goes-on-tos. The scene was fuzzy. He was already several drinks into his cups before he arrived at the rectory. A little pre-Patty's Day celebration, he thought, not really kidding himself.

George shifted in his chair. He checked his watch. Only ten-thirty. God, this was a long morning. He could almost taste his noonday beer. Great with a pastrami sandwich and chips. Maybe he'd have time for two beers. They must get a lunch break. After all, they weren't in jail. Yet!

The coffee hit his stomach like a fireball. Maybe there was a piece of bread or something in the kitchen. Did he dare to get up? The dragon lady was behind closed doors with the red-headed homicide cop. Maybe he'd asked the secretary for something. Charlotte had always appeared harmless.

George's eyes shifted around the room. Everyone in it appeared to be harmless, sitting in their places like so many polite dinner guests. Yet, one of them was a murderer. His nose for news told him that much.

Think logically. Which member of the council had a motive? Mentally, he'd shuffle through the members, but before he could begin the voice of conscience rang through his head.

"You did, fella," it taunted. "You had a very good motive. You were mad enough about Stella's leaving you to have ripped the guy to shreds without a second thought."

George Jenkin felt the color drain from his face. His mouth went dry. His hands felt cold and shaky. "But I didn't!" he shouted mentally at the annoying voice.

"How do you know, wise guy? How can you be so sure?" it mocked him. "Hey! You can't even remember Sunday night, now, can you?"

❧❦❧

"Let me bring in a little snack," Charlotte Wixson said in as cheerful a voice as she was able to muster. "I know we must all be getting hungry and restless from just waiting around."

No one objected, which surprised Charlotte. In light of last Sunday's tea, she wasn't sure that she'd accept anything to eat unless she was fixing it herself. On the contrary, for the most part the group looked relieved. Only Sister Eileen spoke. "That sounds like a grand idea, dear," she said. "Do you need any help?"

Shaking her head, Charlotte went through the pantry door. Thank goodness it's empty, she thought, happy to be alone in the enormous kitchen. Help was the last thing she wanted. She leaned against the counter and closed her eyes. One more minute in that room and I'd have gone mad, she thought, and took four, long, deep breaths. She let each one out slowly the way they told you to in those "Ten Ways to Reduce Stress" articles in the women's magazines. In fact, all it did was make her feel a little lightheaded.

Straightening her shoulders, Charlotte began to arrange an assortment of homemade cookies on a serving plate. Tonight, I'm telling Kip I'm out of this madhouse, she thought, placing a row of macaroons next to the butter cookies.

Yes, sir, my working days are over! From now on, I plan to stay home and be a full-time grandmother! I may even take up bridge or start watching the soaps.

Picking up some paper napkins, she smiled, knowing her husband would be delighted. I'm out of here, she repeated to herself, out of here, before this place is the death of me, too.

❧❦❧

I've had enough of you, George Jenkin, you insufferable old lush! Debbie Stevens thought, studying the tall man across the table.

His liquid brown eyes met hers and Debbie blushed. Thank goodness we can't read one another's minds, she thought, glancing nervously around the room.

No one but George seemed to be looking at her. Surely everyone in the room must have heard what he said about her being so friendly with Joe. Did anyone else suspect that they were more than old friends? That they were sometimes lovers?

Although she'd tried to be careful about when and how she came into the rectory, Eve and Charlotte must have had their suspicions, especially Eve, who made it her business to know everything that went on in the place.

Debbie had had her fill of Eve, too, the acid-tongued old busybody. George and Eve. Eve and George. She visualized the two of them mysteriously disappearing forever without a trace. Would the world be worse for their going? Not at all!

Tears stung Debbie's eyes. What was wrong with her? Never before in her entire life had the thought of making another human being disappear crossed her mind. Maybe of not speaking to them or of avoiding them when possible. Even this simple shunning of people used to make her feel guilty. Today she was daydreaming about making people disappear!

The muscles in Debbie's jaw tightened. It was the anger, she knew, the anger and the hatred which grew together in her like a well-watered vine. Her psychoanalyst had told her that the tendrils would slowly weave and twist around all her feelings and all her actions, this anger and hatred spawned by Joe Higgins.

Now that Joe was dead, there was no place for them to go.

They seemed ready to grab onto anyone. Debbie circled her head, trying to relax her stiff shoulders.

She'd miss Joe. And she would always love her memories, she guessed, despite the fact that he'd merely used her. That was crystal clear now. She'd been so naive when she'd first met him. And she'd been too old to use youth for an excuse.

It was just that Joe was so handsome, so sophisticated. Even now, her stomach churned when she relived her first encounters with the dashing Joe Higgins. He had opened a whole new world to her of stage plays and gourmet dinners, of concerts and drives along the breathtaking California coast.

He had flattered her, pampered her, made her wait eagerly for the sound of his voice. When he'd finally stirred up her deepest emotions and taken her to himself, he'd been gentle and tender.

Oh, how she'd loved him! There was no one else for her, no other life. No way back to the world from which she'd come.

Foolishly, she'd thought he felt the same. How did her psychoanalyst put it? "Women are from Venus. Men are from Mars."

In the peach glow of nostalgia, Debbie remembered the first days of their sabbatical program. From the first moment she'd seen him, she'd known, even then, that her life and the life of the attractive, outgoing priest would be entwined forever. She remembered the autumn day when she returned to her motherhouse in Wisconsin.

An ache closed in on her heart. How brash she had been. Actually, how gullible. She had tried to phone Joe from Wisconsin to tell him what she had done. He never seemed to be at home and it was not the kind of message one leaves with the priest's secretary. Finally, she'd written. She had to wait for what seemed forever, but was only five days for his phone call.

"So, sweetcakes, you leapt over the wall," he'd said. His deep jovial voice gave her goose bumps.

"Have you?" she'd asked candidly.

Joe had chuckled. "My wall is a little more complicated than yours, Deborah. First of all, the Arch has been out of town."

So Sister Superior had been correct, not that it proved anything. Joe had made an honest mistake.

"What should I do now?" Debbie had felt the tears flood her eyes.

"Well, hop on a plane for San Francisco, of course. Get your cute little butt out here, close to me, where it belongs," he'd said.

Debbie's heart had soared. Within the week, she was in San Francisco in a cozy little apartment Joe had rented for her near the Presidio. At first, the wailing of the foghorns outside the Golden Gate had haunted her. Were they an omen? When she'd told Joe about her fears, he had laughed and arranged a couple of job interviews for her.

"What if I get all of them," she'd asked. The thought of being turned down had never entered her mind.

"It's your nun's training," Joe had joked. "You think you'll always get a job, even if you are eighty. But, seriously, Deb. Take the offer that has the highest salary and the best benefits," he advised.

That was, in fact, what Debbie had done. She hated her job but it paid well and the benefits could not be beat.

At first, they rendezvoused almost every night—sometimes at Debbie's apartment, sometimes at the rectory, always discreetly. After a couple of months, "things" came up to prevent Joe's coming. Debbie understood.

Joe was apologetic. "When I get my dispensation, sweetcakes, I promise I'll be with you every night of my life."

By the end of the second year, they were only meeting on Friday nights. Debbie was unhappy with the arrangement, so Joe persuaded her to join his parish council. That way there were some legitimate reasons for "business" dinners and late-night meetings.

"We can't be seen together so much without a reason," Joe had explained. "We don't want people to talk."

"Why not?" Debbie fought back her tears. "If you are going to leave the priesthood to marry me, won't they talk anyway?"

Joe had taken both her hands in his. Fondly, he'd removed her glasses and kissed each of her eyelids. She felt his body harden against hers. "Sweetcakes," he'd crooned, "the archbishop will be much more open to granting my request if there has been 'no hint of scandal.'" He imitated the aging prelate perfectly, and Debbie had laughed in spite of herself.

"Trust me," he'd begged. She had melted into his arms.

Time, ever in flight, turned days and months into years and still Debbie trusted. Like the proverbial moth, unable to resist the flame, she had gone back to him time after time.

It was only three years ago, when the honorary title of "monsignor" was bestowed upon Joe, that her trust faltered.

"A monsignor?" Debbie had exploded. "You are being honored for your work and zeal in promoting the welfare of the Church? That's what a monsignor is, you know, one who is distinguished for those things. How do you have the nerve to accept the honor when you are screwing me every chance you get?"

"You don't have to be crude, Deborah." Joe had looked hurt. "What we have is a relationship based on our mutual zeal for the Church."

"Bullshit!" Debbie spat out.

Joe's eyes avoided hers. "Maybe we should have a time away from each other," he'd said. "Think things over. Reach a new and deeper plane in our relationship."

"You're dropping me, aren't you?" Debbie had shrieked. "You have no intention of leaving the priesthood or of marrying me, do you?"

"Shush," Joe had cautioned. They were in his suite. "We don't want old Eve to overhear, now do we?"

"There is no 'we,'" Debbie had shrieked, "and I couldn't care less who hears!"

"Debbie," Joe had coaxed. "Sweetcakes! This is just a temporary separation. I will always love you. I will always need you. You are my touchstone. Without you I would be—"

"Celibate like you are supposed to be!" Debbie shouted.

She watched as first anger, then righteous indignation, replaced the softness and compassion on Joe's face. It was as if she was watching a chameleon crawl onto a leaf, except at last she saw Joe Higgins's true colors.

At that moment her anger and hatred, like evil twins, had begun to grow in her. Sometimes, especially on nights when the bleating of the foghorn kept her awake, she would fantasize about grabbing the monsignor's shoulders and watching his eyes fill with terror before she flung him, as she had once flung her gold profession band, into the roaring, leaping bank of flames licking out from the motherhouse incinerator. With a sense of satisfaction, she imagined the cracking of the fire consuming him until there was nothing left but his shiny Gucci loafers.

Even her psychoanalyst had been a little shocked when Debbie had told her that.

�֍֍

Without waiting to be invited, Eveleen Glynn plopped down in the office chair. Her "dogs" were killing her already and it wasn't even noontime yet. "Well, Officers," she said as soon as she settled, "what is it you want to know?" It was a good thing to be direct with the police.

Eve noticed the skinny redhead, Murphy, shoot a glance at the fat cop, Gallagher, who had his rump perched on the end of Charlotte's desk. God help him if he breaks off the leg, she thought, the monsignor will have his hide. Then she remembered that *himself* was dead.

Well, he'd better be careful nonetheless. If he knocks over Charlotte's picture of her grandchild and breaks the glass there'll be hell to pay, too.

Why anyone doted so much on an infant was hard for Eve to imagine. In the old country, she'd helped her own poor mother raise the eleven after her that God had sent. Not without the assistance of Da, to be sure. That was before her cousin Padraig, God rest him, rescued her. If she never

174

saw another squalling infant, it would suit her just fine.

"How long have you worked at St. Agatha's?" Murphy asked sweetly.

All that sweetness and light wasn't fooling Eve for one minute. *She wonders if I'm the killer,* she fumed. *She's nearly convinced herself that I did it. Stupid cow! Why, in God's name, does the city allow women policemen, anyway? It isn't natural. It's a man's job. Not that the fat one, Gallagher, looked any more promising.*

"How long? Didn't I tell you that yesterday?" Eve asked innocently. In her head, she was figuring up the years as quickly as she could, hoping her tally was the same as yesterday. *Were they trying to trick her?*

"We'd like to have you tell us again, to make sure we have it down correctly." Murphy seemed unflappable.

We'll see, thought Eve. "Too long," she said.

Both officers chuckled. *Who did they think they were fooling? She'd seen cops do that friendly act hundreds of times on her television.*

"How long is too long?" Gallagher asked, as if it could make any difference.

"About forty years," Eve said finally.

"That *is* a long time!" Murphy said, as if this was the first time she'd heard it. *Maybe the woman was a little dense.*

Eve folded her thick hands and rested them on her lap. *I should have changed my apron,* she thought, noting several unidentifiable spots.

"Did you like the monsignor?" Gallagher asked, as if it were any of his business.

"Like I told you yesterday, you don't feel the same about a

man after you pick up his shorts, but he was the pastor." Eve hoped she sounded pious.

Gallagher slid off the desk. "I'm asking you if you liked him."

Uh, oh! The joviality had slipped from his voice. "He was a good man," Eve said, crossing her fingers. It was not wise to speak ill of the dead, especially to the police.

Obviously aware that there was no use beating a dead horse, Gallagher shrugged and yielded to Murphy.

"Miss Glynn, can you tell us again what you did last night?" she asked politely. At least the woman knew her place!

Quickly, Eve recounted calling the monsignor on the house phone—he was plenty alive then—putting on her hat and coat, meeting Molly Ford, a good friend from the old country, and the two of them traipsing off to the Empire Theater in West Portal.

"The movie was PG," the housekeeper added. No harm letting these two know that she was a decent sort of woman.

"What time did you tell us you arrived home?" Murphy asked.

"I was in my own room by ten," Eve said. She had tried to persuade Molly to stop in at Joxer Daily's after the show for a nightcap, but Molly had refused. Seems she doesn't like to drink after her evening meal, which was probably why, Eve figured, she was always complaining about insomnia. She wasn't sure now whether or not to be grateful to her friend.

"How can you be so sure?" the fat cop asked.

"Because I turned on my television and the ten o'clock news had just begun."

"Will Molly Ford be able to corroborate your time frame?" Murphy asked, as smart as you please.

"Unless she's lost her senses since I saw her last."

"Did you happen to see the monsignor after you came home?"

"I never stop by any of the priests' rooms after they retire in the evening." *What kind of loose woman do they think I am?* Eve bristled. *Furthermore, she was getting tired of answering the same questions. She wished they'd get to the good stuff.*

"About the meeting on Sunday," the Murphy woman began.

Changing the subject, hoping to catch me off-guard, is she? Eve tried not to smile. *They must think me as dull as dishwater. This question was precisely the one she'd been waiting for.*

"Oh, the meeting." She rolled her eyes and hoped she didn't sound too eager. *No one, even the police, likes a gossip.* Eve stared earnestly at the officers through her smudged glasses. "Evil begets evil, they say. A bad deed turns on its doer."

"Were you at the meeting?" that uppity policewoman asked. *She knows bloody well I wasn't.* Eve struggled not to let her annoyance show.

"You didn't have to be in the room to hear their sparks flying. Unpleasant, it was, too," she said, then added, "although I tried not to hear."

Eve felt her cheeks grow hot. *Why shouldn't she listen? After all, what went on in that meeting affected her more than anyone in the room. What guarantee did she have that* if that pompous peacock, Joseph P. Higgins, was removed from the parish, the next pastor would keep her on? Eve was no fool. She knew she was getting old. Her poor aching feet told her that long before the looking glass confirmed it. And the more time passed since the death of her dear cousin Padraig, the less influence his friends would have. Several of his strongest supporters had already passed away.

Murphy was looking at her expectantly. It took Eve a moment to remember what she'd been saying.

"The unpleasantness of the meeting . . ." Murphy prompted.

"Like I told you, Officer." Eve twisted one corner of her apron. "It was awful," she said, trying to sound shocked. "The voices came into my kitchen as clear as if they were in the very room."

The housekeeper checked the faces of the two homicide detectives for their reactions. A couple of poker faces. They must learn that in police school.

She went on. "Someone, Fred Davis I think, accused the monsignor of theft. The whole place got quiet as a tomb and then, himself roared, 'How dare you?' But Fred paid him no mind, just went right on. Then, I heard that Debbie Stevens shout, 'You bastard!' "

Eve wrung her hands. "To the priest, no less! She's a bold girl. Always pestering the man. And George Jenkin shouted, 'Got you!' Sounded like he might have had a bit of the sauce. That nervous little Tina Rodiman started to bawl, and Sister Noreen tried to calm her although I could tell, by the tone of her voice, that Noreen was hopping mad, too. The professor threatened to call the police although the police could have heard him a block away. But, all the while, the maddest was that old milquetoast Fred Davis. I've never heard him holler so loud, calling down fire and brimstone on the monsignor's head.

"Any one of them could have killed him and might have, too, if the doorbell hadn't rung and Charlotte let in the two nuns. I can tell you, Monsignor Higgins was one happy man to see them. Made over them something terrible. Ordering up tea and fixings like I was some kind of slave.

"Then all the parish council members got polite, asking if they could help, but they weren't fooling nobody. Those nuns would have to be blind not to see the tension.

"I'll tell you the truth, Officers, any one of those council members could have done it. And, as for me, I'm not going to miss his 'better-than thou' ways one little bit. You mark my words, there will be many a dry eye at that man's funeral."

Eve was conscious that both police officers were studying her. She felt her cheeks burn. "I didn't murder the man, if that's what you want to know." She patted her already flat hair into place. "As far as I'm concerned, Officers, and this is the God's honest truth, our monsignor wasn't even worth the poison it took to murder him."

Eveleen Glynn stared at the two homicide detectives, silently daring them to contradict her.

❧❧❧

Sister Mary Helen checked her wristwatch. This waiting your turn to be interrogated was driving her crazy. In fact, she could not remember when, if ever, having the time pass so slowly. Inspectors Kate Murphy and Dennis Gallagher seemed to be following no particular pattern in calling the "suspects."

Eve Glynn had been first. Then Charlotte Wixson, the parish secretary. Professor Komsky had marched in with a determined expression on his wide-open face and been followed in quick succession by George Jenkin, then Debbie Stevens.

Sister Noreen had come out of the small office looking as if she might be sick. And from the puffiness of Tina Rodiman's eyes, Mary Helen was sure the woman had been crying.

Fred Davis was in with the homicide detectives now. Actually, he'd been there for quite some time which, in a way, made sense. Since Fred was the head of the parish council's finance committee, he was the one who had discovered that the monsignor was dipping into the collection. Naturally, the police would have questions.

Sister Mary Helen wondered if Eileen or she would be called next. Probably Eileen. Not, she suspected, because they considered saving the best for last.

She hoped they would at least break for lunch before they called her. She was starving. It would never do to answer serious questions about the monsignor's murder with her stomach growling.

As though Kate Murphy had heard her, the dining room door swung open. "It's nearly twelve-thirty and I'm sure you must all need a break for food or fresh air," Kate said with a smile that would make an alligator proud.

Mary Helen watched her fellow suspects. When the inspector suggested that they eat, several turned pale. Regardless of their coloring, Mary Helen agreed with Kate. They all would feel better with some fresh air and a little something in their stomachs.

As soon as Kate finished emphasizing that they were free to roam, but must be back at St. Agatha's rectory at one-thirty sharp, Eileen raised both eyebrows. Mary Helen knew the signal well. "Let's get out of here in a hurry," it said, "so that we can talk."

Cautiously, Mary Helen peeked out the front door of the rectory. She was surprised that the news media hadn't arrived yet. Someone must be keeping the lid on this case, but she was sure they couldn't do it for too much longer. The two nuns made a quick exit.

Their first stop was Guerra's deli. After flirting briefly with the Toscano and Sicilian sandwiches, both heavy with salami, the nuns settled for the Milano, which was a gourmet turkey sandwich, a bag of chips, a low-cal cola, and one chocolate biscotti to split. These last two items were to appease the diet gods, of course. Neither was serious enough to have chosen the vegetarian Napoli sandwich.

Safely back in the car with their paper sack, the two nuns drove along the Great Highway to Ocean Beach where Mary Helen parked the convent Nova, its nose pointed toward the Pacific.

Except for a few senior citizens walking the strand, one jogger, and a curly-tailed beige husky pulling a woman with blue hair behind him, the beach was deserted.

"I was so involved at the rectory, I altogether forgot it was a workday," Eileen commented, spreading out her napkin and unwrapping her sandwich.

Several other cars were parked along the highway. Their passengers seemed to have the same idea as the nuns. And why not? It was a view that even the priciest restaurants could not duplicate.

Below a cloudless blue sky, the flat, camouflage green ocean sparkled with hundreds of whitecaps. A single sailboat bobbed far out on the water. At the shoreline, enormous waves crested and crashed in a deafening roar.

Mary Helen drew in a long salty breath and gazed out to where the sky and the sea met in an unbroken line. The breath of it somehow put things in perspective. She sighed. Despite all the evils that human beings are capable of, God the Creator still orders an immense and powerful universe. Yet that same omnipotent God loves each one of us as if we were the only one. "The very hairs of our heads are numbered," the Gospel's words popped into her mind, "and not one sparrow shall fall to the ground without God knowing it." It was truly amazing.

She bit into her Milano sandwich, savoring the taste of roasted peppers.

"You know what bothers me, old dear?" Eileen asked.

Mary Helen, whose mouth was full, knew that her friend didn't expect an answer. Eileen would tell her anyway.

"Why—if we all drank the tea—weren't we all poisoned?" Eileen's gray eyes were wide as she studied Mary Helen, who finally managed to swallow.

"Obviously, the monsignor had something in it that none of the rest of us did," she said, and took another sip of her diet drink.

"Honey?"

Mary Helen shook her head. "Debbie had honey, too."

"That's why Kate and Inspector Gallagher aren't telling us anything more than the poison was in the tea," Eileen said, thinking aloud. "Anything more only the murderer knows, and they are hoping he or she will make a slip."

"I'm sure we'd know how it was done if we could just remember everyone's exact movements that afternoon," Mary Helen said. "Every murderer makes one fatal mistake." She bit into her half of the biscotti.

"At least in your mystery stories," Eileen added.

The two sat in comfortable silence, chewing. Eileen finally turned to face her friend. "The longer I'm with those parish council members, the harder it is to believe that any one of them is guilty of murder. Actually, they all seem to be really good, generous people."

"What is it you always say?" Mary Helen tried to remember one of Eileen's sayings from "back home." " 'A saint in the face may be a fiend in the heart'?"

Eileen nodded. "That's true, but we've known the professor and Sister Noreen for years. I can't believe either of them is guilty of murder. And Tina Rodiman has children to raise, for heaven's sake. Debbie Stevens told us she was a nun for years. Not the best training for a murderer." Eileen shut her eyes, obviously figuring which suspects she'd left out. "Neither Fred Davis nor George Jenkin seems the type. We know we didn't do it, and Charlotte Wixson wasn't even in the room."

"What about Eve Glynn?" Mary Helen asked.

"What is Sister Anne's latest expression? 'Big hat, no cattle.' "

"Which means?"

Eileen shrugged. "Possibly the old 'bark is worse than her bite,' might better fit Eve's situation."

"There must be something we're missing," Mary Helen repeated. "They say—whoever *they* is—that everything you see or hear is stored in your memory, even if you can't recall it. What we need to know is stored in there somewhere."

"*If* we saw or heard it." Eileen was beginning to sound skeptical.

Sister Mary Helen gathered up their lunch wrappers. "Maybe if we just relax and not try so hard," she said, "it will pop into one of our minds. How about a little stretch? We still have thirty minutes."

Slamming the car doors, the two nuns strode briskly along the strand. Mary Helen tried to follow her own advice by concentrating on the grandeur of the Pacific Ocean as it changed moods in the light. Trying to keep her mind blank, she relished the sharp breeze on her face, enjoyed the grains of sand prickling her legs. She listened to the shrill cries of the seagulls wheeling gracefully over the trash cans in search of food. In the distance, she heard the bark of the seals on Seal Rock, and beyond it the Cliff House perched on the promontory like a miniature mansion.

Still, no matter how empty Mary Helen's mind became or how absorbed she was in the beauty around her, the fatal mistake of the murderer and his or her identity did not pop into her mind.

Judging from the expression on Sister Eileen's round face, Mary Helen guessed that her friend wasn't having much better luck.

Inspector Kate Murphy was relieved when all her suspects took her up on her invitation to break for lunch. After Eve Glynn had announced to the assistant priests that they were on their own, even she had left the rectory. Probably to bring her friend—what was her name?—Molly Ford up to date on the investigation.

Kate was glad that Gallagher and she were alone. They could talk freely. In this old place, with all its doors and cupboards, it was difficult to know who could overhear what.

Before she left, Charlotte Wixson was kind enough to offer them a sandwich. She had put salami, cheese, and sourdough bread on the kitchen table.

"There's coffee on the stove if you want some and mustard in the refrigerator," Charlotte had said. Then she closed the door firmly behind her.

"Salami and cheese and sourdough!" Dennis Gallagher was practically salivating. "Now, there's an offer I can't refuse." He led the way down the hall to the kitchen.

Despite the fact that the kitchen was an enormous, stainless-steel affair, Eve Glynn had done her best to make it cozy. Yellow-checked, ruffled curtains hung on all the windows and picked up the yellow speck in the linoleum. A bright flowered tablecloth covered a small table that she had placed by a triptych of windows, where it picked up both the morning and afternoon sun.

Outside the window, the rectory garden was a commotion of color—white, lavender, hot pink, lemon yellow. Bright sun gilded the camellias, the rhododendrons, the azaleas, all heavy with buds. Even the Japanese plum tree was beginning to bloom.

An unlikely spot for a murder, Kate thought, gazing out at the peaceful setting. But then she'd found herself in many unlikely murder spots in the company of Sister Mary Helen.

She turned to watch her partner building a sandwich. "I thought Mrs. G. told me she was sending you to work with fat-free yogurt," she said.

Mouth full, Gallagher shrugged. "It will keep," Kate thought she heard.

Unable to resist, Kate fixed herself a sandwich, too. The monsignor had kept a fine larder. Apparently, in food, as with everything else, money was no object to the priest. After all, Kate thought cynically, he wasn't spending his own . . . apparently.

"Coffee?" she asked her partner.

"Anything but tea," he said, and Kate agreed wholeheartedly.

When they had finished their nearly silent lunch, Kate felt better. She had needed a break. She knew they shouldn't take too much more time. When they'd left the Homicide detail this morning, the telephone was already ringing and the lieutenant shouting for a quick solution. He was probably spending most of his day fielding calls from prominent San Franciscans wanting "something to be done about the atrocity." Little did they realize what a can of worms this case really opened. If the good monsignor hadn't died, his next assignment could have been Vacaville Prison.

"What do you think?" Gallagher asked, wiping the corner of his mouth with a paper napkin. "We better wrap this thing up soon, Katie girl. The last time the lieut called, which as you know, was less than an·hour ago, he sounded like he could eat human flesh.

"Have you any gut feelings who's the perp? Does anyone give you an itchy feeling? Is that woman's intuition thing kicking in?"

Kate shook her head. "Nope," she said. "I go from thinking they are all innocent to thinking they are all guilty. Except Sister Mary Helen and Sister Eileen, of course. I'm sure those two had nothing to do with the murder."

Gallagher moaned. "Those are the very two I'd like to pin it on."

"You don't mean that, Denny."

"I do. I'd love to get them out of my hair once and for all."

"What hair?" Kate couldn't resist.

Gallagher didn't seem to hear her remark. He must be really preoccupied, she thought.

"All guilty. There's something familiar about.that. Maybe they all got together, decided to kill the good Father, and keep it a secret." Gallagher was warming to the idea. "Wasn't there a movie?"

"If we are going with the movies, maybe the housekeeper did it. You know, a female version of 'the butler did it'?"

"Maybe she did," Gallagher said. Obviously, he was desperate. "There seems to have been no love lost between the monsignor and herself. Maybe she got fed up with cooking his dinner and making his bed and taking his crap."

"Wouldn't poisoning his food be a little too obvious a method for a cook to use?"

Gallagher loosened his tie. He ran his finger around the

collar of his shirt, which had left a flaming red line encircling his neck. "You wouldn't expect a woman her age to learn to make pipe bombs, now would you?"

"No, but neither would I expect her to poison the man she'd fed for twelve years." Kate twisted one lock of her red hair around her index finger, then pushed it into a curl.

"You've been twisting that lousy piece of hair all morning." Gallagher pointed at her accusingly. "Something's bugging you. You always do that when something is bugging you."

Kate felt her face flush.

"And," her partner continued, "I have the funniest feeling what's bothering you has nothing to do with the case."

Kate smiled sheepishly. "I think we've been together too long," she said softly.

"What is it, Katie girl? Tell old Denny. The sooner you get whatever it is off your mind, the faster you can really concentrate on finding the murderer in this case. And the happier we'll all be, especially the lieutenant."

Kate gathered up the remains of their lunch and walked toward the sink. What was bothering her was really too personal to be discussed over salami. Yet, she had known Gallagher since she was a youngster. Her father and he had been on the force together. To be truthful, she thought of him as family. Yet. . . .

"It has something to do with that baby picture you've been staring at on the secretary's desk, doesn't it?"

Kate was startled. Dennis Gallagher really was a good detective.

"Is something wrong with little John?" he asked.

"Yes and no," Kate said. Gallagher looked concerned so she added quickly, "Nothing serious. It seems he wants a baby brother or sister." As soon as she had said it, she was sorry.

Gallagher let out a whoop. "Smart kid!" he said. "Who wants to get all your parents' attention?" He hitched up his pants, ready to get back to work, as though the problem was solved.

Kate's temper began to fizz. "It may seem funny to you, Denny. Your children are grown and have turned out well. I suspect Mrs. G. had a lot to do with that."

The look of hurt on her partner's face made her instantly sorry she'd taken out her frustration on him. After all, it wasn't his fault. It wasn't anyone's fault. She was the one who was grappling with conceiving another child. She softened her voice. "Times are different now. The world is more complicated. There are so many more dangers."

Kate felt the tears flood her eyes. "I work. Jack works. Another child would need our attention, our care. After a day's work, would we have enough energy left to really raise another child? A child is a gift and a sacred responsibility. It is a big decision to bring a baby into today's world."

"You don't have to make the decision alone. Jack should have something to say about it. And God."

"God?" Kate wiped her eyes. God had been the last one on her mind.

Gallagher looked embarrassed. "Katie girl, I read somewhere that every baby that comes is God's message that He's not yet discouraged with the world."

Although she probably would not admit it to Gallagher,

Kate felt her heart leap with a familiar joy at the very thought of carrying another life.

"Not that I'd blame Him if He was fed up. Look at the mess we're investigating today. Nuns and priests doing things they have no business doing. . . . " Gallagher was back to his old gruff self. Off and running.

For once, Kate welcomed the ranting.

❦❦❦

Sure enough, at one-thirty when the group reassembled at St. Agatha's rectory, Sister Eileen was called into the secretary's office. Just as Mary Helen suspected, she was to be the last one questioned.

She glanced around the dining room. Eve Glynn and Charlotte Wixson had taken seats against the wall near the pantry door. Charlotte looked as though she had chosen the spot in hopes of making a quick exit. Eve, on the other hand, looked as if she meant to prevent anyone from doing just that.

For some inexplicable reason, the members of the parish council again arranged themselves around the dining room in the exact same places they had occupied last Sunday afternoon. Undoubtedly, they occupied these same seats at every parish council meeting, the way all groups tend to do. Someone should conduct a study on the phenomenon, Mary Helen thought, studying their faces. Rather than looking relaxed by their lunch break, the group seemed even more tense than before.

The afternoon sun slanting in through the windows caught the crystals in the Waterford chandelier and sent sparks of light through the room. Nothing like the sparks that may soon be flying around here, Mary Helen thought, feeling the electricity in the silent room.

"Did you have a nice lunch?" she asked, hoping to dispel the mood. Immediately, she sensed it was the wrong question.

"Who could eat?" Tina Rodiman asked in a high whine that made Debbie Stevens lower her head and cover her ears.

"Anyone who isn't guilty of murder, I guess," George Jenkin said, slurring as if he'd drunk his meal.

"What in the world are you implying, George?" Sister Noreen's sweetness had all but vanished. "That anyone who has lost his or her appetite is a possible murderer?" She stared at him through her owl glasses, daring him to answer.

"If the shoe fits, dear Sister . . ." George said, his eyes rheumy.

Noreen opened her mouth to speak, but Professor Komsky raised his broad hand, palm out like a traffic cop. "Whoa, George," he began as if he expected to be the voice of reason.

George cut him off. "Don't 'whoa' me, Nick," he said, "and don't tell me you didn't want to see the old bugger dead as much as the rest of us. You told me what he did to Sarah. After that, any father would want to kill him."

Color spread from Nick Komsky's jaw to the roots of his bushy white hair. "Honestly, George," he stammered obviously upset.

"Oh, shut up!" Debbie Stevens shouted. "Why even bother talking to that old lush?" She turned on George with sudden ferocity. "You must be getting a little soft in the head, Jenkin, from all the suds. How dare you accuse any of us of murdering the pastor? How do we know you didn't? After all, he ruined your marriage."

With effort, George Jenkin focused on Debbie. "Excuse me, Ms. Stevens." He bowed his head in exaggerated contrition. "I may be a lush, but I'm an honest-to-God one. At least I'm not a sex-starved 'Ms.' who has to sneak around and get my kicks from screwing a half-baked priest."

"How dare you?!" Debbie sprang to her feet so quickly that she sent her chair over backward.

The crash made Mary Helen jump. Eve Glynn gave a little yelp and Tina Rodiman began to cry softly. Charlotte Wixson looked as if she might faint. Even Eileen's ruddy face lost its color.

"If the shoe fits, Ms. Stevens . . ." George mumbled, ignoring them all.

"This is getting us nowhere." Fred Davis spoke for the first time. He clenched and unclenched his fists, the knuckles white. "This fighting among ourselves is pointless. Someone killed our pastor. If we don't want to be accused of it ourselves, then we had better try to figure out who else had a motive and the opportunity."

"Mr. Logical," George Jenkin taunted. "Murder is not like a cold column of numbers, you know. You can't just add up columns of motive and opportunity and come out with the correct answer. Murder has passion, rage, jealousy, envy."

"What do you suggest then, George?" Fred's face was white and strained. Was it from anger or was it from fear, Mary Helen wondered.

"I think Mr. Davis has an excellent suggestion," she said.

Someone had to bring this group under control before they came to blows.

With a look that would sour milk, Eve righted the fallen chair. "This set belonged to my sainted cousin, Monsignor Concannon. I don't want it destroyed, too," she mumbled to no one in particular, "by a bunch of murderers."

Once everyone was settled and reasonably attentive, Mary Helen spoke. "As Mr. Davis said, we had better figure out who, besides us, had a motive and the opportunity," she began, hoping fervently that Kate Murphy and Dennis Gallagher wouldn't discover her playing detective.

"Dozens of people had a motive." Sister Noreen spoke up. "The monsignor, for all his charm, could be a hard and unyielding man." She surveyed the room for affirmation.

No one said anything. In fact, they looked shocked.

"So, Sister Goody-Two-Shoes isn't blind after all!" Eve Glynn cackled cruelly. "She does have eyes that see."

Noreen's round face was blazing. "Just because I don't say anything doesn't mean that I don't see it." Her eyes swept the group daring anyone to contradict her.

Surprisingly, no one did. In fact, Charlotte Wixson raised her hand. Wondering if she was acting too much like a schoolmarm, Mary Helen nodded for Charlotte to speak.

"I'd like to affirm what Sister Noreen just said." Her voice shook. She stopped, waiting for someone to react, but the room was strangely silent. "As the parish secretary, I hear all kinds of complaints about what goes on." She shrugged. "Some people you can never please, of course, but some of the complaints were legitimate. The monsignor summarily dismissed them all."

Ah, now we are getting somewhere, Mary Helen thought. "Does anyone stand out in your mind?" she asked.

"Well," Charlotte stopped for a moment, "right off the top of my head, Mr. Dooley and Mae Raddish."

Fred Davis groaned. "They're both in rest homes, for God's sake. How could either of them—"

"She asked me who stood out in my mind," Charlotte interrupted, pointing an accusing finger at Sister Mary Helen.

"This line of thought doesn't seem to be getting us anywhere." The professor cleared his throat. "We are all here, friends, because each of us had the opportunity. Our problem, it seems to me, is to figure out who else had an opportunity to poison our—ahem!—*esteemed* pastor. Or . . ."

From the unnatural quiet in the room, Mary Helen knew that everyone was mentally finishing the question. "Or which one of us . . ." She glanced around the room. Since each member of the parish council was sitting in the exact same spot as on Sunday . . . Frame by frame, she tried to play back the events of the afternoon: the tea, the Irish soda bread, the passing of the sugar, the cream, the honey.

There was nothing the monsignor alone had eaten, so where did the murderer put the poison? In the cups? No. They were passed at random.

Mary Helen was missing something, something that was just beyond her reach, like an itch in the middle of your back. She felt relieved when the dining room door opened.

"It's your turn, old dear," Eileen said, "and God bless you!"

❧❧❧

When Sister Mary Helen saw the expression on Inspector Dennis Gallagher's face, she knew why Sister Eileen had sent her off with a blessing.

"No luck?" she asked innocently, slipping into the chair Kate Murphy indicated. Inspector Gallagher turned a frightening red. Mary Helen was tempted to ask him if he had his blood pressure checked regularly, but thought better of it.

"This is not about luck, Sister," he said, loosening his tie and unbuttoning the top button of his white shirt. "This is about uncovering the facts. Now, we could bet the farm on the fact that someone in that room poisoned the priest. And we want to know who."

Mary Helen's back stiffened. "And you think I know? Let me assure you, Inspector Gallagher, that if I did, I would tell you. I have better things to do with my time than sit around all day in a room full of bickering adults." She met Gallagher's glare, just waiting.

Noisily, Kate Murphy cleared her throat, an obvious signal for her partner to back off, which he did. To Mary Helen's surprise, he moved across the small office and became quite absorbed in something outside the window.

"I know this is nerve-wracking for you, Sister, but you have no idea how much pressure we are getting to solve this case and make an arrest. Anything you can do to help us, we would appreciate." Kate smiled sweetly.

"I have every intention of trying to help you," Mary Helen said. Still annoyed, she raised her voice so that Gallagher wouldn't miss it. "I see no need to take out our frustrations on one another."

From where she sat, Mary Helen saw the back of the inspector's neck redden. Fortunately, she could not see his face.

"You said, 'bickering adults'?" Kate asked, getting the interrogation back on track. "What were they bickering about?" Kate paused, her blue eyes expectant, as if awaiting a big clue.

As succinctly as possible, Sister Mary Helen told Kate about the interplay in the dining room. "George Jenkin is, of course, feeling no pain," Mary Helen remarked, "and may be shooting a few blanks. But I think, from her reaction, that Ms. Stevens and the monsignor may have had . . ." Mary Helen hesitated, trying to find a more delicate way to put it, but there was none. "An affair," she said. She could tell from the expression on Kate's face that this was not news.

"According to Sister Noreen and Charlotte Wixson, the monsignor had many enemies. Maybe that's too strong a word. Many dissatisfied parishioners. But I think that's just a smoke screen. Actually, Sister Noreen is the one who really surprised me," Mary Helen said, almost to herself.

Kate jumped on it. "In what way?"

Her question startled Mary Helen. "Only in that she appears so passive until you scratch the surface. Underneath that meek facade, she is a very angry woman. Not that she murdered the monsignor, but she surely didn't like him. Then, who can blame her? He was not very likable."

Sister Mary Helen shoved her slipping bifocals onto the bridge of her nose and studied Inspector Murphy. "What stumps me, Kate, is how the killer did it. I've gone over it and over it. We all have. Only Monsignor took a piece of Irish soda bread, but that did not contain the poison. Both Monsignor and Debbie had honey in their tea. I almost had some myself," Mary Helen said, straining to recall every detail, even the smallest. "But I decided on sugar because it was closer. The only one that didn't take sugar was Tina." Her eyes met Kate's. "I think she must be watching her weight."

Kate nodded and Mary Helen continued. "No one took cream except Sister Eileen. Eve served no lemon slices.

"That leaves only Charlotte Wixson and Eve Glynn," Mary Helen concluded, but added quickly, "it doesn't make sense that either of them would choose a time when the rectory was full of people to poison their employer. Both had numerous other opportunities when they were alone with the man, particularly his housekeeper. Or does it?" Mary Helen wondered aloud.

Kate didn't give a direct answer. "We did question them," she said. "Both women agree that they had tea together at the kitchen table, using the same pot of tea, and eating the same soda bread and goes-on-tos."

Sister Mary Helen saw the frustration in Kate's face. Gallagher, who apparently had gained control of himself, moved from the window and perched on the edge of the desk. Both homicide inspectors looked as dejected as she had ever seen them.

"This is really a 'locked-room' mystery," Mary Helen said, hoping the impossibleness of the situation might cheer them up.

From the expressions on their faces, she knew it hadn't. If anything, they looked even more down in the dumps.

"Remember, you two, even in locked-room mysteries, there is always an explanation." She'd try another tack. "What we need to do is relax, then let our thoughts flow.

Right now, we are trying too hard to think. It's like straining to remember the name of a familiar tune and it's just out of reach." She stopped to make sure they were following her. It was difficult to tell. "If you forget about trying to remember, the title pops into your mind when you least expect it—in the shower or stopped at a red light—for no apparent reason." She knew she was babbling, but they looked so downhearted.

"I know there is something in there." Mary Helen pointed to her temple, hoping to make her point. "If we just let our unconscious get to work, it will come." She crossed her fingers. "I'm sure of it. Why don't we break for the day?"

By now, both Kate and Inspector Gallagher were studying her as if she were foreign matter under a microscope.

"She sounds like that pain in the ass Frenchman on the PBS channel," Gallagher muttered. "The one my wife likes."

"Belgian," Mary Helen corrected, knowing he meant Hercule Poirot.

"Whatever." Gallagher's face reddened and he ran his hand over his bald pate. "In spite of my better judgment, Katie girl . . ."

Kate looked quizzicaly at her partner. "What's against your better judgment, Denny?" she asked, sounding tired.

Gallagher grinned sheepishly. "I think the Sister might be right."

❧❧❧

Only moments after Sister Mary Helen joined the other "suspects" in the rectory dining room, Inspector Kate Murphy appeared in the doorway. "Thank you all for your cooperation," she said as politely as if they'd had a choice. "We're finished for today."

"For today?" Sister Noreen spoke up. "Does that mean we're going to be called back tomorrow?"

"Is there a problem with that, Sister?" Inspector Gallagher stood behind Kate in the doorway.

Noreen looked flustered. "I understand that Monsignor Higgins's body will be released tomorrow morning. The chancery office called and the archbishop scheduled the funeral Mass for Saturday morning. There are a great many things to be done in preparation for the burial of a pastor."

Especially one who has turned out to be such a scoundrel, Mary Helen thought.

The two homicide detectives exchanged a quick glance. "We see no need to call you together tomorrow unless something develops," Kate said. "Please, however—everyone stay where we can reach you if it becomes necessary."

"Just like the cops on television," George Jenkin said. His face was pale, his eyes bloodshot. He looked as if he had the beginnings of a monumental headache.

"This is nothing to joke about, George." Fred Davis pulled himself up to his full six feet, his face the epitome of indignation. Mary Helen half expected to see thunderbolts shoot from his red-rimmed eyes. "Our pastor, no matter what we thought of him, has been murdered. One of us could easily have done it."

Not easily, Mary Helen thought, as the room burst into a riot of sound, all the "suspects" talking at once.

"Enough!" Gallagher shouted over the din. "Enough, all of you!" His face showed that he meant it.

"I swear I'll never come back to this place again." Tina Rodiman's last sentence echoed in the silent room. She shook her head so violently that her dangling earrings tinkled. "Unless you need us, of course, Inspector," she added quickly. Her face was the color of oatmeal.

Kate Murphy smiled indulgently at the woman. "I understand, Mrs. Rodiman. I assure you that we won't call any of you back unless it is absolutely necessary."

"That's music to my old ears," Eileen whispered, heading for the door. Mary Helen followed her lead. She was tired and her head was beginning to ache. The last thing she wanted to do was spend another minute talking to anyone, least of all the other "suspects." Being the first ones out seemed a perfect solution.

The moment she pulled open the heavy front door of the rectory, Mary Helen realized her mistake. Reporters from every major network and newspaper in the city swarmed toward the two nuns, some with microphones, some with cameras riding on their shoulders, some with pads and pencils ready. All had eager and expectant faces. The clamor was frightening.

Standing on the rectory steps, Mary Helen had some idea of how the early Christians felt coming face-to-face with the lions. Eileen clutched her arm. "What now, old dear?" she asked, her brogue as thick as Mary Helen had ever heard it.

"Look concerned, but controlled. Nod wisely and, if you can manage it, say absolutely nothing," Mary Helen whispered.

"Good night, Nurse!" she heard her friend exclaim as questions bombarded them on every side.

That sweet-faced little blonde anchorwoman from Channel Two, Leslie Something, plunged a microphone toward Sister Mary Helen. "Can you tell us what's going on in there, Sister?" she asked.

Mary Helen stared at the harmless-looking black microphone, then at the earnest blue eyes waiting eagerly. "No comment," always sounded as if the person saying it were hiding something.

"Are the police getting anywhere?" Leslie prodded. "Have they any idea who murdered the monsignor? Are there any new developments, Sister?"

Under the pressure, Mary Helen broke her own rule. "The police are working very hard to solve this crime. I feel confident that they will have the monsignor's murderer in custody very soon."

Apparently satisfied, the reporter's swarmed the next "suspect" coming through the rectory door.

"As you viewers have just witnessed," Mary Helen heard Leslie Whoever saying into the camera, "Sister Mary Helen of Mount St. Francis College assures us that the police have nailed down a suspect in this heinous murder of a prominent San Francisco clergyman. And it's about time, too. When even our priests cannot be safe in their own rectories. . . . "

"You said nothing of the sort!" Eileen had taken the wheel of the convent Nova and was revving up the motor.

"I shouldn't have said anything," Mary Helen moaned. "I should have said, 'No comment.' "

Eileen wrinkled her nose.

"As bad as that sounds, it doesn't sound nearly as bad as telling the whole world that the police have solved a case which, at the moment, seems unsolvable," Mary Helen lamented.

"Don't worry, old dear." Eileen was trying hard to sound optimistic. "If I remember correctly, that reporter, that Leslie, is on the five o'clock news. How many people actually watch the five o'clock news?"

❧❧❧

"Did you hear what your friend told Channel Two?" Inspector Dennis Gallagher roared as soon as Kate Murphy and he were safely in the police car. "Put on the siren and let's get out of here before another mob of media attacks us."

Kate obliged and Gallagher peeled out from St. Agatha's parking lot. "Didn't I tell you that the woman should be muzzled?" he shouted over the shriek of the siren.

" 'Bound and gagged,' is what I think you've said before." Kate braced herself against the dashboard as Gallagher took the corner. "Slow down, Denny. You'd think we were going to a riot."

"It will be a riot by the time we get back to the hall. Just you wait until the word gets out that the nun said we will be making an arrest soon."

"That's not exactly what I heard her say, Denny. It was more like we are doing a good job, which is true. And that we will have the monsignor's murderer in custody soon, which is, of course, not true without a miracle. Which you should be praying for instead of bellyaching about an innocent remark."

Gallagher careened the police car around the corner of

Fourth and Bryant Streets, knocking all other protestations out of Kate's mind. When he pulled into the parking lot and parked, she waited for her breath to catch up.

Gallagher glared at her. "Kate," he said, "I'm dead serious. I want that nun . . . both those nuns," he amended, "in fact, any future nuns, out of my hair. Is that clear?"

Kate nodded. She knew he was too upset for her to ask, "What hair?"

Gallagher's grim prediction proved correct. Back at the detail, the phone never stopped ringing. The lieutenant never stopped shouting, and the other Homicide detectives never stopped wisecracking about *Sister Act III* and *The Flying Nun*.

By four-thirty, both Kate Murphy and Dennis Gallagher were happy to pack it in and say good night to both the Homicide detail and each other.

Kate was delighted that it was Jack's turn to pick up John at the baby-sitter. One of the calls this afternoon had been from her mother-in-law.

"I have some homemade ravioli," she announced when Kate answered the phone without even identifying herself. Not that her voice was difficult to recognize. Who besides Loretta Bassetti makes ravioli in this day and age, Kate wondered, but her mother-in-law was leaving no room for questions.

"I made enough for all you kids for dinner. Tomorrow is St. Joseph's Day. A special Italian feast day, as you know."

Kate did know, but with all that was going on, it had slipped her mind.

"I wanted to have you all here at my house, but it's worse than trying to gather the Arab nations together. If I get you and Jackie, then Gina and what's-his-name are terribly busy. Doing what, I wonder? Angie doesn't even answer back her message machine. I hate those machines. What ever happened to real people answering the phone? It's no wonder we have so much unemployment when we have machines answering the phones when people could.

"Anyway, Kate, what I called about is, can you come by about five to pick these ravs up? I made sauce, too. They're no good if they aren't fresh."

Kate had her one chance to get in a word. "Yes!" she said, gratefully. "I'll be there." Mrs. B. had hung up before she had time for a thank-you.

When Kate Murphy pulled up to the Bassetti home on Thirty-eighth Avenue in the Sunset District, she saw her mother-in-law's face between the parted lace curtains in the front window. "In the ready," Jack always teased.

Before Kate had reached the top step, the front door swung open. The tangy aroma of garlic and peppers simmering with onions made Kate realize how hungry she was.

"Come in, come in," her mother-in-law trilled. "You look exhausted. It's that monsignor's murder, isn't it?" She ushered Kate toward the living room couch. Kate noticed the television was switched off. Thank goodness, Mrs. B. had been too busy to turn on the five o'clock news which, undoubtedly, had featured the murder.

"Have a cookie." Loretta Bassetti offered her a plate of chocolate chip cookies, still warm. "I don't know what the world is coming to, Kate. Honestly, I don't. Crazy people murdering priests. Monsignors, for that matter. In all my life I never heard of such things.

"Not that I haven't heard hundreds of Catholics say after Mass, 'If he doesn't make those sermons shorter, I'll strangle him with my own bare hands.' In fact, Jackie's own Papa, may he rest in peace, used to say that. But he didn't mean he'd really do it."

"This priest was poisoned," Kate said, her mouth full of cookie.

"Which reminds me, you came to pick up dinner. Don't get up," Loretta Bassetti called, hurrying toward the kitchen.

Kate took her at her word. Closing her eyes, she let her head fall back against the overstuffed couch. The setting sun streaming through the bank of front windows made the room warm and cozy. In the distance, she heard her mother-in-law puttering in the kitchen. The cookie had taken the edge off her hunger. She felt drowsy.

How peaceful everything seemed. No phones ringing, no perps whining. No dried blood or smells of death. Just the tantalizing aroma of a delicious meal cooking.

Dreamily, Kate pictured herself in her own sunny kitchen—flowers in the window box, gleaming silver pots and pans, rainbows in her soap suds, and she in a clean apron. Little John with his coloring book kneeling on a chair at the kitchen table. The tip of his small tongue sticking out of the corner of his mouth as he concentrated. A chubby-cheeked baby cooing contentedly from a high chair.

For the first time in her memory, Kate didn't view the scene with panic or revulsion. As a matter of fact, tonight, re-laxed on her mother-in-law's couch, she seemed to be relishing it—maybe even craving it. Mama Bassetti's home had this effect on her. She had better get out of here while she still had her head on straight!

᠅᠅᠅

Contrary to Sister Eileen's opinion, it seemed that thousands of San Franciscans watched the five o'clock news. That is, if the phone calls to the convent on Tuesday night were any indication.

Family members of the Sisters, friends, alumnae, students, and staff of the college all were telephoning ostensibly to make sure everything was "all right." Mary Helen suspected that most were also trying to pick up a little insider information to pass on to not-so-well-connected friends. Always a temptation in a crisis.

"Everything would be a lot better if they'd all get off the horn," Eileen said, her good nature wearing thin, as she left the Sisters' Room, once again, to answer the telephone.

"Can't we put the blasted thing on the answering machine?" old Sister Donata growled, the fifteenth time it rang during *Wheel of Fortune*. She gave Mary Helen a fierce look, almost as if this entire murder business was her fault.

Sister Cecilia sat in stony silence while Sister Therese crocheted furiously on a baby blanket. To Mary Helen's great relief, most of the other nuns were busy preparing for tomorrow's feast day. St. Joseph, patron of the Universal Church, was also a special patron of their congregation. They would start the day with a feast day Mass, then follow it with a top-notch breakfast.

Sister Anne, who should really have been at choir practice, was the only one who thought the situation was exciting. She sat cross-legged on the floor in front of Mary Helen's chair. Behind her new wire-framed glasses, her hazel eyes were eager. "Imagine being right there when someone was poisoned," she effused, ignoring a murderous look from Therese. "What did you feel like when you realized you could have accidentally helped yourself to whatever it was that was poisoned?" She smiled with anticipation.

Actually, until Sister Anne put it so clearly, the thought had not even occurred to Mary Helen. She swallowed. How did she feel? As if she'd just stuck her hand in an electric socket. To be honest, if she wasn't already sitting down, she'd make for a chair.

Mary Helen's face must have lost its color because Sister Anne gasped. "You didn't realize it, did you?" she asked, even more enthralled.

"Typical!" Sister Therese blurted out. "These two." Her sharp, dark eyes swept from Mary Helen to Eileen, who had just innocently re-entered the room. "They never do realize the consequences of what they do. They simply rush in where angels fear to tread."

"Please, pipe down!" Donata demanded, straining to hear the television program.

With a sniff, Therese did, which was fortunate because Mary Helen could feel her blood pressure and her own temper smoking like twin rockets ready for blast off. She'd had enough tension for one day. She didn't need it at home, too.

"That's unfair." Anne now swiveled toward Sister Therese.

"They were simply delivering our Irish soda bread. How in the world were they to know someone would poison Monsignor Higgins?"

Stiff and silent, Therese turned her baby afghan and began to crochet another row, pulling the stitches so tight that Mary Helen wondered if the whole thing would end up vee-shaped. "It just seems odd to me, that's all I'm saying," Therese mumbled.

" 'Innocent or guilty, you'll be hanged,' says the judge," Eileen whispered and Mary Helen couldn't help but agree. Sometimes the better part of valor is to simply disappear.

"I've had a long, rather exhausting day," she announced, without giving any more details. "I think I'll make my way to bed."

Only Anne looked the slightest bit disappointed.

❦❧❦

"How about another glass of wine?" Jack asked, filling Kate's glass with dark red Merlot before she'd answered.

Little John was in bed. The television was off and the dishwasher hummed in the background. The house rang with a contented quiet. Taking their glasses into a darkened living room, Jack placed them on the coffee table, then switched on the radio. Mysteriously, the dial was set to a romantic music station.

"Is this a setup?" Kate asked, following him to the sofa.

"Sort of," Jack admitted, sitting close to her. "I'm sorry about last night. . . ."

Before he could continue, Kate put her finger to his lips. "I'm sorry, too. I think I was overreacting."

Her husband was kind enough not to agree.

"I've been brooding all day long about what you said last night." Kate twisted a stand of her red hair.

"I'm sorry, hon."

"No, you don't need to be sorry. You were right."

Jack feigned an expression of shock. "Tell me exactly what I said so I can say it again."

"Don't push your luck, pal!" Kate snuggled closer to him. "I'm serious. You said, and you are right, that a child is a priority."

"I said that?"

"Well, that is what you meant." Kate waved her hand to dismiss any further argument. "Then today Denny said something about babies."

Jack stiffened. "How did you and Gallagher get into babies? Aren't you still working on the monsignor's murder? Don't tell me there's a baby involved, too."

Kate shook her head. "Of course not. There was just this adorable snapshot of a baby girl on the parish secretary's desk. I'm sure it's her granddaughter. And Denny said something about this baby was more than just my decision."

"I should hope so." Jack took a sip of his wine.

"No, not just you and me. Of course, we're essential."

"Right," Jack said warily.

"But God, too, plays a part in it."

Beside her, her husband sat very still. Kate wondered if he was remembering, as she was, the difficult time they'd had conceiving John. At the time, she'd thought God was punishing her. Sometimes she still had trouble believing in a God who loved her personally and unconditionally.

"Let me try to remember exactly how Denny put it." She paused. "Something like, every baby is a message from God that He's not fed up with us yet. Nice, isn't it?"

Jack nodded. Kate leaned her head on his shoulder. She heard his heart beating and felt him kiss the crown of her head. How close she had come to losing him altogether. Unexpected tears flowed from her eyes, but she brushed them away.

"Then, at your mother's, I don't know why, but sitting there listening to her bustle around her kitchen, smelling the delicious smells, feeling her peace, I envied her certainty, her contentment. I almost wanted to be her."

Kate felt rather than heard her husband laugh. "Be my mother? I bet it's the ravioli," Jack said finally. "I love her, but the woman is impossible, Kate. We both know that. Most Italian mothers make St. Joseph's bread for the feast tomorrow, but my mother makes ravioli. I wouldn't put it past her to have put something in the sauce."

"Like what?"

"A love potion of some sort. Some ancient Italian secret brew. I know her, she's been concocting something since the other night." He touched her.

"Is it working?" Kate set her wineglass on the coffee table.

Jack raked his fingers through his thick hair. "You tell me," he said. "How do you feel?"

Kate answered by putting both arms around her husband's neck and giving him a long, loving kiss. "It's a start," she said at last.

"Maybe Mama should patent it." Jack grabbed Kate's hand and quickly led her upstairs to the master bedroom.

Once again, after a long hot soak in the bathtub, Mary Helen crawled wearily into her bed. Her bedside lamp cast a warm glow over her bedstand. The large luminous numbers on her clock read 9:00. Time for sleep. She was even too tired to replay all that she had heard that day.

Reaching over, she picked up her half-finished mystery and opened it to her marker. She wondered just how long she'd be able to keep her eyes open. That is until she read the phrase, " . . . that was totally out of character."

Then, as unexpectedly as a hiccup, the "thing" that she had been chasing all day, the "thing" that she had been trying to recall, the "itch" that she had been unable to reach, came to her as bright and as luminous as a star in the clear March night sky.

Knowing that tomorrow would indeed be a busy day, Mary Helen slept the sleep of the just.

Wednesday, March 19

❧❧❧

Feast of Saint Joseph
Patron of the Universal Church and
Foster Father of Jesus

Several minutes before her alarm was scheduled to go off, Sister Mary Helen awoke full of energy and full of assurance. Dressing quickly, she chose her new pink blouse, the one Sister Anne gave her last Christmas. It would brighten up her navy blue suit.

Why not? she thought, cutting off the tags. Today was a special feast day. Besides, as sure as she was of the murderer's identity, she felt bright! In the pink, if you wanted to get corny!

Tying the blouse's large bow under her chin, Mary Helen checked her reflection in the mirror, then ran a brush through her short gray hair. She paused at her bedroom door just long enough to say a quick prayer that things would turn out as well as she fully expected they would.

The Mount St. Francis College campus glittered in the

morning sunshine. Rows of stiff golden jonquils greeted her along the path to the chapel. Multicolor patches of saucy-faced pansies amid the spring green grass added to her euphoria. Today would be a day of celebration.

Pulling back the heavy chapel door, she was welcomed by the familiar odor of incense and candle wax mingled with wood polish. After a few quiet moments with God, Mary Helen noticed the choir beginning to assemble. Sister Eileen slipped into the pew next to her.

"You're looking very chipper this morning, old dear," Eileen said. "What's up?"

"I know who murdered the monsignor," Mary Helen whispered. Bending close to Eileen, she told her what she had remembered.

"By Jove, I think you've got it!" her friend exclaimed.

The two old nuns beamed at one another as the organ intoned "O Blessed St. Joseph." Heartily, both joined in the familiar hymn.

The feast day breakfast was a real treat. The dining room tables were decorated with spring bouquets and colorful napkins. A small package of note cards tied with ribbon were at each Sister's place. A feast day gift, no doubt, from Sister Cecilia.

Ramón, the chef, had outdone himself. Besides the traditional bacon and eggs and sausage and homemade biscuits, Ramón had prepared cheese blintzes with raspberry and his own version of crepes Suzette.

Being once again in full appetite, Sister Mary Helen moved her tray through the buffet line, deciding to try a little of everything. Who knew when she'd eat again?

Besides, it was too early to call Kate Murphy. After break-fast, Kate would surely have arrived at the Homicide detail. Mary Helen could scarcely wait.

Her frame of mind must have showed. "You're looking much better this morning," Sister Cecilia remarked, clearly fishing for the reason.

On the other hand, the night had done little for poor Ce-cilia. Her eyes looked as if someone had punched her. She must have lain awake for hours.

Feeling guilty, Mary Helen wanted to tell her what she had remembered. She wished she could put the poor woman's mind at ease, but thought better of it.

She was nearly ninety-nine percent sure she was correct. There was still that one percent, her prudent self warned. "I am feeling better," Mary Helen said, quickly taking her place at a table.

"What's up?" Sister Anne asked, sitting down across from her. "That blouse looks great on you. When you didn't wear it, I was afraid you didn't like it."

"I was just waiting for the right occasion," Mary Helen said, checking the bow for raspberry stains.

"Is it the color, or are you onto something?" Anne asked. "You are positively glowing."

Mary Helen felt her face flush. At her age, "glowing" surely was an overstatement, but nice to hear, nonetheless.

"Well?" Anne's eyes sparkled with eagerness and interest.

Mary Helen might have been tempted to confide in her if Sister Therese hadn't arrived at the table.

"Happy Feast Day," Therese called, sounding cheerful for Therese, and the conversation took off in another direction.

Only the sound of the bell for the first class broke up the party.

❦❧❦

Her telephone was already ringing when Kate Murphy arrived at her desk at the Homicide detail in the Hall of Justice. Shoving her purse into her bottom drawer with one hand, she answered the phone with the other. She half expected it to be her boss. She was surprised when, without even saying hello, Mary Helen told her who she thought the murderer was and why.

"Whoa, Sister," Kate said, cautiously. "Would you just repeat that." After she had, Kate was even more cautious.

"What we don't have, Sister, is any solid proof. I'm not saying you are wrong. Actually, you are probably right on target, as usual." Kate hoped her partner wouldn't walk in. "But how are we going to prove it?"

There was a disappointed silence on the other end of the line. "Could we all meet at St. Agatha's rectory?" Mary Helen suggested. "Re-enact last Sunday's meeting. Put in every detail, if you know what I mean."

"We could," Kate conceded reluctantly, "but this is not a 'Perry Mason' show on television. In real life, the murderer is apt to be too smart or too terrified to break down and confess."

"There is always the chance that the killer might want to tell someone," Mary Helen offered hopefully. "After all, these are basically good people. The burden of guilt must be horrific."

Kate Murphy twisted a lock of her hair in thought.

"Are you still there?" Mary Helen asked.

After a grunt, Kate said, "I'm just thinking. I'm not sure what Denny will say."

"About what?" Gallagher appeared at the adjoining desk, a scowl on his full face. "What I'll say about what?"

It was only after thirty minutes of heated argument that Gallagher reluctantly agreed to the plan. Kate didn't flatter herself that she had won him over by her logic or her persuasiveness. To be honest, what turned the tide was the appearance of a frowning lieutenant shouting about getting their asses in gear before the pressure from the big brass got any hotter!

❧❧❧

When Fred Davis opened his front door, the telephone began to ring—an unusual sound in his quiet house now that Mildred was gone. Who in the world can that be, he wondered, taking off his woolen jacket. Despite the morning sun, there was a nip in the March air, especially here near the beach.

Fred was just returning from Mass at St. Ignatius Church. He'd stayed a few minutes after to speak with one of the Jesuit priests. The man had given Fred his solemn word that he would say the Masses for Mildred. He had even refused the stipend at first, until Fred insisted. What was the use of saving his money now? Really, he had no one to spend it on.

Feeling happy with himself, Fred picked up the phone on the fifth ring. Maybe it was one of those telemarketing people. Well, he wasn't buying. His heart dropped when he recognized the voice.

"Inspector Murphy, here, Mr. Davis," the woman said.

"We would appreciate it if you could be at St. Agatha's rectory this morning by nine-thirty."

From the tone of her voice, Fred knew it was an order, not a request. His mouth went dry. Without thinking, he clenched his fist. Would this thing never be over? Although he dare not say so aloud, he'd like to tell the inspector that he considered ridding the world of the monsignor an act of kindness rather than a crime. He realized that officially she could not share his opinion, but she might if she truly knew the man.

Fred cleared his throat. "Yes, Inspector, I can be there." He replaced the receiver as if it were hot. Staring at it, he hoped he'd sounded calm despite his churning stomach.

Checking the kitchen clock, Fred was happy to see that if he hurried, he had just enough time for a cup of coffee and a bowl of cold cereal. It would never do to be late.

On this kind of a morning, Mildred usually made him hot oatmeal with brown sugar and butter melting on top and slithering down its miniature mountains. Since she had gone, he had tried to make it himself, but only once. The mess he produced was burned and so lumpy it choked him. He had soaked the pot for three days and finally had to throw it in the garbage can.

Fred poured milk over his bran flakes. Mildred deserved better than he had been able to give her. But he had fixed all that now. Mildred would be in the heaven she so richly deserved.

❧

George Jenkin was in the process of mixing his second Bloody Mary when his telephone began to ring. Who the hell is that? he wondered, wiping his hands on a soiled dish towel. Don't they know that 9:00 A.M. is an uncivilized time to call a drinking man?

George had really tied one on last night. This morning his whole body craved "the hair of the dog that bit him."

His hand trembled slightly as he reached out for the phone. "Hello," he barked into the line.

"Mr. Jenkin?" a faintly familiar voice asked. "This is Inspector Kate Murphy. We would appreciate your being at St. Agatha's rectory this morning by nine-thirty. Do you have a problem with that?"

George hesitated, for appearances, if for nothing else. It was none of the woman's damn business that he hadn't had an assignment for months. After the paper had canned him, he had decided to go freelance. He was, as they say, between assignments. His money was running low. With Stella working and his occasional paycheck, they had just been able to make it. With her gone now, George didn't know how much longer he could hold on.

He smiled scornfully at the thought of the recent police and the Cal-Trans workers' sweeps of homeless camps in Golden Gate Park and under the freeways. Soon that might be he. Maybe he'd write a "first person" account and sell it to the *Chron*. Wouldn't Stella feel bad when she read it.

"I'm checking my appointment book," Jenkin said. He'd always been quick on his feet. "I see that I am free this morning. I'll be there, Inspector."

When George hung up, he stared at the half-filled glass. Should he finish it? No sense wasting good vodka. Besides, a bird cannot fly on one wing alone, he thought. He'd always liked that old saw.

To be honest, George knew he needed it to calm the shaking in his arms and the quaking of his stomach. He couldn't meet the police with the whips and jangles, now could he? They might mistake his nervousness for guilt.

George took a long gulp of his drink. The spicy tomato juice burned his mouth, but he felt his nerves begin to settle. That old familiar glow was coming back. Much better! Maybe with the monsignor gone, he could talk Stella into coming back.

Good old Stella! She'd always been a sport. George guessed that she'd want to know who had poisoned her friend, the monsignor. A cramp grabbed his empty stomach. Was it the tomato juice or was it fear?

George had started this murder business. That much he knew for sure. Getting old Fred and his beagle nose on the case of the missing money.

But who had finished it? Fred? Maybe. Debbie? Could be. Noreen? Not likely. Then again, it's always the most unlikely. At least in the detective shows he watched, or half watched, on television. Most of the time, he dozed off in the middle.

Who was the most unlikely? He was, actually. He was a drinking man, not a killing man. Poison would not be his style, if he had a style.

I probably would have strangled him, George thought, with my bare hands until I saw his cold eyes bulge. Sweat broke out on his forehead. He had never considered himself a violent man. He had shocked himself when he had actually beaten Stella. It was the last thing he had ever expected to do. He had hit her, maybe once or twice over their thirty years together. When he saw what he had done to her, he couldn't believe it. And he probably wouldn't have, if his knuckles hadn't been bruised.

George's whole body was hot and clammy. Had he done it? Would the police accuse him of it? How would he answer?

What frightened him most was that he really did not remember. How could you kill someone and not remember it? George emptied the vodka bottle into his glass. There wasn't much room left for tomato juice.

❧❧

Tina Rodiman had just dumped another load of laundry into her washing machine when her telephone rang. "Hello," she called cheerfully, half expecting it to be her husband.

Since her blowup at the beach, Tony had been surprising her with small acts of kindness and Tina was revelling in them. She had been right to take things into her own hands. Her only regret was that she hadn't thrown a fit sooner.

As a child, she'd been punished for her temper tantrums. She still remembered, despite the consequences, how good it had felt to lie on the floor and kick and scream and bang your fists in protest. She always suspected that the rage was still there, buried deep inside.

Even her children were behaving better. This morning they had all finished breakfast without anyone spilling milk. Tony had fixed her a piece of toast and spread it with her favorite jam.

When their hands brushed, Tina had wanted to invite him back into the bedroom and would have, except that he

221

was running late. If this was him on the phone, she might ask him to come home for a quick lunch.

Tina's heart dropped when she recognized the voice of Inspector Kate Murphy. "Nine-thirty will be fine," Tina said, her lunch plans dissolving.

Now she hoped Tony wouldn't call. She didn't know how he'd feel about her going to the rectory again. Not that he had anything to say about it. The monsignor had been murdered. Done is done!

Tina hurried to the bathroom and examined herself in the mirror. Thank goodness she had showered. It would take all the time she had left to put on her face.

Instinctively her stomach lurched. The laundry! Tony will be angry if it isn't done when he comes home. Tina calmed herself. That was the old Tony. She giggled. The new Tony wonders if I'll poison him if he makes a fuss. And I'll never tell!

Smiling at her secret, Tina applied the foundation, then chose a light blue eye shadow. She applied mascara to her lashes until they reminded her of two spiders sitting on her eyelids.

When she was done, her lips were red and waxy, just the way Tony liked them. She slipped dangling turquoise earrings into her pierced earlobes. I look exactly like a gigantic Barbie doll, Tina thought, resisting the urge to wash her face clean. She wondered how Tony would cotton to that. Time would tell. Better not to press her luck and ruin everything.

Slipping several bangle bracelets over her wrist, Tina listened to their merry jingle as she slammed the front door behind her. She headed for the rectory on foot. It was better for the figure. Besides, she needed time to compose herself. Her intuition told her today was the day she must prove to the police that she was totally innocent.

❧❧❧

Professor Nicholas Komsky, retired, had just finished telling his daughter, Sarah, that he'd planned to spend the day gardening. He didn't know who was more surprised, his daughter or himself.

"Dad, you never garden," she'd said, as if he didn't know.

The thoughts of all that dirt under his fingernails and in the cracks on his hands, of grabbing hold of a prickly weed that filled his fingers with invisible slivers, or of the unexpected appearance of a fat black bug usually repelled him.

He'd told her that, for some reason, today he felt like running his fingers through the moist earth, pulling up weeds by their roots and throwing them into a ragged pile. Even the feel of turning over big, heavy shovels full of soil and breaking it up with the tip sounded good.

Maybe it's male menopause, he'd explained to Sarah, although he knew what it was—the frustration that came from sitting in the rectory dining room for days. Maybe it was only two days, but it felt a great deal longer.

He stared out his kitchen window at his yard. There was enough work to keep three men busy. He was foolish to have let the gardener go, thinking he could handle it himself. He should have known better. Now it was a mess like so much else in his life. Overgrown. Out of control.

The pressure of this daily police interrogation was beginning to get to Komsky's nerves. He knew the police would keep it up and keep it up until the murderer finally cracked.

Sweat broke out under Komsky's arms and he felt it run down his ribs. Within the hour, he knew, his clean shirt would stink with the odor of fear. He had never realized that fear gave off such a distinctive smell.

He rinsed his hands under the cold water tap in the kitchen sink. Like Pontius Pilate, he thought crazily. "I am innocent of the blood of this just man," the old Roman fox had declared, but had that made him innocent?

Komsky wondered how long it would be before that police inspector, that Kate Murphy, would get around to asking him about Xenophon and the poison. Someone was bound to tell her that he'd said it.

As soon as the words had left his mouth, Komsky could have cut his tongue out. Why did he have to be such a show-off? It was one of his worst shortcomings. Surely, two or three other people in the room must have known that fact. Anyone would who had taught ancient Greek history. It was one of those stories that most good teachers throw in to keep the class awake.

And it would wake them up, too: the thought of an entire army poisoned on the nectar of a harmless-looking—indeed, magnificently beautiful—flower, particularly one that grew in such abundance in San Francisco in the springtime.

Now is too late for regrets, Komsky thought, rummaging around on the back porch for an old hat to garden in. Not surprisingly, there wasn't one there. Maybe an old dish towel would do to cover his head. Like a 'do rag some of the football players wear. At least it would keep the sweat from running into his eyes and matting his bushy eyebrows.

Komsky had just tied the faded cloth around his head when the telephone rang. Probably Sarah warning me not to overdo, he thought, picking up the receiver.

When Komsky heard the voice, his legs felt like rubber bands. He leaned against the kitchen counter and closed his eyes.

"Yes, Inspector Murphy," he said, despising the forced cheerfulness of his voice. "I see. Yes, I can be there right away." His words rang in the empty kitchen.

Gently, he placed the damp receiver in its cradle and stood for a few minutes getting his breath. Here we go, he thought, mopping his face with the dish towel. Here we go! God help me to keep my big mouth shut!

🖙🖙

Ms. Debbie Stevens woke up with a throbbing headache, which should have been no surprise. She had spent most of the endless night crying.

She examined her ashen face in the bathroom mirror. Her short auburn hair stood on end as if she'd run a lawn mower over the top of her head. Her eyes were red against her blotchy angular face. Her chin protruded, making her look more sure of herself than ever, which was the exact opposite of how she was feeling.

Debbie rummaged in the medicine chest for a couple of aspirins and swallowed them quickly with cold water. Carefully, she climbed into her rumpled bed and put her head down on the damp pillows.

For a moment she stared at the ceiling, but even that made her wince with pain. She closed her eyes, trying to think.

How in the world had she gotten herself into such a mess? Everything had seemed so right when she'd first met Joe Higgins. She was a good nun, an intelligent woman with an active ministry, teaching high school and having many friends and acquaintances. Then, he fell out of nowhere into her life like a bomb, and everything exploded.

Without warning, she felt incomplete, vulnerable, stirred-up emotionally. How could she have been so stupid as to make a snap decision to leave the convent without thinking it through? She had never in her life done anything so impulsively. Why hadn't she listened to Sister Superior when the woman tried to warn her?

Why had she ever believed Joe Higgins? It was clear now, when it was far too late, that he had never meant anything he had said. He was a liar! The bluntness of her realization shocked even her. Debbie's face burned as she remembered all the times she'd believed him like a gullible, moonstruck adolescent. She'd trusted him so completely.

How could he have done this to her? How could he have done it to anyone? And she'd bet there were others. He was too good at it to be a beginner. She wondered about Sister Noreen. Was she one of his trophies? Or Tina Rodiman?

Debbie Stevens felt tears run from the corners of her eyes over her ears onto the wet pillow. What had he turned her into? A shrew, a hard hateful shrew who thought of hating people as easily as she'd once thought of loving them.

She who had all her life hated cruelty and violence, who as a child had wept over a dead goldfish. . . . Now look at her. Where had the rage come from? Now that it was unleashed,

Debbie wondered how she would ever be able to get it back into the infamous box. The ragged jingling of the telephone startled her. The now-familiar voice of Inspector Kate Murphy asked her to come to the rectory.

"I'll be there, Inspector." Debbie's pulse began to throb with sickening speed. "Just give me twenty minutes."

❧❀❧

Sister Noreen was in the school office on the telephone. She was going over, yet again, the last-minute details for Monsignor Higgins's funeral with the chancellor of the Archdiocese. She had left strict orders with Sister Bernice that no one was to disturb her.

When she saw Bernice's gray head peek cautiously around the corner, Noreen knew it meant trouble. In this case, only one group could outrank the chancellor and that, of course, was the police.

"Excuse me for a moment, Monsignor," she said. "May I put you on hold?"

The man's flat silence clearly indicated that "hold" was not his usual button.

It's your own fault for not keeping a better eye on what's going on with your priests, Noreen thought, giving the red button a fierce jab. She was glad to shift the blame to someone else—anyone else.

"What now?" she whined at Bernice, who smiled sympathetically.

"Police, on the other line. They want you at the rectory, A.S.A.P."

Noreen tilted back in her desk chair and watched the red light blink importantly. The high sound of children laughing and playing drifted in from the schoolyard.

Fear gripped her stomach and she reached into her pocket for a Tums. She stared, half seeing, at the familiar package, waiting for the burning pain in her esophagus. She studied the silver foil not quite covering the white pill on the end.

Her eyes glinted with tears, remembering once again every detail of that final scene she and the pastor had had on that fateful Sunday afternoon.

Sister Noreen had completely lost control. Thinking back on it, she was not quite sure who had been the more surprised.

She had asked to see him after the meeting. Her only motive was to reason with him, to support him in confessing the truth and making restitution for what he had stolen.

Noreen wanted to let him know that, due to his indiscretions, his affair with Debbie Stevens was pretty much common knowledge. She had prepared a few words—nothing preachy or condemning—in which to assure him that she was not sitting in judgment. That, like God, most people forgive and forget if you admit your mistakes and say that you are sorry.

Patiently, she'd waited for all the others to leave. Then, for maximum privacy, she had followed him to his suite of rooms.

Even now, Noreen was not sure exactly what went wrong. It had started out calmly enough—quite civilly, considering the subject matter. She could still picture Monsignor in the back glow from his study window. His stark white hair stylishly combed, his sharp blue eyes appraising her unfavorably, as usual, making her feel like some lesser specimen unworthy of his gaze. That tan face, "smoked Irish" some called him. Those thin lips saying sarcastically when she'd finished, "So, Goody-Two-Shoes, you know more than your prayers."

He'd even offered her some of his damnable scotch. She had swallowed a mouthful, struggling to control herself, watching his face twist, hoping to numb herself against his cruelty.

"Who do you think you're talking to?" he'd asked haughtily. "What do you know about love? What do you know about anything?" Suddenly, his insults flew at her like stones. "You can't even control the gossip in your own schoolyard, Sister. This is none of your business. None. You can't take any pressure. You're a poor excuse for an administrator eating those antacids like candy. Grow up, Noreen!"

Sister Noreen covered her blazing ears, but not before she heard him shout, "I want you out of my parish by morning. Do you understand me? Out by morning."

Noreen remembered closing her eyes. Her stomach imploded. Then something erupted in her brain and when she opened her eyes again, the entire room glowed a splotchy red. It was out of focus.

She remembered screaming. She remembered an emptiness as all that was pent up rolled out of her, like boiling lava, covering everything. Noreen said words she never realized she knew, calling the priest names she would never allow in her schoolyard.

Her loathing for the man bubbled up and foamed out of her mouth as if she were a creature possessed. She could not stop. The terror in the monsignor's eyes only made her laugh and ridicule his foppish ways.

For a moment, Noreen feared the priest would lunge at her. Let him try it, she thought flippantly. She hadn't hit anyone since she was a five-year-old fighting with her older brother, but let him try. She would love to give him a good hard punch in his stuck-up nose.

Instead, she had thrown the only thing she had in her hand, her Tums. Wasn't it just like Eve to find them and give them to her.

Sister Noreen felt weak all over. What must the police think? She'd find out soon enough.

"Sorry, Monsignor," Sister Noreen said, picking up the receiver. "What is it you wanted me to do about the honor guard?"

❧❧❧

Eve Glynn didn't feel herself this morning. She clutched her thick hands together to keep them from trembling, which didn't help. She was trembling all over. Her stomach quaked.

Was the room moving? she wondered, lowering herself into the padded rocking chair in the corner of her suite. The housekeeper's suite! She had to laugh at such a grand-sounding name for two dingy rooms joined by a narrow bath.

When she'd first seen these rooms, she'd thought they were grand. She'd been a child really, and they were such a far cry from her home in Ireland, sharing a bed with two of her sisters. Then, she'd thought of her cousin Padraig as her savior come to take her to the Promised Land.

She'd had such great hopes, such great dreams and aspira-

230

tions. First, she'd get herself an education. Many women did in America. Then, a good job, a little later she'd marry a caring man and have a houseful of well-fed youngsters.

Somehow none of it had ever happened. She'd been so busy learning to cook and to clean the rectory to Padraig's expectations that, before she knew it, she was too old to go to school and most of the Irish girls she'd played with were married. Was there no one for her?

When Padraig died, he'd left her a small inheritance, but not enough to really retire, so she stayed on with the next pastor, and the next. Living at St. Agatha's at their whim. Playing at politics, jockeying, scheming to keep her power and her position.

Eve surveyed her suite, actually seeing it for the first time in years. Cream drapes hung limply from the window, a brown stain where water had seeped in. The hems were uneven with time. A small worn sofa covered in a chintz of faded cabbage roses was pushed against one wall. In front of her was her powder blue vinyl hassock, torn at one end from years of holding tired feet.

Her shiny, new twenty-four-inch television set held a place of honor. It was a gift to herself from herself last Christmas. One large rhododendron picked from the monsignor's precious garden floated in a small flat vase on top of the scarred bookcase.

Fading family pictures of relatives she'd never seen in person hung on the walls. Her favorite picture of Our Lady of Knock was over the television set.

Rocking back in her chair, Eve could see the corner of her bedroom. Her blue slippers, worn at the heels, were next to the bed where she had left them when, dead tired, she'd crawled in. From where she sat, it was obvious that the mattress dipped in the middle and that the flowered spread, once so bright and cheerful, was old and shabby. A few wash dresses hung in her closet with her winter coat and her Sunday hat. Even the sunlight streaming in from the window was full of swirling dust motes.

Tears welled up in her eyes and ran unheeded down her cheeks. She felt their wetness on her hands. Her heart ached with the icy cold realization that she was just like her suite— old, worn, tired, nothing special. No longer was she something to behold, a force to be reckoned with. Her nose began to run and she dug in her apron pocket for a tissue. Her smooth wooden rosary, a gift Padraig brought her back from Rome, was wrapped in it.

Where would she go now? What would she do with the rest of her years? Who would have her and her television and her old faded pictures and her Sunday hat?

Slowly, Eve rocked back and forth, back and forth, keening now in her misery. Back and forth, she rocked for the years—the long, sad, hard years—for the lost life, for all the hurts and heartaches. Back and forth she went, like an infant sucking his thumb.

She pulled the tiny beads through her fingers. "Holy Mary, Mother of God," she rocked and prayed over and over, "pray for us sinners."

The room blurred. Sweet Mother, Eve thought, maybe I should just tell the police I killed the dreadful man. I'm an old lady. I was insane. Old and insane. Then, wouldn't someone have to take care of me?

This morning, Charlotte Wixson had brought her letter of resignation into St. Agatha's rectory with her before she realized that there was no one to give it to. She had tried to make her position clear to the energetic red-headed detective but before she could, Charlotte was pressed into service.

"But, Inspector," she found herself trying to explain to a fleeting back, "I quit."

Inspector Kate Murphy did not appear to hear.

This is it! Charlotte thought, slamming into her office. As soon as this day is over, police or no police, I'm out of here. I'm history!

With a burst of newfound energy, she began to clear her personal belongings from her desk drawers and pile them into an empty paper box. She stopped just long enough to plant a kiss on her sweet granddaughter's picture, then wrap it carefully in a copy of last Sunday's bulletin.

❧❧❧

Just before ten o'clock on Wednesday morning, all the parish council members had managed to make their way through the handful of reporters still lingering outside St. Agatha's rectory and were assembled in the dining room.

Like a frozen photograph, they had all taken their assigned seats around the mahogany table. Charlotte Wixson and Eve Glynn were in their usual places doing their usual tasks with as much ease as possible under the circumstances.

Sister Mary Helen was there with Sister Eileen and a stale loaf of Irish soda bread she had managed to find in the college kitchen. This performance had to be as authentic as possible.

Inspectors Kate Murphy and Dennis Gallagher sat sphinx-like in the spot vacated by Monsignor Joseph P. Higgins.

"When is this ordeal going to be over?" Professor Nicholas Komsky asked peevishly. His uncombed mane of white hair stood out around his face, making him look more than ever like an aging Einstein.

"You know, Inspectors, some of us have jobs that we need to get back to. I don't know how much longer I can keep taking 'sick' days," Debbie Stevens said; her Hershey's kisses eyes had the anxious sheen of one who had been up all night fighting demons.

Sister Noreen nodded in agreement. Her round, dimpled face was nearly as gray as her hair. "The teachers have all pitched in to run the school for about as long as they can. Besides, with the funeral Saturday . . ." She sounded on the verge of tears as she let the words trail off.

Tina Rodiman jingled her bangle bracelets nervously but said nothing.

George Jenkin, his eyes closed, squirmed in his chair. "Does this whole thing strike anyone else as a little theatrical? Everyone sitting in state. What is it? A scene of the crime re-enacted?" he said in a droll tone. "Don't we have civil rights or something that protects us from this kind of harassment?"

"Why can't you just keep quiet for a change?" Fred Davis clenched his fists, his knuckles white. Obviously, he was near the end of his rope. "Can't we get this over with and get back to our lives?"

"All of us but one can." Jenkin smirked, waiting for a reaction. He was not disappointed.

Mary Helen watched carefully as the room exploded. Everyone was talking, no one was listening. Hearing the racket, Eve Glynn stuck her head in from the pantry door to watch.

Sister Mary Helen's murderer was acting no differently from the rest of the council members. Her mouth went dry. Was she wrong about the person she suspected? Would this turn out to be nothing but an embarrassing fiasco? It took Kate Murphy several minutes to settle everyone back into his or her place.

"Mr. Jenkin was right," she explained quietly. "Inspector Gallagher and I would like to re-enact as closely as possible everything that happened in this room last Sunday afternoon. What you said. What you did.

"Let me assure you that we are even more eager than you are to have this case solved, so that you can get back to your lives. If you can just bear with us for another hour."

Grudgingly, the group settled down. Kate Murphy motioned Eve Glynn back into the kitchen. The silence in the room was as thick as Sister Mary Helen remembered it.

"I understand that when the Sisters arrived and were seated," Kate said, looking to the nuns on either side of Gallagher and herself, "you began by introducing yourselves."

On cue, Fred Davis, his eyes red-rimmed behind his wire-framed glasses, began. "Fred Davis, Sisters," he said in the same strong clear voice Mary Helen remembered. "I'm the head of the parish finance committee." He looked to his right.

"I'm Debbie Stevens," Debbie said in her high nasal twang. The muscles in her square jaw were working. "I'm the chairperson of the outreach committee."

Sister Mary Helen remembered the monsignor saying, "Really, I don't know what I would do without Debbie." In the light of what she now knew about their relationship, it took on another, crueler meaning. She shuddered with disgust.

Debbie gestured to her right. Tina Rodiman slid to the edge of her chair, teetering precariously. She squeezed her small jeweled hands together. "My husband Tony and I head the bingo committee." She nibbled at her waxy red lower lip. "They call us the 'Two T's,'" she said with a tone of resentment that Mary Helen did not remember hearing last Sunday. Quickly, Tina looked to her right.

"George Jenkin, here," Jenkin said without glancing up. "Communications." Slumped in his chair, he presented the picture of nonchalance, except for the pencil eraser he bounced nervously on top of the mahogany table.

"Then I said I knew Sister Noreen." Mary Helen spoke up.

Noreen gazed at her from behind her owl-eyed bifocals. "That's right," she said, folding her chubby hands on the tabletop.

"And I also acknowledged that I knew Professor Komsky." Mary Helen smiled at the man to Noreen's right.

The tension in the room was palpable. Mary Helen could hear the professor breathing. His blue eyes shone as hard as glass. "You asked if I was enjoying my retirement," he said.

"And you said, 'I was,'" Mary Helen recounted, "then

stared, not without cause I know now, at the monsignor." Komsky reddened and Mary Helen turned away.

"At that point," she said, "Eve Glynn came into the room."

The housekeeper must have been listening for her cue. She burst noisily through the pantry door, her slippers scuffing, with a tray. The china cups rattled, the teaspoons jingled. "I'll get the rest," she said, leaving again.

Like a sleepwalker, Noreen stood and began to pour the tea and pass around the cups.

"Were you the only one passing out cups?" Kate Murphy asked.

Noreen froze. "Yes," she said, her voice quivering. "Why do you ask?"

"I just wanted to make sure everything was as exact as possible," Kate said, her voice friendly.

Eve swung through the pantry door, rear end first. "Enjoy!" she said sharply, placing a plate of the Irish soda bread, a cube of butter, and a plate with a lump of berry jam down next to Eileen.

Mary Helen felt the same chill zigzag up her spine as she had on Sunday at the sight of the way Eve had butchered the bread.

Inspector Gallagher, apparently resigned to playing the monsignor, was served first. Did he look nervous when the bread was passed to him or was Mary Helen imagining it?

Eileen stood to help Noreen as she had last Sunday. The room was extremely warm and Eileen seemed to be having difficulty trying to remember what she had talked about on

Sunday afternoon. Mary Helen noticed her friend's thicker and more pronounced brogue.

Soon, she hoped, this charade would be over. She felt the perspiration break out on her forehead.

Once more, the pantry door banged open and Eve entered the dining room. She placed a silver tray on the table. All the "suspects" stared at the contents. A Belleek creamer and sugar bowl and a plastic honey bear with a nick in its green plastic top. The spout was as sticky as it had been on Sunday.

The group began to pass the sugar, the cream, the honey bear. Cautiously, they began to sip the tea.

"Wait!" Mary Helen tried to keep her voice steady. "We forgot one thing."

All eyes were on her. "Debbie helped herself to the honey first, then complained that the top was sticky."

Debbie Stevens rose awkwardly from her chair, her bony body stiff. All the color had fled her square face. Her eyes, like rabbit eyes, shifted nervously from one to another.

"I did not," she shouted. "I took honey, then I handed the bear to Joe. We both took honey from the same container!"

Sister Mary Helen shook her head. "No," she said softly. "I remember, Debbie, because I was going to try it instead of sugar. Less fattening and all," she said self-consciously. "But you took it to the kitchen to clean, although I don't remember seeing the nick in the spout when you came back, not that I had any reason to examine it at the time."

The strain filled the room like an air bag, smothering all sound. No one spoke. No one moved. All eyes were on Debbie.

"You have no proof," Debbie shouted. "It's my word against yours!" Her eyes were wild. "I had no reason to kill him," she pleaded with the group. "I loved him. I left everything for him. Everything!" she shrieked. The word echoed in the silent room. "I gave up *everything* for that lying, cheating bastard!"

No one seemed to be breathing. Debbie's face twisted with rage. "You can't know, Sister. You can't be so damn sure," she taunted.

Mary Helen shrugged. "As I said, I was going to try the honey, too, so I was waiting for you to return. At the time, I thought that you were probably having trouble getting the spout clean. But you were switching bears. Hiding the rectory's, the one with the nick, and substituting one you must have brought from home. After Monsignor Higgins helped himself, I was going to ask him to pass it, but the sugar was closer and there was so much tension in the room, I could hardly wait to drink up and get going. Had I asked . . ." Mary Helen's knees felt weak.

Debbie's head twisted from side to side, desperately looking for a pair of friendly eyes. Finding none, she swept the room with a look of such rage and hatred that Mary Helen's heart pounded.

"I wish you had," Debbie said through clenched teeth. "I wish you all had!" she shrieked in an unnatural voice and reached toward heaven. "As God is my witness, I wish I had killed you all."

With an animal roar, she collapsed into her chair, folded her arms on the mahogany table, buried her face in them, and wept.

Impulsively, Mary Helen patted the woman's heaving shoulders.

All eyes were focused on her. She knew the group needed a fuller explanation. Just because someone leaves the room for several minutes does not necessarily mean she is a murderer.

"What really stuck in my head was Eve Glynn saying that washing off the top was unusual for Debbie. Out of the ordinary," she said to no one in particular. She was debating the wisdom of telling them that she'd come across that phrase in a mystery novel and that it had jogged her mind, making everything fall into place. But Eveleen Glynn spoke up.

She was beaming. "I knew it was her the whole time," she confided to Charlotte Wixson, who had rushed into the room at the sound of Debbie shrieking. "All the time, I knew no good would come of them two hanky-pankying around like we were all blind, deaf, and dumb. No good at all!" Eve repeated. "And, I was right, wasn't I, Charlotte?"

Charlotte Wixson looked as if she might faint.

Saturday, March 22

❧❧❧

Fifth Week of Lent

Sister Mary Helen woke up tired, not so much from lack of sleep, but from dread of the day to come. Since Wednesday when Debbie Stevens was arrested for the murder of Monsignor Joseph P. Higgins, Sister Mary Helen had spent most of her time successfully dodging reporters and their never-ending questions.

Sister Anne had suggested that she wear sunglasses, but that had seemed somewhat too dramatic for Mary Helen's taste. Instead, she had found exits in the college building that hadn't been used in years.

During those days, she had even looked forward to her visits to the Hall of Justice. No matter how persistent Inspector Gallagher and Kate Murphy were in their questioning, they didn't hold a candle to the media.

Within hours after the scene at St. Agatha's rectory, the detectives had procured a search warrant and were able to find the missing honey bear in the Dumpster behind Debbie's apartment. Thank goodness, the Sunset Scavengers only collect garbage once a week, Mary Helen thought, or a crucial piece of evidence would have been lost at the dump.

Slowly she pulled herself up and sat on the edge of her bed. This morning she was feeling every one of her seventy-seven, or was it seventy-eight, years. It may as well be one hundred, she thought, wishing the convent had room service. What she needed to get going this morning was a good strong cup of hot coffee. Pronto!

At first, she thought she imagined the soft tap on her bedroom door. "Are you awake, old dear?" Eileen's whisper floated into the room along with the aroma of freshly brewed coffee. "I thought you might be able to use this," she said, settling a tray with steaming mugs on the small square table beside Mary Helen's easy chair.

Holding a mug, Eileen waited for Mary Helen to fluff her pillows and sit up in bed. When she'd finally handed Mary Helen her coffee, Eileen settled into the easy chair and began to sip from her own mug.

"Is everything all right?" Mary Helen asked suspiciously. It was quite unusual for Eileen to serve her coffee in bed. In fact, she hadn't done so since Mary Helen was recovering from the flu several years ago.

"Everything is fine, if you call the hubbub about Monsignor's murder fine. I, for one, could not face one more word, howsoever well meaning, about the man's death. 'There is no tax on talk,' they say back home." She rolled her eyes for emphasis. "So I got a tray from the dining room and left, important as you please, as though I were Florence Nightingale gone to serve the sick."

Sister Mary Helen groaned. "I suppose the others will think that I'm the one who is sick."

"It will give them something new to fret about," Eileen said with uncharacteristic sharpness.

She must be tired, too, Mary Helen thought, noticing the deep lines on her friend's round face as she removed the small silver dome from the dish on the tray. "Hot raisin scones," Eileen announced like a magician who had just pulled a bouquet of flowers from her sleeve, "with butter!"

In companionable silence, the two nuns savored the warm, rich, yeasty taste of the bread. Another nice day, Mary Helen thought, watching a patch of sun brighten a square of flowers on the edge of her comforter. Too nice a day for a funeral, although she'd be glad to bring some sense of closure to the tragedy.

"There'll be a big crowd at today's Mass," Eileen said, obviously thinking about Monsignor Higgins's funeral, too. She checked her wristwatch. "If we want a seat, we had better get going. I've signed out one of the cars for nine."

"The Mass isn't until ten," Mary Helen began.

Eileen put up her hand. "It's early, I know, but I thought we just might get in without anyone spotting us."

"Say no more." Mary Helen swung her feet from the bed. "Give me fifteen minutes to get body and soul together."

When Eileen had gone, Mary Helen chose her black suit

and a white blouse with just a touch of lace along its stand-up collar. She dressed quickly, trying not to think about what the morning might bring.

Funerals, no matter whose, were difficult affairs. They served as stark reminders to all present of their own mortality and the uncertainty of the time they had left.

"Remember, Sister, that you are dust and unto dust you shall return." Father Adams had said the ritual words on Ash Wednesday when he'd traced a sooty cross on her forehead. Here it was already the day before Holy Week. Where had Lent gone? she wondered, running a comb through her short gray hair. Where had life gone?

Precious life, how we cling to it. How we fear death. "Yet, it is in dying that we are born to eternal life," St. Francis of Assisi, patron of the city and of the college, had declared in his famous Peace Prayer.

She slipped into her tight black leather pumps, her funeral shoes, and wiped the dust from the toes. "Guide my feet into the way of peace," Mary Helen prayed, straightening the collar of her jacket. "This morning I'm banking on it, Lord," she said, shutting her bedroom door on her unmade bed. "Positively banking on it."

❦❧

"It was pure luck. Nothing but pure dumb luck," Inspector Dennis Gallagher shouted, loosening his tie and glaring at his partner, Kate Murphy.

She faced him squarely. "Why is it you never give Sister any credit?" she needled. "And don't you think for one minute that your shouting and blustering intimidates me."

"Intimidate you? I'm not trying to intimidate you, I'm trying to reason with you." Gallagher scowled. "Which might be more impossible than trying to intimidate you."

"Sarcasm doesn't become you, Denny." Kate smiled, then turned back to the paperwork on her desk. Both she and Gallagher had arrived at the Hall of Justice at about eight-thirty, hoping to get the necessary files on the Monsignor Higgins murder case finished before the funeral.

Despite the early start, this morning Kate felt too good to let anything Gallagher might say ruffle her. In fact, she felt as if she glowed. Jack and she had talked long into the night, finally making gentle love. Kate knew that their decision to have another baby was right.

Not that deciding to have a baby made it happen. But she knew that if God sent a child, Jack and she would both welcome it with joy.

"We had better not tell my mother," Jack had teased.

"Why not?" Kate asked sleepily, not that she had been considering it.

"Because she'll pray for twins and any time my mother prays for something, it terrifies me." He shivered.

Filled with desire, Kate had kissed her husband on his shoulder, then his neck. Her body tingled when his hands found her and he pulled her to himself.

"What the hell's wrong with you this morning?" Gallagher growled. "You look as moony as a teenager on the morning after the prom."

Suddenly aware that her partner was studying her, Kate felt her face redden. "None of your business, Denny! And let's get this done without any more grousing."

Kate checked the clock on the wall of the Homicide detail, which was always ten minutes fast. "The funeral is at ten. It will be packed. Let's try to get there early enough to get a seat."

"I still can't figure out how the perp knew about the poison. It's not something everyone knows about," Gallagher said, seeming to growl like a dog that wouldn't let go of his favorite slipper.

"In the convent she was a history teacher. Apparently, the Greek general Xenophon and the honey story are common knowledge among history teachers."

"I never heard of it," Gallagher said.

"You're a cop. History teachers probably never heard of, of Ninhydrin." She'd picked the name of the general-purpose fingerprint reagent for paper and other porous surfaces out of the air.

Gallagher grunted. Clearly still unconvinced that they had the right perp, he ran his hand over his bald pate. "What about the motive? First of all, why would she leave the convent for this guy? Was he that attractive?"

"There is no accounting for taste," Kate said, pulling her gaze back from the Saturday traffic on the James Lick Freeway.

"And, why would an intelligent woman like Debbie fall for all that crap the monsignor fed her once she did leave?"

"I guess love is not only blind but deaf," Kate said, eager to get finished. She'd planned a picnic in Golden Gate Park for tomorrow and hoped to get to the Safeway to pick up some things after the funeral Mass.

"How did she know to bring the poisoned honey on that particular Sunday? How did she know they'd have tea?"

"According to Eve Glynn, the monsignor always served tea at the parish council meetings."

"Then how could she be sure no one else would take the honey?" Gallagher asked stubbornly.

"She couldn't. And Sister Mary Helen almost did take some." Kate stared at her partner. "Don't you dare say it, Denny, even if you're only kidding. Do you have any idea how long it might have taken us to solve this case if Sister Mary Helen hadn't goaded the woman into an admission?"

"Like a goddamn Perry Mason, if you ask me," Gallagher said. "I don't know why those two nuns can't stay out of our business and in the convent where they belong. Swear to God, Katie girl, if either one of them shows up on another one of my cases, I'll run them in on . . ."

"Spoil sport!" Kate poked her finger at her partner.

His face flushed. "You know as well as I do the chances of a hare-brained scheme like that working are zero to none."

"But it did work." Kate was not going to let him badger her. "And the woman confessed and we found the evidence and the phones stopped ringing. The lieutenant looked as if he might have had a good night's sleep, and best of all, tomorrow we have the day off!"

Gallagher considered. "That's another thing I want to ask you. If we go to the funeral Mass today, which I can imagine will last a good two hours, can we count it for Sunday Mass tomorrow?"

"Now, Denny, that is something Sister Mary Helen might really know. Why don't you ask her? I'm sure she'll be at the church."

"I'd rather go twice," Gallagher grumbled, focusing all his attention on his paperwork.

❧❧❧

St. Agatha's Church was already half-filled by the time Sister Mary Helen and Sister Eileen arrived. And the school honor guard was in place along the avenue.

Using the front side entrance, the two nuns slipped into the dim church. Thank God, Catholics notoriously sit in the back, Mary Helen thought, sliding into one of the vacant front pews.

"We were lucky to find a parking place," Eileen whispered, surveying the quickly growing crowd.

The hum of conversation rose to the vaulted ceilings. The morning sun shone through the stained-glass windows, skittering miniature rainbows along the pews and on those seated in them.

Bright spring flowers banked the main altar and a priest, fully vested, was testing the loud-speaking system. Freckle-faced altar boys and altar girls, like a parcel of penguins, strutted around the sanctuary trying not to look at the monsignor's casket which, closed and covered with a white pall, had been placed facing the altar.

A couple of pews ahead of the nuns and across the main aisle, Mary Helen noticed that seats were reserved for parish council members. Professor Nicholas Komsky and Fred Davis were already seated. Turning sideways, the professor raised his bushy white eyebrows in recognition and gave them a wave, while Fred Davis, with his long narrow face stiffly set, made no effort to even look in their direction.

"Somehow I get the impression that Fred feels this whole thing is my fault," Mary Helen whispered.

"I'd like to go straight over there and tell him where the whole bunch of them would be without you." Eileen steamed, and she may have, too, if Sister Noreen hadn't suddenly appeared at the end of the pew.

For the first time in a week, Sister Noreen looked as if she'd had a good night's sleep. Behind her owl-eyed bifocals, her hazel eyes were unclouded. She patted Mary Helen's shoulder.

"Thanks for everything you did, Sister," Noreen whispered. "I'm so relieved it's over. Father Calvo, you know, our assistant pastor . . ." It was more a statement than a question. "He was appointed administrator for the time being, and he's asked me to stay on as principal. Of course, I will." Noreen's soft voice had its lilt back. "There is no sense in upsetting the parish any further if we don't have to," she said, inviting Mary Helen and Eileen to agree, which they did.

Noreen might have gone on except that someone beckoned her to the back of the church. "The archbishop must have arrived," she whispered excitedly. "I hope I'll see you at the reception afterward."

Not on my longest day, Mary Helen thought, turning back toward the altar with its draped casket.

Tina Rodiman and a tall, thin man whom Mary Helen assumed was Tony, her husband, slipped into the church through the same front side door as the nuns had. Tina waved one bejeweled hand at them and led her husband to the parish council pew where he shook hands with Fred and the professor. Tina, fresh in her bright peach spring suit, looked like a fashion model.

"Now, there's a woman who seems to have come into her own," Mary Helen said, studying Tina closely.

"Gold, tested by fire?" Eileen suggested.

"In her case, I think it's more like steel," Mary Helen said.

Near the front of the church, behind the pews reserved for the clergy and in the place where family and close friends usually sat, were Eveleen Glynn and Charlotte Wixson. Charlotte sat stiffly, her brown eyes conscientiously studying her missalette. It was obvious, even from where Mary Helen sat, that Charlotte did not want to talk to anyone about anything, nor even make eye contact. Period.

On the other hand, Eve in her Sunday hat might as well have been in a touring car. She smiled and waved to all who'd respond and beckoned another woman of her vintage to come join her.

"She's trying to tell us something," Eileen said, squinting. "I can scarcely read her lips, but I think she's saying 'Father Calvo wants me to stay on.'"

"No wonder she looks so happy," Mary Helen said, wondering what Father Calvo would look like in six months.

"What is it?" Eileen was still straining to read Eve's lips. "Oh, dear! She's saying, 'When you're in the neighborhood, drop in for tea.' I'd sooner drop into a lion's den at feeding time." Eileen sighed and sat back in the pew. Mary Helen agreed.

A scuffing noise drew Mary Helen's attention to the middle aisle. George Jenkin, a silly grin on his face, weaved toward the sanctuary. Professor Komsky reached out to grab him, but George dodged his grasp with an alacrity that any Forty-Niner running back would envy. Then, for no apparent reason, he stopped and with bloodshot eyes, surveyed the quickly filling church.

Sister Mary Helen held her breath as George teetered to balance himself. He drew in a deep breath and opened his mouth like a practiced orator about to begin a major speech.

"Friends, Romans, Countrymen," he bellowed.

Luckily, the opening chords on the massive pipe organ drowned out both him and the nervous giggles of the altar servers. The congregation rose.

Mary Helen felt Eileen nudge her to move over and make room in their pew for Inspectors Kate Murphy and Dennis Gallagher. Both homicide detectives looked much happier than they had the last time she'd seem them. At least, Kate did. To be honest, Inspector Gallagher looked his usual grumpy self without the bags under his eyes.

"I am the Bread of Life," the choir and congregation sang. "You who come to Me shall not hunger." A priest holding the Easter candle aloft led the long procession of clergy up the center aisle. Mary Helen estimated that there must be, at least, one hundred priests in white cassocks and stoles preceding the archbishop.

Feeling a twinge of sympathy for the prelate, whose face was as white the miter he wore, she closed her eyes. She didn't envy the man his task. What would he say about this once good priest gone wrong? What could he say about a priest who had been all too human without sounding judgmental or, what's worse, pharisaical? And if he chose to ignore the whole mess, he'd be accused of whitewashing.

The only thing he could say that made any sense was that Joe Higgins had gone to God in whom all us sinners find

mercy. Then beg the God who loves each one of us unconditionally to forgive the man.

"Dear Lord." Mary Helen sighed. "It is so much easier on
us human beings to bury a saint than to bury a sinner."

"Isn't that what all this Lent and Holy Week business is
about?" the Lord answered gently. "That I died to save sinners? Saints and sinners, I love them both. And, dear Mary
Helen, when all is said and done, you may be very surprised
to find out who is which!"

"Who is who," Mary Helen corrected softly. She couldn't
help herself.